WILD
WIND

WILD WIND

BY
TEMPLE BAILEY

Jacket by
Charles D. Mitchell

GROSSET & DUNLAP, *Publishers*, New York

COPYRIGHT 1930 BY TEMPLE BAILEY

MANUFACTURED IN THE UNITED STATES OF AMERICA

WILD WIND

CONTENTS

PAGE

Chapter One
"This is the Way we March to War!" 9

Chapter Two
London Bridge 36

Chapter Three
Kit's World Crashes 61

Chapter Four
Alarm Bells Tolling! 83

Chapter Five
An Impregnable Tower 108

Chapter Six
"My Heart is Like a Singing Bird" 134

Chapter Seven
Five Years 152

Chapter Eight
Life and Little Things 177

Chapter Nine
The King of France! 193

Contents

	PAGE
Chapter Ten *O Happy Wind!*	207
Chapter Eleven *Yolanda Takes the Center of the Stage*	236
Chapter Twelve *Crumbs From the King's Table*	261
Chapter Thirteen *A Call to Adventure*	279
Chapter Fourteen *An Angel on the Stairs*	306

WILD WIND

Wild Wind

CHAPTER ONE

"This Is the Way We March to War"

I

"WAR IS drums beating and flags flying and pipes playing," said Jacqueline, when her lover went overseas.

Of course war is more than that — blood and brutality and horrors and hatred, and Jacqueline knew it.

"But I won't think of it that way," said Jacqueline to herself, "or my heart will break."

It was a very young heart, for Jacqueline was seventeen and she really had no right to a lover. But there he was, and what were you going to do about it?

So she kissed Christopher good-bye, and told him how brave he was, and how handsome in his ensign's uniform, and how glad she was that he wouldn't have to fight in the trenches.

"For when the sea is blue as blue, I shall be thinking of you all nice and clean, with your buttons shining."

Christopher held her close and she clung to him, for

he knew and she knew that the sea wouldn't always be blue and that even when it was, Christopher might not be seeing it, for there might be smoke screens, or orders that would keep him below decks, or he might even be sinking to unfathomable depths among the fishes.

So he went away as a gallant lover should, with his head in the air, and the prayerbook Jacqueline had given him against his heart. And the Star-Spangled banner fluttered in the breeze and Jacqueline's eyes were wet with the beauty of it.

She felt that the way she had sent Christopher off entitled her to say things to her sister, Mary.

"I shall die if Joel leaves me," Mary wailed, when Jacqueline, having been sent for in hot haste, arrived bag and baggage in a station taxi, and was met at the door by Mary's small daughters, who were five and nine, and who adored their aunt.

"Don't be an idiot," Jacqueline bent and picked up the brand-new baby, "he'll be back before you know it."

"He may be killed."

"Nonsense, Mary."

"I don't see how you can take it so lightly, Jackie."

Jacqueline knew that she dared not take it any other way, but all she said was, "They'll come back with flags flying."

Mary sat up and looked at her, "What do you mean by 'they'?"

"Christopher. He went — a week ago."

For just a breath's pause, the eyes of the two women met, and Mary — saw!

"This Is the Way We March to War" 11

But she wasn't sure a moment later that she had seen anything, for Jacqueline was flapping the baby's hand against her cheek, and was saying, "Does he love his Auntie Jack? And is he going to be the only man left in the family?"

Well, of course Joel went, and Mary held on to him until the very last, sobbing and begging him to stay.

And in the front room, the two small girls and their Auntie Jack talked about the war. "Mother's crying because Daddy's had to go," said Yolanda, who was the older and had a straight-thinking mind.

It was not easy to sidetrack her, but Jacqueline did the best she could: "She'll laugh when he comes back."

"But he might get killed," Yolanda was pale with the thought of it.

"Nonsense," said Jacqueline, as she had said it before to Mary. "He'll come back with medals pinned all over him, and we'll be as proud as proud, and we'll have turkey and ice-cream for dinner, and you and Patsy can have the drumsticks."

The thing sounded to the children enchanting. Medals and turkey and Daddy coming back! "Will it be like that?" Yolanda demanded.

"Yes, and the band will play and you and Patsy will wear your white dresses and carry bunches of roses," Jacqueline was breathless with the ardor of invention.

"What will the roses be for?"

"For Daddy and the other men with medals. And then we'll eat the turkey."

"And we will have drumsticks, drumsticks," Yolanda sang in a lilting voice.

And Patsy echoed, "D'um'ticks!"

Over their heads Jacqueline saw Joel coming out of Mary's room. White-faced he closed the door behind him and leaned against it heavily, his arm across his eyes.

She kept the children with their backs to their father. "Daddy's coming. Now — don't look till you get in line! Show him how you can march. One, two, one, two — ! See them, Joel, they are going to march like that when you — come home."

She saw him straighten up. Square his shoulders.

Her gay voice ran on. "And we are going to have turkey, Daddy, when you come back with your medals; and bunches of roses — and drumsticks!"

She hardly knew what she was saying, but she drove herself to it, "Won't it be — corking, Daddy, when you — come home?"

He had Patsy in his arms, Yolanda clinging to his hand! And now he, too, was playing the game! Thank God, he, too, was playing — ! He began to sing to the tune of "Here we go round the mulberry bush":

> "This is the way we march to war,
> March to war,
> March to war.
> This is the way we march to war,
> All on a Monday morning!"

The children sang with him, and when he had them laughing, flushed, heedless of the shadows which had hung about them, he caught them up and kissed them. "Save me a drumstick," he said, and said it, smiling.

Then he kissed Jacqueline, "You're such a darned good sport! I'll never forget it. And look after Mary."

II

Looking after Mary meant more than Joel had dreamed. In the first place it meant that Jacqueline must give up college. She had had only her freshman year, and now the whole thing must stop. But then, she told herself, no girl had a right to as much happiness as four years in college and a real lover. And she still had Christopher and his letters.

Christopher was ten years older than Jacqueline, and before he left for his war-time training, he had had an office in his uncle's warehouse down near the docks in Boston harbor. His uncle had inherited the business from Christopher's grandfather, and back of that had been a great-grandfather whose ships had brought from the Far East picturesque cargoes of teas and spices and silks and sandalwood. The liners which had replaced the sailing vessels were, perhaps, less spectacular, but they, too, yielded strange and splendid wares, and Jacqueline visiting his office with Christopher, would bring away with her packets of tea, and jars of ginger, and things in ivory and things in jade; and once she had said to him, "I believe it's because of the ships that I fell in love with you. It's like something out of a book — Keats and Coleridge."

Christopher, less fervid in his literary passions, had smiled at her: "No man named Christopher was ever a part of a poem." And she had tucked her head against his arm and had said, "You're a part of my poem."

It was a very pretty head, though all this happened years ago, when America went to war with Germany. Jacqueline's hair wasn't bobbed or permanently waved. It was just beautifully braided and wound about her head with curls breaking through here and there, and bronze lights all over it, and the face that it framed was wistful and charming, with a narrow sweep of black brows above the blue eyes. Her skin was fine and white, and her lips as red as the lacquer box which Christopher had just given her.

They were in his office at the time. It was a very interesting place and Jacqueline adored being there. On the walls were models of the Company's old ships, boxed with glass over them. There were quaint compasses, brass spyglasses, a ship's clock with its chiming bells. There was a portrait of Christopher's grandfather in the uniform he had worn when he commanded a ship during the Civil war. He was sturdy and upstanding, with a thatch of rough curls like Christopher's, and the same gay, flashing glance. And Jacqueline, looking up at the portrait, had said, "You're like him, Kit," and Christopher had said, "I wish I were half as fine."

It was then that he had given her the lacquer box and had said, "You're to keep my letters in it."

It was a long time, however, before letters came, and meanwhile Jacqueline went about her task of taking

"This Is the Way We March to War" 15

care of Mary. It seemed strange to be doing that, for Mary was the elder, and had been the beauty of the family, and had always had her way about things. But her way had been a lovely way, and when their parents had died and the two girls left without an adequate income, it had been Mary who had worked and slaved and looked after little Jack, and when Mary had married she had insisted that her young sister go to college, even if she and Joel had to live somewhat scantily to accomplish it.

But now that Joel was gone, Mary seemed to have lost her moorings, and it was Jacqueline who took the helm, as it were, and guided the family ship.

And guiding the family ship meant packing up everything and moving from the roomy, rented house in Brookline to a tiny cottage in a sleepy seaport town where the rents were cheap because the season was over, and where Mary and Jacqueline could do the housework and take care of the children, with only one maid or perhaps with none at all.

All the women of the sleepy town had waked up for the moment and were busy making surgical dressings. They went every day to the Red Cross rooms, and Mary went with them, for she seemed to find in this service a sense of nearness to Joel. But Jacqueline stayed at home and looked after small Joey and the two girls, and did a thousand things that she had never done before, and some nights when bedtime came she was so tired, that it seemed as if she could never get up again.

She wrote about it to Christopher, however, as if it

were all a joke and a joy. "When the wind roars about us on these autumn nights, we are cozy as birds in a nest. We have a great fireplace, and a peach of a furnace. And outside there's the sea, stretching away between you and me, and every morning I blow a kiss to you across it. I miss you more than I can tell, but you mustn't worry about me. For while life isn't all cakes and ale, we have our moments. Last week there was a dance at the yacht club for the officers who are stationed here, and I wore blue taffeta, and I am sending a snip of it in this letter. It is like a periwinkle and matches my eyes."

And Christopher, writing back, said, "Your letter was all putting-your-best-foot-forward, and I love you for it. But you needn't think I don't know what you are up against, my dearest, and how brave you are. And I am wearing the snip of taffeta as a talisman. And if it is periwinkle it doesn't match your eyes for your eyes are sapphire."

That was, Jacqueline decided, the lovely thing about Christopher. He always understood. Beneath all those shallow sparkling things she had written him, he had discerned the hurt that the hard days brought.

As the weeks went on, Jacqueline decided that it might not be as dangerous to take care of her sister's children as it was to fight in the front line trenches, but it was, none the less, work which belonged to the saints and martyrs. And as Jacqueline was neither a saint nor a martyr, she was sometimes put to it to know what to do with Mary's children.

"If only I could spank 'em," she said to herself in tense moments.

But of course she couldn't, although now and then Mary did it. But only mothers have the right to discipline their children. Mary had told her that, and of course Mary knew, but there were times when Jacqueline felt that only a spanking would make it possible for her to live another day in the same house with Patsy.

Patsy was adorable. She wore primrose rompers which stuck out on each side like Dutchmen's breeches, her hair was a bronze mop of beauty, her eyes were gray and black-irised under long lashes, and when she wanted a thing she wept for it.

And she always sat down to weep, and nobody could move her, not even if she were in the middle of the street, except her mother, who would say, "Get up, Patsy," in a quick voice, and Patsy would scramble to her feet at once, and stop crying.

Jacqueline might say "Get up" forever, and Patsy would stay glued to the ground. Mary protested, "You're not firm enough with her, Jack. She minds me." But Jacqueline knew what Mary did not — that Patsy, with uncanny wisdom, had divined Jacqueline's limitations in matters of punishment and had acted accordingly.

Yolanda was more tractable, but she was none the less disturbing. She had a logical mind and faced facts. Her aunt, whose philosophy had to do with making things easy for everybody, talked about pleasant things to Mary, and wrote pleasant things to Kit and Joel, and tried not to think of the awfulness of everything, because she felt that if she let her mind dwell on it for a moment she would go mad.

But Yolanda with her flair for realism, softened nothing. She talked with the children on the street and at school and repeated to her mother and aunt, stories of men drowned in submarines and caught in barbed wire, and blown to bits by bombs, until the two women, blanched and breathless, would beg her to stop, and Yolanda would fling out at them, " Well, it's true, isn't it, Mumsie? " and her mother would cry, " Jacqueline, take her away."

So Jacqueline would go off for a walk with her niece, and the two of them would have it out. And Jacqueline would say, "You mustn't tell such dreadful things to your mother."

And Yolanda would say again, " Well, it's true, isn't it? "

" My darling, yes. But we are trying not to think of it."

Yolanda was not convinced, however, nor was she credulous in matters of dogma.

There was the morning, for example, when they went into the old church.

It had been Jacqueline's suggestion. "Let's stop in and say a prayer for Daddy."

So they had entered and knelt down together, and Jacqueline had prayed first for Christopher, and then for Joel, and then for all who fought.

"*This Is the Way We March to War*" 19

Yolanda, kneeling beside her, had prayed for Daddy and had let it go at that. The other soldiers had their own families to pray for them and enough was enough. So she put her chin on her folded hands and looked up at the window over the altar. It was a wonderful window and showed the resurrection of Christ, and the heavens in a glory.

When they came out, Yolanda talked of the window. "When you're dead, you're dead. How can you come alive?"

"My dearest, look at the trees. There's not a leaf on them now. But in the spring they'll be budding and beautiful."

"Well, why don't the Lord do that to old people. Just let them lose their hair and their teeth for a little while, and go to sleep, and wake up young again?"

"They do wake up young — in Heaven."

But Yolanda was not satisfied. "I'd rather wake up here."

There were times, however, when the children were enchanting. At night, for example, when you put them to bed and they lay curled up in infinitesimal pajamas, like warm kittens. And you told them about Santa Claus, and about the little wax angel that was to hang on the tree.

It was a saving grace in Yolanda that she liked the idea of the wax angel better than she did that of Santa Claus. She liked to hear about its golden wings and its golden trumpet and the message of peace that it brought to a war-sick world. Of course Jacqueline didn't call the world "war-sick" when she talked to the children. And as she sat there in the tranquil, lamp-lighted room, with Yolanda and Patsy, lovely and lovable in their bedtime mood, it seemed as if the things happening in France must be a nightmare and that presently she would wake and find Christopher safe by her side, and her wedding bells ringing.

But Christopher was not safe, nor Joel. And it was just after Thanksgiving they had news that Joel was wounded. Jacqueline got the message and it was she who had to break the news to Mary.

Mary, after the first moment, took it calmly. "In a way I'm glad, Jack. At least he isn't in the trenches."

The two women clung together for a moment, then Jacqueline whispered, "I wish Kit were there with — Joel."

But Christopher was somewhere at sea, and at the mercy of those great gray sharks, the submarines. In his letters, he never spoke of the dangers which confronted him. He said, indeed, that he bore a charmed life. "It is because of the talisman. That bit of blue silk goes with me everywhere."

The children had to be told, of course, of their father's wounds, and it was Yolanda who asked, "If he dies, will he go to Heaven?"

Jacqueline, stabbed by the thought of Joel dead, demanded, "How can you doubt it?"

Yolanda persisted, "If I only knew more about it."

"About what?"

"Heaven."

"This Is the Way We March to War" 21

Jacqueline tried to explain. And Mary. Helplessly. For Yolanda was still skeptical. She was sure Daddy wouldn't be happy. Not without the rest of them. Not without Mother.

Patsy, untouched by doubts, broke in: "There'll be a pink wax angel waiting for Daddy, and it will have gold wings an' a gold trumpet, and it won't be on top of a tree, and it will come walkin' up to him and hold out its hand, and it will say, 'Are you Patsy's Daddy?' An' my Daddy will say, 'Yes, but you can be my little girl while I'm in Heaven.'"

"Patsy!" Jacqueline remonstrated.

But Mary who was knitting, knitting, endlessly, raised her anguished eyes and said, "Oh, let her talk, Jack. If — if anything happened to Joel, I'd want to have her think of him like that."

III

That night the wind blew down strong from the north, and as Mary and Jacqueline sat late by the fire, the little house was filled with the roar of it. Mary still knitted, but Jacqueline's hands were folded in her lap. It was the first time all day that her hands had been quiet. They had been busy since early morning. They had dressed the baby and made the toast and coffee, and had set the table for luncheon and dinner, and had peeled the vegetables and wiped the dishes for old Hannah, and had given Yolanda and Patsy a final rub-off in their baths.

But why go over it? The day was done.

Mary talked as she knitted — about Joel and the children, and the high prices, and the need for retrenchment. "We might let Hannah go. I could give up my war work and help more about the house."

Jacqueline wouldn't hear of it. They must keep Hannah. "They need you at the Red Cross. Who else could they get to instruct in surgical dressings? And you are so lovely, Mary, in your uniform."

Mary smiled and went on with her knitting, "Darling, will you ever grow up?"

Mary was beautiful. There was no doubt about it. Even as she sat there, worried and weary, you were aware of her golden fairness. She was tall and had a grace of bearing like that of the Duchess of Towers in an old book, or of the lissome ladies in the *Idyls of the King*.

Jacqueline was not a tall and lissome lady. She was small, her figure childish. As she leaned back in her chair and looked at Mary knitting in the firelight, she wondered how it had come to pass that her sister, with all her poise and previous training in the hard things of life, should lean now so heavily on others. For it was Jacqueline who in these days assumed the bulk of responsibility.

Mary's thoughts were running in the same direction. "I've been such a slacker, Jack. And you're marvelous! But if Kit were your husband and there were babies, you might not be so brave. Loving them all so much weakens me."

"This Is the Way We March to War" 23

Leaning a little forward, Jacqueline spoke with a sort of tense passion: "I love Kit as much as you love Joel—"

"I know. But as yet you haven't had any of the realities—the sharing of everyday things. All that means—so much. I thought I loved Joel all I could before I married him. But now—"

Mary couldn't go on. She began to cry. Jacqueline soothed her, and at last put her to bed, then she got a book and sat alone by the fire. She found, however, that she could not read. Mary's words blazed up in her mind. She had wanted to cry out that no woman had ever loved any man as she loved Kit. And Kit was finer than Joel. In many ways. Joel was a good husband and father, and he adored Mary. But Kit's head touched the stars!

And oh, how she wanted him! She was restless, and at last she rose, opened the door, and gazed forth. The moon was shining, and the sea was a raging, restless expanse. Light clouds flew across the sky like birds in a flock. The air was icy. And singing, shrieking, shouting, the wild wind came down from the north!

Wrapped in a warm coat, Jacqueline made her way up the hill to the edge of a high bluff. The wind blew her hair about her face and beat her back as she pressed against it. She felt her blood warm to the struggle, and when at last she stood looking out over the illumined waters, she was aware of a sense of exaltation. For the first time in weeks her cares fell from her. She forgot Hannah and the dishes, Mary's depression, the baby's food, the unceasing demands on her of Yolanda and Patsy. She forgot, too, the gray sharks lurking in dark waters. For on the other side of that illumined sea, she seemed to discern a shadowy figure, which grew brighter as she gazed. Laughing, triumphant, his head thrown back, Kit was holding out his arms to her.

So real was the vision, that she put her hands to her mouth and called to him, " Christopher! "

She seemed to catch his answer, " Jacqueline."

When at last she tore herself away and went into the house, it was as if she and her lover had kept a sacred tryst; as if they had met and parted. There on the bluff she had had a sense of his actual presence. And it was not until the next morning, when the glamour had faded that she wondered if the visitation might not have been an omen. What if Kit were dead, and she had been granted, at the last, one radiant moment?

But Christopher was not dead. For letters came and more letters, and in December one which seemed to Jacqueline the most wonderful of all, for in it Christopher said, " There's our old house in Salem. It has been closed since Mother died. Four generations of Howlands have lived in it, and you and I are going to live in it when I come home."

The key was, he said, at the bank. She was to go there and get it and have a look at her future home.

When she read that, Jacqueline held the letter against her beating heart. How sure he seemed of their life together. How sure he seemed of — coming back.

"*This Is the Way We March to War*" 25

The next day she went to Salem. She took Yolanda with her.

The child was full of curiosity, "Whose house is it?"

"Christopher's."

"Why are you going to look at his house?"

"Because I am going to marry him, Yolanda."

"Oh, I know that. But why can't you just keep on living with Mother and Daddy and me?"

"People have houses of their own when they are married."

"But Mother and I want you."

"So does Christopher —" and so lighted was Jacqueline by the rapture of it all that when she came to the bank the clerk who gave her the key thought he had never seen anyone so gay and glowing.

Christopher's house was a fine old Georgian residence on a wide old street. It was of brick and its sturdy white door had a brass knocker. The knocker was tarnished and the steps unswept, but in spite of this there was a benevolent air about the entrance as if it brooded over the days when carriages drew up to it, and there was much going in and out.

It was flanked by other residences no less imposing, but these other houses had occupants; there was smoke coming from their chimneys, and a stir of life about them in keen contrast to the somnolence of their neighbor. The trees along the street were elms, and their stark branches stretching up towards the steel-blue sky were coated with ice. It was very cold, and Jacqueline, turning the key in the door said, "We should have had a fire built, Yolanda."

The hall as they entered it was dim and deep. Yolanda drew back. "I'm frightened, Aunt Jack."

But Jacqueline was not frightened. It seemed to her that the arms of all the friendly folk who had lived there enfolded her. It was as if their spirits crowded about her to welcome her as the wife of one of them. She ran up the stairs swiftly and unlatched the shutters of the great window on the landing. The winter sun streamed in, and as she turned and looked down she was aware of Yolanda staring up at her. "Shall you like being a bride in this house, Aunt Jack?"

"My dear, of course."

"I'd hate it."

"Why?"

"It's too old—" Yolanda shuddered. "When I have a marriage house, Aunt Jack, I shall have everything new."

Jacqueline, descending the stairs, said cheerfully, "It will be your house, and you can do as you please. I adore all this, because it is Christopher's."

Yolanda weighed that for a moment. "Do you like him as much as that?"

"I don't like him. I love him."

As they went into the drawing-room they found themselves facing a long gilt-framed mirror. Jacqueline would have passed on but Yolanda stopped her, "Look, Aunt Jack, I'm almost as tall as you."

"You'll be taller some day."

"Like Mother?"

"Yes. And you will have her good looks."

Yolanda's face in the mirror betrayed a sort of startled ecstasy. "Not really?"

"Yes, really."

"Will it be like the ugly duckling?"

"But you're not an ugly duckling, dearest."

Yolanda shrugged a skeptical shoulder, "I'm not much to look at."

She did not turn away, however. She stood for a moment surveying their mirrored figures in silence. She had taken off her hat, and her hair, floating free about her shoulders, was like spun gold. There was little light in the room, so that the reflection had the depth and darkness of an old painting. Yolanda wore a wide rose-colored ribbon in her hair, and there was a certain flamboyancy in her youth and coloring, which threw into delicate contrast the bronze of Jacqueline's braids, the whiteness of her skin, the fathomless sapphire of her eyes.

Yolanda said unexpectedly, "Aunt Jack, I'd rather look like you than Mother."

"My darling, why?"

"Because you're so young."

"Mother isn't old."

"I know, but she will be some day. And you won't — ever."

Yolanda's precocity was sometimes startling. "How do you know I won't?" Jacqueline demanded.

"Well — you wait and see — "

They returned to the examination of the room, which was charming with its crystal chandeliers, its carved white-painted woodwork, its tarnished gildings, its sofas and tables in Empire pattern, its chairs in faded brocade. The library beyond was lined with books, and it was here that Yolanda stayed, buried deep in a volume of Dürer's engravings while Jacqueline made her way to the upper floor. She was glad she could go alone, for the old house spoke to her of a thousand things which Yolanda would never understand until she, too, had lived and loved and waited for her bridegroom. Here other men and women had loved and lived. Here men had brought their brides, here, too, had been the tragedy of parting, when death claimed a husband or a wife — Christopher's mother had been left alone. . . .

But then she had had her happiness with Christopher's father. She had given him a son. . . .

Jacqueline climbed finally to the attic, and found there the toys which had been Christopher's — tin soldiers in a box, a train on a track. There was the little trunk which held his baby clothes, each garment marked with his mother's fine script. There were photographs of Kit. Jacqueline did not have time to look at them all, and as she laid things back in the trunk, she had a feeling almost of awe that this boy Christopher had lived through all the years that he might one day be her lover.

Continuing her search, she found under the low attic window, a cradle in which had been rocked all the babies of bygone Howlands. An antiquated, out-dated bit of furniture. Babies in these days were never rocked.

They told you that at the hospitals. They had told Mary, and Yolanda and Patsy and little Joel had been put to bed by rule of book . . . !

But if there was ever another Christopher Howland, he should be rocked in this cradle! Nurses and doctors notwithstanding. What did nurses and doctors know of angelic influences. Might not a child gain something of strength and wisdom from those who hovered about him? The attic even now was filled with welcome as the hall had been. Jacqueline, kneeling there beside the cradle seemed to face the friendly spirits with a question, " Do you want me? "

And the spirits answered, " Yes."

IV

Yolanda was calling, " Come down."

When Jacqueline joined her in the lower hall, the child said: " There's some one in the house."

" What do you mean, Yolanda? "

" They opened the kitchen door."

" But, my dear, how could they? "

" I don't know. And I was scared and ran up to you."

They searched the rooms with no result. " Do you think it was a ghost, Aunt Jack? "

" Nonsense, darling."

But Yolanda insisted: " Some one came in."

They had stopped near a window in the upper hall, and Jacqueline, looking out, saw a girl standing on the stone walk which led to the gate. She was wrapped in an army cape, and the wind whipped about her head the long blue veil of the canteen worker. The blue was in strong contrast to the locks of bright auburn which curled over her ears. She was a rather dazzling creature as she stood in the strong light, with her red hair and her red cheeks and the wind blowing her about.

They went down at once and let her in.

"I'm sorry," she said, smiling, "but I live next door. And we try to keep an eye on the house. I saw the shutters open and came to investigate."

"I got the key at the bank," Jacqueline told her, succinctly. She felt no need of further explanation. She might, of course, have said that Christopher had given her permission, but she didn't. She simply stood there, silent.

The other girl, unaware of any concealment, went on, "I hope Kit isn't thinking of selling. I've always been next door neighbor to Kit Howland, and I'd hate to have anyone else."

Yolanda, sweeping suddenly into the conversation said, "Aunt Jack's going to live here. She's going to marry him."

Jacqueline remonstrated, "Darling."

"Well, you are — "

A change had come over the girl in the blue veil. She still smiled, but she was less dazzling. "Is that why you came in to look at the house?"

"Yes. Kit told me to ask for the key."

The eyes of the girl in the blue veil seemed to weigh Jacqueline in the balance — bronze hair, white skin, red lips, youth and slenderness. Pretty. More than pretty. Mind and spirit. Kit would like that, more than youth or slenderness.

"Look here," she said, suddenly, "I wish you'd come over and have a cup of tea with us. This cold is perishing. I'm Sue Gilman. The Gilmans and the Howlands have known each other forever."

Jacqueline hesitated, "We ought to be getting home."

"It isn't late. And there aren't any 'oughts.' And I like having my own way."

Yolanda begged. "Let's do it, Aunt Jack."

There was a big fire blazing on the hearth in the Gilman living-room, its flames flickered on flowered chintzes, and there were jade green curtains and Chinese porcelains, and the silver teaset was Queen Anne.

Three women sat about the fire, and laid down their knitting when Sue presented Jacqueline, "She's going to marry Kit Howland."

As the three welcomed Jacqueline, they too had their moment of appraisal. One of the three was Sue's mother She was ample in figure, gracious in manner and prideful in spirit. The other two women were Sue's aunts and single. Aunt Phoebe was small and unassuming. Aunt Paula had red hair like her niece's, and a burnt-out, thoroughbred sort of beauty. And the appraisal of the three of them amounted to this: All of them thought her a lady but too young for Christopher. Mrs. Gilman considered her not sufficiently imposing to take her place with the Howland women. Paula envied her youth and freshness. Aunt Phoebe envied her nothing.

Aunt Phoebe liked being middle-aged and comfortable, and delicate and well-bred.

Aunt Paula, too, wore a canteen uniform, and had just come in. When she shook hands with Jacqueline, she said, " Kit has stolen a march on us. None of us knew he was going to be married."

" We decided not to say anything until he came back. And Mary thought I was too young."

" Mary ? "

" My sister. Mrs. Joel Hutchins. I live with her."

" Oh — I think I've met her — at the Red Cross — " she dropped that, and began again, " How long have you known Christopher ? "

Her questions were assuming the proportions of a catechism. Jacqueline flashed a smiling glance at her, " Long enough — "

" Long enough for what ? "

" To get engaged . . . "

She turned from Paula, and began to talk to Mrs. Gilman. Her manner was not rude, but it was definite. She did not know then, and would never know, that the slight passage of arms had won Paula's admiration. Paula hated acquiescent people. She went through life wanting sword play, and she was disappointed when she did not get it.

The tea, brought in by a trim maid, was delicious — hot chocolate for Yolanda, toasted muffins, little spicy cakes.

" Kit always adored these," Sue said as she passed the cakes, " he used to eat dozens of them."

"This Is the Way We March to War" 33

Aunt Phoebe remonstrated, "My dear, *dozens?*"

"Millions, then, Aunt Phoebe," Sue's eyes laughed down at the pale little aunt who was pouring the tea. Aunt Phoebe had gray eyes and gray hair and wore gray dresses. She had beautiful rings and beautiful hands, and a beautiful complexion, but no one had ever looked at her when her sister Paula was about. To Aunt Phoebe her niece's modern extravagances of speech and manner were a constant source of agitation. Sue's "millions" had floored her, so she went on silently pouring tea.

Yolanda was enchanted by her surroundings. "This house is much nicer than the one next door."

"Why?" Paula Gilman demanded.

"Oh, I like the flowers on the furniture and the green curtains. Everything over there is old. But Aunt Jack loves it," Yolanda stirred the whipped cream into her chocolate, took a long and foamy sip and elucidated, "She says she loves it because she loves Kit."

Jacqueline remonstrated, "My darling . . ." and they laughed at her blushes.

Sue laughed with them, but when she spoke there was an edge to her words. "Kit wasn't always so crazy about it when he was a youngster and he got out of it as soon as he could. If he talks about it now he's probably sentimentalizing."

Paula Gilman glanced at her niece. So Sue was taking it hard? Well — the Gilman women had a way of losing the men they loved — Sue would have to take her turn at it.

It was getting late when Jacqueline rose. She had enjoyed her hour with them and told them so. "It has brought me nearer Kit."

Sue insisted on driving them home in her car. "I can learn where you live. I shall be wanting to come and see you."

When a little later the two girls parted, Jacqueline felt that she and Sue were friends. She did not know that Sue's friendship was founded on an almost morbid desire to hear Christopher talked about. Even if it hurt, she wanted to hear. He had written her a letter or two from France. But the letters had been brotherly, and he had talked about her aunts and her mother. She wondered what he said in his letters to Jacqueline.

Three days later she drove over and asked Jacqueline to help in the canteen. But Jacqueline couldn't. "I look after the house. Mary needs the war work to help keep her mind steady."

"Don't you need it?"

Jacqueline shook her head, "No, I'm not restless. I won't let myself think that anything can happen to Kit."

Sue's breath was short. "But if anything did happen?"

Jacqueline sat staring into the fire. "Kit would still be — mine."

They walked later on the bluff. It was a gray day and the wind buffeted them. Sue's veil was like a bright banner in the breeze. She talked of her work. "I wonder what we'll think of ourselves ten years hence?"

she said, "shall we know then whether we did it for the sake of our fighting men, or simply as another form of excitement? I serve sandwiches to the boys and adore having them smile at me. And I like my uniform, and looking like a Botticelli angel in it. But suppose the boys were sullen and flung their sandwiches back at me and I had to work in old clothes and didn't have time to curl my hair? We are all trying to live up to the Red Cross posters. And for the moment it suffices—"

They had come to the edge of the bluff and were gazing out across the gray ever-moving waters. Along the horizon was a band of gold, overhung by blue-black clouds. "There's wind in those clouds," Sue said, "we'd better be getting down."

Jacqueline did not speak for a moment. Then she said, "I like the wild wind. And when I am here with only the sea between us I seem nearer Kit."

Out of the ensuing silence, Sue said, "You women who have men over there are the happy ones. You are afraid you'll lose them, but it is better to have love and lose it, than not to have love—at all—"

Jacqueline pondering afterwards on Sue's words, found herself wondering how it happened that Sue Gilman had no lover overseas. She was attractive, charming. Men must have cared a lot about her. It was strange that Christopher hadn't . . .

She stopped there, warm with the thought, that of course Kit couldn't. He had been kept for her. From the beginning of the world. She was his and he was hers throughout eternity.

CHAPTER TWO

London Bridge

I

IN ALL the weeks since Joel had been in the hospital there had been no letter from him.

Mary fretted: "He may be dead."

But Jacqueline was hopeful. "We'd have heard of it. Everybody is having trouble with overseas letters."

"You are not having trouble with yours, Jack. You hear from Christopher every day."

"Not every day, Mary."

"Oh, well, he writes every day, even if they arrive in batches."

When Christmas was at hand, the cloud of Joel's silence still hung over the little house. Mary went around hollow-eyed and unhappy. But when she talked to the children of Daddy there was no hint of her unrest. "I won't have their lives shadowed, Jack. This war is dreadful enough without letting it leave its mark on my babies."

But Yolanda had her own point of view of the war and expressed it. "If I were God I'd stop it."

"Men must stop it," Jacqueline told her.

"Then why don't they?"

London Bridge

Jacqueline's and Mary's eyes met, "Why?"

"I stopped two dogs fighting yesterday," Yolanda stated with a sort of superior calmness, "I threw a dipper of water over them. . . ." Her tone indicated that somebody ought to stop the war by a similar simple expedient.

There was to be a party for the children on Christmas Eve. Nothing elaborate, just thin bread and butter and hot chocolate and the little jam tarts which Hannah made to perfection.

Jacqueline wore her blue taffeta, and Patsy was enchanting in an above-the-knees frock of apple-green, with her bronze mop tied up with a green ribbon.

Yolanda, thin and long-legged, voiced her discontent. "I wish I was pretty like Aunt Jack."

Her mother said, "You should have seen Aunt Jack at your age."

"Wasn't she pretty?"

"Not very. She was all eyes like the wolf in Red Riding Hood."

Patsy, always ready to improvise, took up the theme, "An' Red Riding Hood said, 'Oh, Grandmother what big eyes you have,' an' the wolf winked at her and said, 'The better to see you, my dear!'"

Yolanda remonstrated, "He didn't wink."

"Aunt Jack said he did, didn't you, Aunt Jack?"

Jacqueline admitted it: "It's such a gruesome tale, that I tried to soften it."

"What's 'gruesome'?" Yolanda demanded.

The two women knew what gruesome was — war

was gruesome. But Jacqueline said, "Oh, tragic things, like wolves eating up little girls and their grandmothers."

"But he *didn't* eat them up," Patsy triumphed, "the woodman came, an' he said, 'you're a naughty wolf, and just for that you'll have to go without your supper.'"

"*Patsy!*"

"So he didn't eat Red Riding Hood, and he didn't eat her grandmother," Patsy further elucidated, "an' he was put to bed with bread and milk, an'—"

She was cut short in her rapturous tale by the arrival of the party. There was a dozen or more of the neighborhood children, and some of their mothers came with them. Most of the women had husbands overseas, and a few of them were disillusioned.

And it was after the children had had their supper and were playing games that one of the mothers said to Mary, "When did you hear from Joel?"

And Mary said, "Not since the first letter from the hospital. I don't know what to think of it. He may be much worse — or dead —" her cheeks were blanched by the thought.

The other woman shrugged her shoulders. "I wouldn't be worried about *that*. There's probably a pretty nurse in the ward. And you are a thousand miles away."

Mary seemed to freeze, "Joel isn't — like that."

"How do you know? The war changes men. And I wouldn't trust the best of them."

London Bridge

Yolanda had come up and stood leaning against her mother. "I should think it would be nice for Daddy to have a pretty nurse. He likes pretty people, doesn't he, Mother?"

There was a dead silence, a stillness on Mary's face, a flutter in Jacqueline's throat, a flush on the cheek of the other woman. Then Jacqueline said, "Come on, Yolanda, we'll all play London Bridge. And you and I will hold up our hands for the children to march under."

So presently she and Yolanda were making an arch of their white arms, and marching beneath it went the singing children:

"London Bridge is falling down,
Falling down,
Falling down —"

Jacqueline sang with the rest of them, but all the time her heart was like lead. She knew that more than London Bridge was falling down. The world was falling — when women ceased to trust their men, there came chaos.

That night after their guests had gone and the children were in their little beds, Mary came into her sister's room: "I can't sleep, Jack."

Jacqueline knew why Mary couldn't sleep. "My dear and my darling," she said, "lie down beside me and we'll talk about it."

But Mary couldn't talk. She sobbed and sobbed. "I

mustn't *think* it of Joel. But it keeps coming into my mind."

"Joel loves you, Mary. You know that?"

"Yes."

"Then trust him."

"But you heard what she said?"

"Yes. It was a dreadful thing to say. Things like that are worse than — murder."

"But war makes men different. And some of them have lost their heads."

"Not Joel."

"Suppose you hadn't heard from Christopher. Not for weeks and weeks."

Jacqueline flamed, "When the time comes when I can't believe in Christopher I won't believe in — God!"

Mary's voice was shocked, "Jacqueline!"

And now it was Jacqueline who was sobbing, "I didn't mean it the way it sounded. I was only trying to say that Christopher — couldn't."

They clung together, and presently Mary said, "I'd rather hear that Joel was dead."

"Any woman would."

They lay for a long time in silence, appalled by the visions they had conjured up. Of Joel dead, of Christopher dead, of Joel and Christopher proving unfaithful to their high trust in matters of love and constancy.

The days that followed were desperate days. In January there was influenza. Mary had it and Yolanda, and little Patsy. Jacqueline worked like an automaton, nursing Mary, nursing Yolanda, nursing Patsy.

London Bridge

The neighbors were wonderful. They came in and helped. They brought soups and jellies and made beds and swept rooms, and insisted that Jacqueline and tired old Hannah should rest and relax. There were no nurses to be had for any money. They were all overseas or in the camps, or tied up in hospitals in cities.

The neighbor who did the most in heavy ways and hard ways was the one who had said the dreadful things to Mary on the night of the Christmas party. She was in black. Her husband was dead. And she had told Mary when she first came over, " My dear, I've never forgiven myself for the things I said that night. And I have had my punishment. I had a letter from my husband, written just before he went — West. All the time I had been thinking bitter thoughts, he had been loving me. Yet out of my bitterness, I had tried to make you, too, unhappy."

Mary reached out a hand to her, " He knows now that you love him."

" Do you really believe that? That he knows? "

" My dear, we must believe it."

II

Sue Gilman's friendship was a great source of comfort to Jacqueline. Sue sailed in and out of the sick rooms, absolutely unafraid, and seeming by her vivid presence to bring life with her. She brought, too, all sorts of delicacies from the three women in Salem. She came back and forth in her little car, carrying Jacqueline off with her when she could for a breath of fresh air.

On the morning little Patsy died, it was Sue who held Jacqueline in her arms, "This is a dreadful world," she said, "but we've got to make the best of it."

"If only Kit were here—"

Sue's arms loosened, "If he were here you wouldn't want me—"

"I should want both of you."

"No. He would be enough."

It was Sue who took Yolanda home with her and kept her through all the tragic days of the funeral, and who thought of everything.

Mary speaking of her to Jacqueline said, "She seems to adore you, Jack."

"She's a darling."

And neither of them knew that it was Christopher that Sue was adoring, and that she loved Jacqueline as it were, by proxy.

In February, however, Sue was called to Washington. The National Red Cross knew her work and needed her. She said she would write often and she did, but Jacqueline missed her vivid presence.

In May, too, Mary went back to her surgical dressings. Now and then Jacqueline would go down to the rooms and help a bit. The women, in their white veils, showed resolute faces. They were being trained in fortitude and were trying to measure up to their men. To Jacqueline, looking on, it seemed as if Mary and the other women were, in these days, like abbesses in convents, or vestals serving at a sacred altar.

Yet, quite strangely, it was not from these exalted women that Jacqueline got strength to go on, but from Hannah.

Hannah was a native of the old town. She looked like a Cruikshank drawing — just as grotesque, just as unbelievable. She always wore a bonnet, even when she worked, and the bonnet had a feather in it and strings that tied under her chin. Her dresses were long in the late Victorian fashion, and swept the ground in the back. She pinned up her skirts with safety pins, and achieved thereby something of the general outline of Little Buttercup in Pinafore.

Hannah was a famous cook, and the history of her acquirement of the art was not uninteresting. "Where did you learn it?" Jacqueline had demanded when she first came to them.

"Well, our men, Miss Jack, have always followed the sea. And my grandfather was a ship's cook. Nothing fancy about it in those days. But the next generation had to do better, and the next. I learned what my father had to teach me and my grandfather, and then I went and married a French chef."

She was peeling onions, and she laid down the knife to go on with her story. "He and my father met on the docks, and he came home to learn my father's way of making chowder. And there I was in a pink dress and a hat like a pink plate."

Jacqueline had a stabbing realization of the awfulness of change. Once Hannah had been a girl in a pink dress and a hat with roses. And now what had that girl to do with the old woman in the awful bonnet?

But Hannah had, evidently, no melancholy reaction to her own story. "We lived happy," she said, "and I miss him. He taught me nice manners, and he always wanted me to dress like a lady. People around here laugh at the way I dress. But he liked it."

She went on cutting vegetables for soup. She was serene in her memories. She cared not a bit what the world thought of her. Her own world was in her heart.

When Patsy died, it was Hannah more than any other who knew what to do with Yolanda. For Yolanda would not let anyone talk to her of Patsy in Heaven.

"I want her here, Aunt Jack," she would say, with her eyes streaming, "and I think God is dreadful."

And Jacqueline and Mary were helpless before her. But old Hannah was not helpless. "You come on down in the kitchen, honey, and watch me do my baking."

And Yolanda went, and old Hannah gave her some dough, and showed her how to make jam tarts, and while the child worked, the old woman talked to her. "You make a nice jam tart for your mother," she said, "and don't talk about Heaven and God."

And when they had finished the jam tarts, they made cookies with raisins in them and nuts, and Hannah told Yolanda stories of the sea and ships. And the things she told had to do with a race of men who fought the elements, the rain, the wind and the stormy waters, and who took life as it came to them, getting something of fun and flavor out of the hardness, and holding on to a sort of rough idealism in the midst of it. And Yolanda listened, and found in the wise old woman a quality of candor which suited her own straight thinking.

"I love Hannah," she said that night when her mother was eating the jam tarts, "I am going to have her for a friend."

And Mary said to Jacqueline, later, when they were alone, "How can she stand the bonnet?"

And Jacqueline said, "She sees beyond the bonnet."

But even Hannah couldn't always cope with Yolanda, and as the days went on, she shot up straight and tall, and in June she was ten, and she had a will stronger than her mother's. And one morning when Yolanda had worn Mary out with arguments, Jacqueline said, "She needs her father," and Mary said, "We all need him," and laid her head on the table and sobbed as if her heart would break.

In June the roses climbed down over the sea-wall till they almost touched the blue, and the wind blew soft on the bluff. And Mary, sitting out amid the checkered shadows of a trellised arbor with Joey at her feet, had a face like the Mother of Sorrows.

And Jacqueline, her heart torn by it all, wrote to Christopher, "The war has made the world over. And it's not as nice as it used to be. Perhaps I've been made over, too, Kit, and you won't like me when you come back. Do you love me because of my butterfly wings and my dancing feet? Because if you do, my wings are broken and you should see my shoes!"

That letter was not sent, however. She tore it up and wrote another. The second was serene and cheerful and all that a letter should be that one sent to a lover in the wars. And Kit, reading between the lines, guessed the truth. "She's lying and she doesn't know it." And he laid that night with the letter under his cheek, for he knew that he might never have another letter, nor indeed another night of sleep — for the gray sharks were prowling and before tomorrow morning he might be at the bottom of the sea.

So the summer passed and September came, and it seemed as if Joel must be dead. They never spoke of him as dead to Yolanda, and the child talked of his coming, "Will he have all of his medals, Aunt Jack?"

"Yes, dearest."

"Will there be a lot of them?"

"I am sure there will."

When Yolanda had gone away satisfied, Mary said, "How can I ever tell her?"

"Tell her what?"

"That he isn't coming —"

"Oh, but you don't know that, Mary."

"I do know, Jack —" there was despair in Mary's voice. "If he were alive he would have written."

October had a golden beginning with sunshine and warmth and a shining sun. One morning Mary got up early and went downstairs and opened the front door. The fresh sweet air blew in, and red leaves from the

London Bridge

maples in the yard flew all about her like little crimson birds, and the sky was a shimmering spread of amber silk.

But Mary, looking out, saw nothing of the morning's beauty. She saw only that winter was at hand. "How can I bear it?" she said in her heart, and went through the darkened house into the kitchen, and began to slice bread for toast, for Hannah did not come until nine, and Mary always got the breakfast while Josephine bathed the baby.

And when Mary had sliced the bread she broke eggs for an omelet, and it was just as she broke the last egg into the bowl, that she heard a queer sound on the porch. It was a bumping sound as if some one were dragging a box and setting it down — Bumpety, bumpety, *bump* — like the farmer in the nursery rhyme.

At last there was a final bump right in front of the door, and the bell rang, and Mary went at once to see who was bringing her a box. She had on a blue gingham dress and an apron that covered her up, and her hair was swept back from her tired white face.

And she opened the door!

And there stood Joel, and the thing that had bumped up the steps and across the porch was not a box — it was CRUTCHES! But at first Mary didn't see the crutches. All she saw was Joel's face, and a world back of him that was as bright as if a thousand rockets were going off to welcome him.

"Joel," she said, with all the rockets falling about her.

"Mary, my darling," she saw him drop his crutches

and catch at her with one hand and with the other hand at the door frame to hold himself steady, then he drew her down with him to the porch seat, and held her close, and for a long time there was no sound but the broken murmur of his voice and of Mary's sobbing.

And after a while Mary sat up and said, "But Joel, did you hurt your leg?"

And Joel said, "Darling, the old left leg's gone . . . !"

And as she sat there on his knee, white and staring, he said, "Oh, I shouldn't have told you like that. But you see, I'm used to it. Mary, *Mary* . . . !"

But Mary had fainted.

III

Yolanda was very proud of her father's artificial leg. She talked about it a lot to the children. "He has to use crutches now, but after a while he won't, and you won't know the difference between that and a real leg."

She was also very proud of her father's medals. She wanted to show them to everybody. But her Daddy wouldn't have it. "I'd rather not, old girl," he told her.

"Aren't you proud of them, Daddy?"

He wanted to say, "No," as became an officer and a gentleman, but he was too honest for that, "Well, yes," he admitted, "I'm proud of them, Yolanda, but I don't want to go around talking of it."

"Oh," she said, and left him on the porch, and went

London Bridge

into the kitchen to have it out with old Hannah, "why can't he be proud of them to other people?"

"Men are like that," old Hannah told her, "they are afraid they might be called vain."

Yolanda considered that, "I don't believe Daddy's vain."

"All men are vain," said wise old Hannah.

"Even Daddy?"

"All of 'em," Hannah slapped the iron hard on the napkin she was pressing, "bar none. Your Daddy's better'n the rest. But he'd hate it if you didn't think he was the bravest man in the world."

"Well, he is," said Yolanda with conviction, and went upstairs to have it out further with Aunt Jack.

Jacqueline was writing a letter to Christopher. She was telling her lover about Joel. "Mary is growing young again, and she is lovelier than ever. But when I see them together I am mad with envy. I want you as Mary has Joel — away from the dreadfulness and danger — "

She laid down her pen as her niece came in. "What is it, darling?"

There was a flush on Yolanda's cheeks. "Aunt Jack, you said when Daddy came home that we'd wear our white dresses and carry bunches of roses — and it hasn't been like that."

"I know," Jacqueline drew the child to her, "but we couldn't, could we, without — Patsy?"

"No. But I thought you said there'd be bands playing,

and flags flying. And that he'd be marching on — two feet."

Jacqueline showed her surprise. "I thought you were proud of his leg."

The flush on Yolanda's cheeks deepened. "I am proud when I talk to the children. But last night I heard him saying things about it to Mother — and Aunt Jack — *he cried!*"

There was a dead silence, out of which Jacqueline said, gently, "Darling, we must try not to think about it."

Yolanda protested wildly: "How can you help thinking about things that are in your heart?"

When the child was gone, Jacqueline sat weighing it in her mind. Was Yolanda right? Were they all trying to gloss things over? Would it be better if the world spoke out and said what was in its heart? What would happen if it knew that its brave men wept in secret at what the war had done to them? Would it stop all the snarling and snapping, the maiming and blinding? Or would it still go on?

Well, men had endured to the end, and would still endure, and their women had helped. She and Mary must fight through with Joel.

Yet fighting through with Joel was not easy. There were days when he was desperate and depressed. And late one night Mary came into her sister's room to talk about her husband. "He isn't my old Joel," she said, and cried as if her heart would break.

And when she could speak she went on. "He lies

London Bridge

awake and talks to me, endlessly, of how useless he is, and when he goes to sleep, he dreams that he is back in the trenches."

The two women looked at each other, dread in their eyes. And at last Jacqueline asked, "What are we going to do?"

"Make him forget," Mary said, with a sudden fierce passion, "Jackie, that's what you and I have got to do — make our men forget."

But with all their passion and their planning, things did not improve with Joel, and at last Mary took him to Boston for a medical examination, and the doctors decided that between a bit of shock and some complications with his leg Joel had better stay for a while in the Hospital, and so it happened that when November came in all gray and grim, that Mary and Jacqueline and Yolanda and small Joey and old Hannah were once more alone by the sea. But now Mary went up every day to Boston to see Joel, and Jacqueline found herself busier than ever, and sometimes she was so tired it seemed as if she could never again get up in the morning.

And old Hannah scolded her, "You're burning the candle at both ends."

"Oh, well, I must save Mary, she's so dreadfully worried, Hannah."

"Somebody ought to be worried about you, Miss Jack."

But it seemed as if no one was worried about Jacqueline but Christopher who was far away in hidden waters and whose letters came through only at long intervals.

And Mary grew whiter and whiter and as thin as paper, and Jacqueline begged her to rest, and Mary cried nervously and said she couldn't.

Then all at once, like a shining meteor from the sky came the news of the Armistice! Everybody went about laughing and crying and there were speeches and flags flying and bands playing, and Christopher wrote that he was coming back!

In the ecstasy of that anticipation, Jacqueline achieved a sort of flashing beauty. Whichever way she turned, she seemed to glint with radiance.

Even Yolanda noticed it. " I've never seen you like this, Aunt Jack."

"Like what?"

"Oh — shining —"

Every night Jacqueline wrapped herself in her warm coat and went out on the bluff to keep her tryst with Christopher, and always there was the wild wind singing, and sometimes she would sing with it, but at other times she was silent as it swept strong arms about her as if it would lift her up and carry her across the sea to her lover, and again it seemed as if the arms were Christopher's, and that the two of them were rushing through endless space like Paolo and Francesca in the famous painting.

Sue Gilman coming up from Washington for a week-end walked one day on the bluff with her. " So Kit is coming."

" Yes."

London Bridge

"And are you happy?"

"So happy that I'm — afraid."

Sue glanced at her. So this was the way that Kit would see her — when he stood beside her on the bluff, slender, swayed by the wind, her bright hair blowing about, her face illumined —

"Why should you be afraid?" she demanded.

"The war has made me a coward. Seeing Joel come back and so many of the men killed. How dare I expect to have more happiness than other women?"

Sue spoke sharply, "Don't bother about other women. We've got to be a bit selfish in this world, Jackie."

"Have we?"

"Yes. Take what we can get and hold on to it. That's my rule."

"I don't believe it —"

"That's because you don't know me, my dear," Sue lifted Jacqueline's left hand; "Is that the ring he gave you?"

"Yes."

It was a square cut sapphire flanked by diamonds.

"It matches your eyes," Sue said. "My eyes are blue, too. But men never see them."

Jacqueline stared at her, "What do you mean?"

"Just what I said. Men don't fall in love with me."

"Nonsense."

"But I mean it, Jack. I'm a good fellow, a comrade. But I don't appeal to their sense of romance."

She walked on — and asked, presently, "When do you expect Kit?"

54 *Wild Wind*

"He can't tell, of course. He may be here at any moment."

"You'll be married at once?"

"Kit wants it that way."

"And you?"

"Of course."

IV

But Christopher's coming was delayed, so that it was December before he could be definite. He wrote then that he would surely be there on Christmas day, and they might as well begin the New Year with a wedding, and she was not to buy many things for her trousseau. He'd take her down to New York for the honeymoon and they'd make a tour of the shops.

On the night after Kit's letter arrived, Mary came home late from Boston. She ate scarcely any dinner, and sat later by the fire in silence.

"Tired, darling?" Jacqueline asked her.

"Yes," she rose and stood looking out of the window. "Any mail?"

"A letter from Kit."

"When is he coming?"

"He hopes to get here by Christmas, and he wants the wedding on New Year's day." She got his letter and read the part which had to do with plans for their marriage. When she finished, she asked, "Do you think I can be ready?"

Mary did not answer. She had turned from the window and her face wore a strained look which struck against Jacqueline's heart.

"Mary," she cried, "what is it?"

And Mary said in a stifled voice, "Jack — do you think you and Kit could — wait?"

Jacqueline sat like a frozen image, "Wait? For what? What do you mean, Mary?"

Mary with the gray light back of her seemed very white and tall. Jacqueline had a sense of something almost spectral in her bearing. "Oh, Jack," she said, "I'm very ill. I have to have an operation."

Jacqueline sat, stricken, "Why didn't you tell me?" she demanded.

"I didn't know — until today. I went to a doctor. It's simply got to be done, Jack. As soon as possible."

Then, dropping into the nearest chair she began to cry. "Oh, Jack, I used to be so brave — but I'm such a coward. . . ."

It was an echo of Jacqueline's words on the bluff. Was that what the war had made of women? Jacqueline flew to her sister's side, knelt beside her, "Darling, darling, you are brave. And I won't leave you, Mary. Kit and I will take care of you."

When Mary was composed again, they talked it over. There wasn't much money. Of course Joel's pay would help, but there would be enormous bills. "And even if I had all the money in the world, I couldn't leave Yolanda and little Joey to be cared for by hired help. You've always been like a mother to them — and if anything should happen."

Jacqueline had a wild feeling that Mary was going to ask her to promise something — to look after the children always, if their mother should be taken from them. But she wouldn't promise — nothing could make her — the future was hers and Kit's, not Mary's, or Joel's or Yolanda's or Joey's. She was willing to do what she could at the moment. But the years ahead belonged to Kit. To Kit and the old house in Salem and the cradle in the attic.

But Mary asked nothing except delay. "Kit won't mind when you explain. And I shall be perfectly well in a few weeks. And spring is the loveliest time in which to be married."

Jacqueline wanted to say that any time was the loveliest time to marry Christopher. But she did not. For Mary was in such desperate need. So the next morning she gave to her sister some of the delicate garments she had made for herself, the nightrobes and a negligee, and when Mary protested, Jacqueline said, "I'll get others when you are well."

Mary's operation was not entirely successful, and she was not sent home so soon as she had hoped. Little Joey, too, was not well, and Jacqueline sat up nights with him. She looked pale and thin, the glint was gone, and the flashing beauty. She was like a candle burned out, and Yolanda asked her one morning, "Why don't you sing any more?"

"Don't I sing?"

"No—"

Jacqueline tried to make a joke of it. "Oh, I'm waiting to pipe for Christopher."

London Bridge

She had written to tell Christopher of her change of plan. She hoped the letter might reach him. But it did not, and it was late on Christmas Eve that he rang her up from New York. His boat had just arrived, and he would not be able to get a train out until morning. Would she meet him in Boston. . . . They must be alone together —

"Kit, I can't. Mary's in the hospital and Joel, and the baby isn't well."

Christopher said something strong and imprecatory about babies and other barriers which kept him from his love. Then his quick mind jumped to the next best thing. "There's a two o'clock train out to you from Boston. I'll get that, and be with you by four. I'll eat Christmas dinner with you, darling."

From that moment, the heavens opened and all their glory shone round about Jacqueline. When Christopher's call had come, she had been trimming a tiny tree for Yolanda. She went back to her work, and so rapturous was her mood that every bauble she swung from a branch seemed a golden bell to ring out her happiness — *tomorrow* and *tomorrow*.

In the morning she told old Hannah. And old Hannah took her in her arms and kissed her. "I'll cook you such a dinner, dearie."

"He'll be here at four —" there was hesitation in Jacqueline's voice — "do you think we could be alone for a bit — without Yolanda?"

Old Hannah understood. "If she knows, she'll stick around forever."

"She'll have to know."

"You let me manage her, my lamb. And I'll sit by the baby. It won't be the first time that old Hannah has minded a baby and cooked a dinner. You just get busy making yourself beautiful."

They had an early luncheon and then Jacqueline set the table and brought the baby up to her room where she could keep an eye on him, and Yolanda went into the kitchen.

Then Jacqueline took a bath and brushed her hair until it was luminous, and braided it and wound it about her head, and touched her lips with perfume and the tips of her ears, and passed a soft puff over a face whose whiteness seemed scarcely to need any powder. And with these preliminaries finished, she went to a closet and got out her dress. It was the blue taffeta from which she had snipped Christopher's talisman, and the crisp silk rustled as the gown went over her head. It had a wide skirt and a tight little bodice, and the slippers which presently carried her lightly down the stairs were blue.

At the foot Yolanda met her. "Gee, Aunt Jack, you look like a princess."

"Kit's coming."

"Hannah told me, and she says I'm to read my book and not bother you. I don't see why I'd be a bother."

"Oh, well, you'll know some day, Yolanda. And I haven't seen Kit for a long time."

Yolanda was hugging the newel post. "Hannah's put me on my honor not to come down till she rings a bell.

If I come before she rings a bell, she won't ever let me stay in her kitchen. She says she hates people who break their word, and the kitchen is her castle —"

Jacqueline, sweeping on out to the kitchen, said, "You're wonderful, Hannah. I couldn't have made her promise."

"No, you couldn't, because when it comes to love, Miss Jack, you're as soft as mush. You let Yolanda walk over you, but she knows she can't walk over me. I told her she could take me or leave me, but that I wouldn't be her friend if she broke her promise. You and her mother cry over her and pray over her, Miss Jack, but I haven't any time for tears and prayers."

Jacqueline, poised like a blue butterfly, in the middle of the room said, "We can't help what we are, Hannah."

"I'm hoping your young man's got good sense," Hannah was stirring gravy, and she emphasized her remarks with a swirl of her spoon, "he's the only one that can save you."

Jacqueline laughed light-heartedly, as she left the kitchen. Kit would take care of her of course. And he was coming!

She went into the living-room where a big fire on the hearth made the north end ruddy. There were some lacquer-red cushions on the couch, and the chintz which covered both couch and chairs had a pattern of pomegranates. As Jacqueline moved about, the delicate blue of the taffeta was shot across with flame, so that it seemed opalescent, and she became a part of the picture, as if she had been painted against the glowing background with a brush.

She glanced at the clock. It was almost time for Christopher. Another moment and she would hear the whistle of his train. Yet when she heard it, it seemed to drive the blood from her heart. She wondered if she would be able to endure the exquisite agony of the meeting. She had a sense almost of panic, and she found herself suddenly running up the stairs, to get a warm wrap and overshoes to cover the blue slippers. She would keep her tryst now with her lover as she had so often kept it!

When she went down, she peeped into the kitchen and spoke to Hannah. "When Mr. Kit comes, send him up to the bluff."

There was snow on the ground, but the sky was clear — a deep sapphire that matched Jacqueline's eyes, and the sea was sapphire when at last she looked out on it. It was very cold, but Jacqueline felt only a beating ecstasy.

And now she saw him coming — tall and splendid, striding up the hill — He took off his cap and waved it. The wild wind ruffled his curly locks. Oh, darling Kit . . . !

She went flying down the path to meet him.

CHAPTER THREE

Kit's World Crashes

I

"THE WHOLE thing is — preposterous."

Christopher flung out the words at white heat. "Preposterous. Do you think I am going to stand for it?"

He and Jacqueline had had their high moment out there on the bluff. Kit had caught her up in his arms when he reached her, and it had seemed to her as if he would never let her go. And she had cried, "Kit, Kit," and had clung to him. And when he had set her down it had been only to catch her up again and say with a sort of fierce breathlessness, "If you could only know how I've wanted you."

And then they had come back to the house — to the bright living-room, where the fire leaped and sparkled, and where, presently, Kit was raging and ramping on the hearth-rug as Jacqueline told him that she couldn't and wouldn't marry him until Mary was better.

At first he had laughed at her, but after a while he had not laughed: "Do you think I'm going to let you put me off like that? I've come back to marry you, and I'm going to do it now."

"But Kit — I've promised Mary — "

"You promised to marry me before you promised Mary."

"But — how will she manage without me? And Joel? And the children?"

He dropped down beside her on the chintz-covered sofa. "Don't I know what they've done to you?" he demanded.

With her bronze head in the hollow of his shoulder, the wide folds of her blue taffeta flowing across his knee, she answered, "I've done it myself."

"They've made a packhorse of you."

"No . . . no! What else could they do? Think of it, Kit — suppose you had come back to me as Joel came to Mary?" she shivered in his arms, "I should have died."

"I know. But you're mine, Jack. Can't you understand? The thing that swayed me level through the months overseas was the thought that I was coming home to — my wife. And now you tell me to wait."

"Only a little while, Kit."

"A little while will seem — eternity."

"Really, Kit?"

"Really, dearest."

It seemed to her incredible that he should care so much. He was such a marvellous person with his military carriage, his bronzed handsomeness, his alert and laughing manner. She wondered that she could set herself against him. But there was no way out of it — "We'll be married in the spring, Kit."

Kit's World Crashes 63

"We'll be married before that. You're going to have a honeymoon in March — in India."

She raised her head and stared at him with startled eyes. "In India?"

"Yes. The war has done a lot of things to our business. And I've got to go out to see what's left of it. Uncle Timothy is needed at this end . . . so that's that. And you are going with me."

"In March, Kit?"

"Yes."

She sighed with content as she leaned against him. She liked his masterfulness, and by March Mary would be better. . . .

Christopher had her hand in his and was turning the ring he had given her back and forth on her finger. It caught the light and glimmered with little mystic fires. "I have your wedding ring in my pocket," he told her, "I had hoped in a day or two that you'd be wearing it."

She pressed her face against his coat, "Kit, darling."

He had to bend down to hear her, "Yes?"

"Let's not argue. Just — love me. It has been — so long."

II

Yolanda, coming in to announce dinner, stood poised like a pink flower on the threshold. She had on a pink dress and a pink hair ribbon and pink socks and slippers. Her little face was eager and illumined.

"Hannah said to tell you."

She came farther into the room and looked up at Kit, "I didn't think you'd be like this."

He had risen, and stood smiling down at her, "Like what?"

"Well, Daddy didn't have any leg."

"Did you think I wouldn't?"

"I didn't know. And you're so tall and Aunt Jack's so little."

"That's why I'm going to marry her. You see, I can pack her in my kit bag and carry her off."

Yolanda adored that. "Would you really?"

"I might."

"Would you cut holes in the bag like we did for our kitty?"

"Yes."

"And carry milk in a bottle to feed her?"

"Of course."

Yolanda laughed rapturously. Here was a man after her own heart. "Will you tell me more about it at dinner?"

"Yes."

"Then you'd better come on. Hannah said the turkey was on the table," she tucked her hand in his confidingly, and drew him toward the dining-room, "You're to sit at the head and Aunt Jack's to sit at the foot, and I'm to sit in between."

The table was charming, with red candles in old silver holders, with holly and mistletoe in a bowl of gray pottery, with the turkey on an old blue platter. Hannah, who had exchanged her bonnet for a huge cap with a frill, passed the plates and beamed on everybody.

Kit's World Crashes   65

Kit carved, and Jacqueline served the scalloped oysters. It was all very domestic, and Yolanda was enchanted. "Next to Daddy," she told Kit, "you're the nicest man in the world."

"How do you know?"

"Because I feel it."

"You must tell your Aunt Jack that, so that she'll think so too."

"She does. They teased her about it at Sue Gilman's. I said she loved your house because she loved you, and they laughed."

"They would," he smiled across the table at Jacqueline. "How did my dove get along in that nest of starlings?"

"What makes you call them that?"

"Well, they all talk a lot — and they're hard and handsome."

"Sue isn't hard — "

"She's a good enough sport," he said, carelessly, "but Paula would walk over anyone's dead body to get her way."

Yolanda, deeply interested, demanded, "Why would she have to walk over a dead body?"

"My dear child — " he was helpless until Jacqueline rescued him. "Uncle Kit didn't mean a real dead body. It was just his way of saying it."

After dinner, Yolanda had her presents from the tree, and Kit produced a lot of parcels. Things from Paris — a superlative doll for Yolanda, and for Jacqueline a bracelet which matched her ring. "It was to have been your wedding present. But I want you to have it now."

Yolanda had gone to show her doll to Hannah, and the lovers were alone.

"Oh, Kit, you're too good to me."

"I couldn't be," he bent and kissed her. "In exchange I want you to give me something."

"What?"

"Your promise. That no matter what comes, you'll love me always."

"Kit, darling, you know it."

"I want you to say it and say it again. Jack, you can't know the hell I've been in over there. And you were always the star in the blackness. I used to think of you in the dark; then I'd light up and read my Bible to find words lovely enough to describe you — my dove, my fair one, my lily among thorns."

She laughed a little to hide her deep feeling, "Your dove among the starlings?"

But he did not laugh. "No matter what comes, you are mine always. Oh, I know that plenty of men say things like that. But I mean it — these years have taught me. There was never anyone — in France. Whether you marry me or not, Jack, there shall never be for me another woman."

"Oh, Kit, Kit, don't put it that way. I'm going to marry you, darling."

He held her to him in silence. She felt that he could not speak. She could only murmur that she was his and he knew it. That there must be no doubts between them.

He told her, after that, of what their life would be in India. They would go into the remotest parts, look-

Kit's World Crashes 67

ing after the tea plantations of his company, coming into close touch with the natives. "There will be temple bells and ivory towers, dearest, and strange and wise old men and young and eager women emerging from centuries of seclusion. And we'll make the trip on a slow-going boat to prolong the honeymoon."

A smile flickered across her lips, "Will it end when we leave the ship?"

"Our honeymoon? It will never end."

She settled back against his arm and stared into the fire, "Paula Gilman says that no sensible woman will ever take a wedding trip on a boat."

"Why not?"

"Because she'd be bored to extinction before the end of it."

"Paula might be bored, but not you. You're all moonshine and starlight. You would feel that you were sailing straight to Paradise. Paula would be sailing straight into the arms of the British Colony, and wondering what they would think of her."

It was not the India of the English, he went on to say, to which he would first introduce his wife. "We can come to that later. Just at first I want you to find the romance — with me."

As she listened, Jacqueline felt that this land to which her lover would take her was a land of richness and color, like one of its own rare shawls. She saw it all in a pattern of vivid loveliness, she felt wrapped in it as if Kit's dreams and hers were woven into a garment.

It was late when at last he called up Sue Gilman.

"You must do it," Jacqueline told him, "they are all so fond of you."

Christopher, running his fingers through his ruffled hair, disputed that. "I am not sure they are fond of anyone. They are a queer lot."

"I like Sue."

"Sue's the best of them, and Paula next. Mrs. Gilman is a bit of a snob, and so is Phoebe in a negative fashion. But Paula was a great beauty and a great belle before she lost the man she was going to marry — and some of her charm still lingers."

"How did she lose him?"

"Nobody knows. She went to visit his people, and one day she came back and said that the engagement was broken. That was the last word. Nothing more could be gotten out of her. Nor out of him. He is still unmarried, and lives in London. I saw him when I was there, and he spoke of Paula. He's sixty if he's a day and she's in her late forties. She hates men, and lets them know it. It's a great mistake. Why blame all the world for what one man may have done to her? That's the trouble with all of them. They're one-sided. Prejudiced."

He was calm in his analysis. Judicial. For the first time Jacqueline had a peep at the man Christopher, who was not her lover. "I am not sure," she told him frankly, "that I like to have you talk of them that way."

He had been leaning back in his chair, but now he sat up and looked at her, "You darling child, you wouldn't. You'd decorate all their faults with the little frills of your charity and hide the ugliness."

He smiled at her as he rose to go to the telephone.

Kit's World Crashes 69

"You must always decorate my faults with your little frills."

Sue answered the telephone. She asked a great many questions, which Christopher relayed to Jacqueline, "She wants me to come over there tonight instead of going back to Boston, and you're asked to breakfast. Sue and I will ride over and get you."

"I'll do it, if Joey is better."

He told Sue that, then hung up the receiver. "What do you think she said to me?" he asked Jacqueline, his eyes bright with laughter.

"What?"

"'Kit, how did you have sense enough to pick out that pretty child?'"

Jacqueline flamed, "I'm not a pretty child."

He laughed again, and swung her up to him. "You're more than that. . . . You're — everything."

There was a discreet cough as old Hannah appeared on the threshold. "Miss Jack, I'm sorry. The baby's worse."

"Oh, Hannah —!" Jacqueline had a horrible feeling that she had neglected the baby — little Joey — hot with fever and choked with cold. "I shouldn't have left him," she ran on swift feet up the stairs, and Kit followed her.

They found things very bad. The change had come suddenly. Christopher telephoned, Hannah heated water, the doctor came, and a nurse was sent for. Jacqueline donned a blue kimona in place of the blue taffeta, and sat with the baby in her arms while he struggled and fought for breath.

It seemed hours before the nurse arrived, and by that time the doctor had eased things up a bit. Jacqueline went down then to Christopher who still waited. Her bronze braids had loosened and hung down to her waist. In her blue robe with her hair unbound, she looked to her lover like a pre-Raphaelite angel. " I can't stay a moment," she said, " But I must say 'Goodnight.' "

His arm went about her, " If only you'd let me take care of you," he said, with a sort of fierce tenderness.

She made a sudden turn towards him, and laid her cheek against his coat: "You are taking care of me, Kit. Just to have you here is — heaven! "

He was moved by that: "My dear one. . . ." He kissed her gently. He felt that she was in need of his gentleness. She was so young and brave and burdened.

III

The next morning the baby was much better, and the nurse proved a treasure, so it was with a free mind that Jacqueline made her plans for the day. She and Kit would spend an hour after breakfast with the Gilman's, then go to Boston to see Mary.

Over the telephone she and Christopher talked about it. He and Sue would be there at eight. It was raining but that need not stop them.

Yolanda protested when she found that she must eat her egg and toast in solitary state. "Didn't Sue ask me to breakfast?"

Kit's World Crashes

"No. Just Uncle Kit and me."

"He isn't my Uncle Kit yet."

"Don't you wish he were?"

Yolanda was honest, "I wish it, if he won't take you away."

Jacqueline had a sudden impulse for confidences: "What would you say if I were to sail — to India . . . ?"

"Oh, you *couldn't*. Not while Mother is sick, and Daddy."

"But when they are well? And back here with you and Hannah?"

"Why can't you live in Salem in his house?"

"Because, he's going out to buy tea in India, and he wants me to go with him."

Yolanda, fire in her eyes, flung out, "I'm never going to be in love with anybody."

"Why not?"

"Oh, it changes people, Aunt Jack. It has changed you. You don't like to be with me as you did. You just want to be with Uncle Kit."

And how could Jacqueline lie before the look in those candid eyes? "Well, anyhow, I love you, darling," was all she could say as she went away to get ready.

Yolanda took her loneliness out to old Hannah. "She didn't ask me."

"Your turn will come, dearie."

"When?"

"When you are a young lady, and men fall in love with you."

"Do you think men will fall in love with me, Hannah?"

"Why not?"

"Did anybody ever fall in love with you, Hannah?"

"Yes, and indeed, my lamb. I wore a pink hat and a pink dress, and he brought me roses."

Yolanda took Hannah's love affair seriously. She saw nothing incongruous in the bonnet and the bunched-up gown. Hannah had been young and had been wooed and won. All the grown-ups had been young, had loved and been loved, her own turn would come.

"Tell be about it," she begged Hannah.

And Hannah who liked nothing better, rehearsed her romance while she seeded raisins for a white fruit cake, and Yolanda, curled in the kitchen rocker, the morning sun shining on her daffodil locks, listened and forgot her wrongs.

And when Hannah had finished, the child said, "May I bring my book and read in the kitchen?"

And Hannah said, "Yes." So Yolanda brought her book, and the fire burned bright, and Hannah baked her cake, and there was a great smell of spiciness, and at last Yolanda looked up from her book and said, "Aren't we happy, Hannah?"

And old Hannah said: "As happy as clams at high tide, my lamb."

Sue Gilman, driving Jacqueline and her lover through the rain was not happy. She wished she had let Kit come over alone. He could not, of course, have suggested it, but the chances were that he would rather

Kit's World Crashes

have had Jacqueline to himself. The night before he had said little about her, but that little had shown how he felt. It was, Sue had realized, a kind of adoration. The kind that men who are virile yet idealistic give to women who meet them in mind and spirit. Kit had always been like that — a vigorous, dauntless youngster, harboring a flock of dreams. . . .

The whole family had waited up to welcome him, and they had done it with open arms. He had kissed Mrs. Gilman and Paula and Phoebe, and then he had kissed Sue. She still felt the touch of his lips on her cheek. . . .

And now here he was, sitting in her little car with Jacqueline between them, and for all that she meant to him Sue might have been a thousand miles away. He saw only Jacqueline — had eyes and ears for no one else. . . .

She broke in on her thoughts, "I hope you two aren't crowded."

"We would be if Jack wasn't so thin. I'm going to fatten her up, Sue. You won't know her when I bring her back from India."

"*India?*"

"Yes. Our wedding trip."

"How soon?"

"As soon as I can get this child to drop her family cares."

Sue's tone had a note of sharpness. "You needn't flatter yourself that she'll ever do that. She has a self-sacrifice complex. What we used to call in the old days 'unselfishness.'"

She saw Kit's hand close over Jacqueline's. "Perhaps we'd better still call it that."

Sue shrugged her shoulders. "Call it what you like. She'll go through life making a door mat of herself. . . ."

She left the subject then to talk of other things. She talked well, and lighted as she was by an inner flame of excitement, her wit and humor sparkled.

She sketched the fortunes of the family since Kit had left them. "Their reaction to the war was priceless. . . . Mother, having no sons, played *grande dame* to the doughboys. Aunt Paula played up to the officers, and Aunt Phoebe played her own little game of being comfortable."

She embroidered the theme, telling how Mrs. Gilman had brought lovely manners to a lot of roughnecks and got no thanks for them. "You should have seen her dining them in six courses. They didn't know what to do with their hands and feet and forks and fingerbowls, and they went right from our house to Skipper Barnes' old joint down by the docks, and had a roaring time with drinks and poker. Mother didn't know that, of course. We kept it from her, and got her to play hostess at the Barrack dances, where she shone upon the warriors from afar.

"Aunt Paula flirted with everything in gold braid and buttons. She always had a lot of young officers about her. And she was never better looking. The whole thing pepped her up. As for Aunt Phoebe, except for the food regulations, she didn't know that the war was on. She had enough to eat and enough to wear, and the rest

Kit's World Crashes 75

of the world might go hang for all she cared. But when they began putting us on war rations, she hid little bags of sweets everywhere. She loves them and she wouldn't be without them. I found chocolate drops under her pillows, and sugar in her jewel box. She was like a wee gray mouse — nibbling."

The gay voice rattled on. Jacqueline, listening, was not sure she liked the things that Sue was saying. It was all very funny, of course, but her own code included silence as to the faults of her family. She wouldn't have talked about Joel and Mary for worlds — not to anybody. But, then, Sue was different. She believed in frankness. She was, in a way, like Yolanda, without Yolanda's deeper sense of values.

At breakfast Kit sat on one side of Mrs. Gilman and Jacqueline on the other. Sue was opposite Kit. She wore a simple morning frock of cinnamon brown. She had taken off her hat and her red hair blazed. It was very beautiful hair with a wave of its own. Her cheeks were flushed, her eyes shining.

Paula, watching her niece, saw the change in her. She had not been lighted up like this for ages. " It is because Kit is here," was the older woman's shrewd deduction. " And he hasn't eyes to see it."

Sue was saying, " He's going to take Jacqueline to India with him."

There was a chorus of exclamations, out of which Jacqueline's voice was heard: " I'll go if I can leave Mary."

Paula weighed that last sentence. Sue was, it seemed, to be reprieved for the moment. And who knew what might happen if Kit went out alone? Men forgot at long distance, and Sue might still have her chance. And why shouldn't she? There might even be a trip to India, with Paula playing chaperone. They had often talked about such a trip, and Sue had been keen for it. "We both have adventuring spirits, and I don't want her to suffer as I have suffered," was Paula's mental defense as her conscience questioned her. And anyhow that child wasn't the mate for him. Anyone could see that. She was charming, but not spectacular. And Kit would need a wife who was a bit spectacular. He had a position to maintain and Sue had money. The Howland house was the place for her. Paula having settled all this to her satisfaction, and having finished her breakfast, lighted a cigarette. Smoking was one of the accomplishments she had acquired during the war, and she was proud of it. She was a pioneer, as it were, of sophistication, in her home town. It gave her a sensation of daring, of youth renewed.

It had been a wonderful breakfast — honey-dew melons, crisp ribbons of bacon, hot rolls and honey, but Jacqueline had eaten little. She had been glad to sit at her ease, her eyes roaming the table, noting the exquisiteness of the linen, the heavy, old-fashioned silver and cut glass, ugly, but adding none-the-less, a touch of elegance. She knew as well as if she had seen it with her own eyes, that this was the way Kit had lived in the house next door, he and his mother with their Canton and Sheffield, and with trim maids moving about the table.

Kit's World Crashes 77

Yet, as she weighed the Gilmans in the balance against the Howlands she was aware of the difference in the two families. Both had pride of race and lived up to it, but Kit had what none of the present generation of Gilmans possessed — an understanding of the fine meaning of democracy. In him was the spirit of the men who had made America — men who, banded together, could make the laws of a nation, who could vote, administer and represent intelligently. Only a weak people needs a dictator. Democracy is the ideal of the strong.

They were all talking together now, leaving her out of it. It seemed to Jacqueline, all at once, as if everybody wanted to claim Kit, to make him theirs, while she, who was to be the wife of his heart, was shut out. She knew she was unreasonable to be thinking such thoughts. It was her own fault since she had been too tired to exert herself as she might — but, oh, she wished that she and Kit were alone — shut away from the world — together.

Then suddenly, as if he *knew,* Kit glanced at his watch: " Great guns, do you know what time it is? And Jack and I are due in Boston by noon." He rose and laid his hand on Jacqueline's shoulder, " Can you tear yourself away? "

The look he bent on her was the answer to all that Paula had been thinking. She was stirred to anger by the sight of his devotion. Here was a thing she had lost in her life, and now Sue was losing it.

But to Jacqueline the touch of her lover's hand was a

glory — like that of the moon at night! And when Kit got her at last into the train, he said, "I wanted you to myself."

"Did you, Kit, really?"

"My darling, yes."

IV

Joel and Kit! Army and Navy! Both of them hating war. Yet both ready to fight again for a worthy cause!

Jacqueline loved to see them together. Joel was to lunch with them, then drive with them to the Hospital to call on Mary. He limped down the corridor beside Christopher. He had done away with his crutches. The two men towered tall. Joel was big and bulky and handsome, his dark hair brushed straight back from his forehead, his little black moustache, his brown eyes with their quick glances. Kit's slenderness and freshness of skin stood out in almost boyish contrast to Joel's swarthiness. Many eyes were upon them when, having been whirled along the snowy streets for a few moments in a taxi, they entered the big hotel in Copley Square and made their way to the dining-room. Many eyes rested also with appreciation on the slender child between the two tall men. She wore a not-so-new coat of gray squirrel and a small round hat that matched. But the ends of a sapphire scarf knotted in the opening of the coat, brought out the color of her eyes, and there was about her as she looked up first at one big man and then at the other, an air of soft radiance that was enchanting.

Christopher was host. The two men got on very well

Kit's World Crashes

together although their acquaintance had been short. They matched experiences, eagerly, as they scanned the menu. "Go to it, Joel," Kit said, "these are the days we eat. Shall we have onion soup and an omelette in memory of our days in Paris? And new asparagus? Vinaigrette?"

Joel thought not. "If you'll leave it to me, I'll have an English mutton chop. Heavy and hearty. They've been giving me fluff at the hospital."

"Jacqueline?"

"May I have what I want?"

"Yes."

"Chicken salad and chocolate ice-cream."

"My dear...."

"Oh, I know ... it's bromidic, Kit. But it was always what Mary and I had on high feasts and holidays — and this is such a high feast —"

Joel broke in, "If only we had Mary with us ... !"

"When she's well enough," Kit said, "I'll give a party. We'll all doll up and dine here and go to a play afterwards...."

At the end of the feast they drank Mary's health in little cups of coffee. Their hopes were high. There in the rose-lighted dining-room, with its Yuletide decorations, its mirthful music, its laughing crowds, the shadows which had hung over them lifted. Mary would be better soon; they would bring her here, and she would make a quartette of their trio. Life would swing back to its old careless happiness. The things that the war had brought would be forgotten....

So a little later, they came to the Hospital, bringing into Mary's white still room, a sense of vitality which lifted her for the moment out of the languor which had chained her for days, and enabled her to welcome them with a sort of smiling ardor. " Merry Christmas, my darlings," she cried.

" Are you including me? " Christopher asked her.

She reached out her hand to him, " Why not? You are one of us."

He kissed the hand, " You are being very good to me."

Joel had the other hand, and now bent over her, " Better, sweetheart? "

" I'm not sure," she seemed to sink deeper among her pillows, " they said it was all right for you to come today. And that's a step forward. Yesterday — they wouldn't. But they gave me your flowers and showed me my presents. . . ."

Yolanda had made her mother a handkerchief, helped by Hannah, who had washed and ironed it. It lay beside Mary on the bed and she spoke of it. " Wasn't it wonderful of her . . . such a little thing . . . my little . . . little girl . . ." she broke suddenly into wild weeping. " Oh, I want to go home, Joel, to see my children. . . . Ask them to let me go . . . home. . . ."

Joel could not soothe her, nor Jacqueline. The nurse came in: " I think you'd better leave her."

" Let Joel stay — a little longer," Mary begged.

Jacqueline and her lover waited outside. " Oh, Kit, she's worse."

" What makes you say that? "

Kit's World Crashes

"Oh, there's a look about her . . . different. . . ."

Joel joining them, presently, confirmed Jacqueline's fears. "I'm going straight to the surgeon. The nurse says he left word I could see him at his house. And I want the two of you with me."

The surgeon's house was on Beacon Hill. The butler who opened the door for them showed them into the great drawing-room. Kit and Jacqueline were left to wait there while Joel went into the doctor's study.

Jacqueline, sitting with Christopher on one of the brocaded sofas was aware of children in the hall. They were going up and down the stairs, the little girls like puff-balls in their white dresses, the little boys in snowy blouses and velvet shorts with shining pumps on their twinkling feet. They were playing a game which involved much running about and much laughter, and now and then a youngster would rush in and hide behind the curtains of the drawing-room, yet so absorbed were they in the adventure that they had only cursory glances for the two grown-ups on the sofa. Jacqueline thought of Yolanda. How she would love such a party! They hadn't had a party since Patsy left them. The last had been the one when they had sung "London Bridge," and Mary had been so unhappy. And now Joel was back . . . and Mary knew that he loved her. . . .

Joel was gone a long time, and when he came out the surgeon was with him. The look on Joel's face made Jacqueline's heart stop beating. She stood up as if to receive a judge's sentence. And Christopher stood up with her.

It was the surgeon who spoke. "I've been telling

Mr. Hutchins," he said, "and he has asked me to tell you, some rather distressing news. We find that Mrs. Hutchins' trouble is likely to be chronic."

Jacqueline felt a sudden lift of spirits, "Oh, then . . . she isn't going to . . . leave us? I was afraid of . . . that."

"No. But there's little hope that she will ever be well. The trouble is with her spine. She will have to stay in bed. It is hard to say how long. Perhaps — always. . . ."

Mary in bed . . . ALWAYS!

Jacqueline began to tremble. Oh, she couldn't stand a thing like that. She couldn't . . . !

Kit was holding tight to her hand, but suddenly she dragged it away from him. There was poor Joel. . . . Joel who had dropped into a chair and was sobbing, his head bent upon his hands. She went to him and put an arm about his shoulders. "Joel," she said, "Joel . . . I'll stay with you and take care of Mary. I've got to take care of — Mary."

Christopher stood alone in the middle of the room. His world crashed about him. She had gone straight to Joel. Her love for Mary transcended everything. It transcended her love for him who loved her so dearly, so desperately, as he now saw her slipping away from him.

Yet when she lifted her head, and he saw her groping in the blindness of her tears, he went to her and held her to his breast. "Hush," he said, "my dearest. Things will work out for us. Things will work out. . . . They must."

CHAPTER FOUR

Alarm Bells Tolling!

I

INDIA? The rich garment in which life was to wrap herself and her lover? The honeymoon on the high seas? The old house in Salem, and the angel-guarded cradle?

Dreams all of them! Never to be fulfilled! For Mary was going to be ill — forever! Never well! Years and years to pass away without ever a touch of her foot to the floor, or to stand tall and straight in her golden beauty.

Mary with pillows back of her! Mary with nurses always about her! Mary . . . !

Jacqueline stopped there . . . perhaps there wouldn't be nurses. Perhaps Joel couldn't afford it. Perhaps there would be only herself and old Hannah. Perhaps Hannah would grow too old, and there would be just herself!

And Yolanda! Yolanda growing up! Yolanda taking her place by her mother's bed! Yolanda the head of the house. . . . Yolanda!

For the first time a glimmer of hope. . . . Yolanda!

How many years before Yolanda could take her place? The child was ten. Eight years more — nine? And then Jacqueline and Kit could have their happiness. She would be twenty-six, Kit in his late thirties. But why should that matter? Many men and women didn't marry before that? And Kit loved her. He would wait till the end of the world. He had said it, but there hadn't been much hope in it. "I'll go out alone, Jack, if you think best . . . and I'll wait — forever. . . ."

That had been the afternoon when they came back from the Hospital. They had had to leave Joel at *his* Hospital, but they had promised to go up the next day and talk things over. There would be so much to talk over. "Great guns," Joel had said, "I've got to get well. I've got to get into business. There'll be no living on this infernal pension and making Mary comfortable."

He had had only one idea — that Mary must be comfortable. It had brought him out of his depression, steadied him, swung him away from the things the war had done to him. "And you needn't think I am going to let this spoil your life for you, Jack. If you'll just help out until I get started. She can do that, can't she, Kit — help until I get started?"

"She can do," said Kit, "anything she wishes."

It was then that, for the first time, Jacqueline noticed the change in him. Something gone of the flashing laughter in his eyes; something gone of that carefree cock of his head. Nothing gone of his tenderness, but something out of his voice. . . . She couldn't quite de-

Alarm Bells Tolling!

fine it. It was as if a bird in a cage still sang, but had lost some thrilling note.

They had talked about it on the train. "If the business hadn't smashed up, I'd put them all in my house in Salem, hire nurses for Mary, and carry you off to India."

"Joel wouldn't let you do it, and anyhow nurses couldn't take care of the children."

Kit had flamed, "They're not your children."

"They'll need me, Kit."

"I need you. . . ."

Her hand had crept into his, "I know. . . ."

They had been silent after that, and it was not until they reached home and had dined, and were again in front of the living-room fire, that they thrashed the thing out to the end.

"I shall never ask you," Christopher said, "to go against your will. Perhaps I could make you do it. I think I could. I could so press upon you my need of you that you'd be sorry to see me — suffer. . . ."

He was leaning forward, staring into the fire, his face stern. "For I shall suffer — have no doubt of that. And I shall suffer not only because you would not go, but because your first thought today was not of me, but of Joel and Mary. If you call that selfish, then let it stand that way. But if you think it best to stay, you must stay. I'll go out alone, Jack . . . and I'll wait — forever."

She had been sitting on the other side of the fire, but now she came over and knelt beside him. "Kit, look at me."

He did not look at her, but his arm went round her. "Kit, are you blaming me? Don't you know that I, too, suffer?"

"God knows I do. That's why I hate it. Do you think all my fear is for myself? It's because I know you're made of the stuff of saints and martyrs. It's because I know you love every little helpless thing. It's because I know your tenderness." He held her to him. "It's because I know you'll lose youth and joy in an unequal battle. . . ."

She tried to explain. "It's something in me, Kit, that won't let me go, and leave them. And if I went, I shouldn't be — happy."

His arm relaxed. "Not with me?"

"Kit — try to understand." Her face was white and troubled.

She was still kneeling beside him, and now he put his hands on her shoulders and looked down at her. As long as she lived, she was never to forget that look. "You are what you are," he said, "I am not sure I would have you — different. You are what God made you — dear one."

II

The next afternoon they went up to see Joel. Kit was still staying with the Gilmans. "They asked me about Mary. They sent much sympathy."

"Did you tell them that I wouldn't go out with you?"

Alarm Bells Tolling! 87

"Yes. Sue was waiting last night when I got there. I felt a bit broken up, and we sat by the fire and talked. I told her that we would have to put things off."

"What did she say?"

"Oh, that we were dead wrong. She made me feel that a man wasn't red-blooded who wouldn't pack a woman in his old kit bag and run away with her."

"Oh, Kit, if we only could — run away."

They were having lunch together in Boston. Not this time at the big hotel, but at Christopher's pet club in Park Street, where you had lobsters fresh from the sea, and a huge and superlative kind of macaroon with a special and superlative ice-cream, and where the windows at the back looked out on an old cemetery and the graves of the distinguished dead.

"I'll run away now," Kit said, "come on."

She shook her head, "What did Sue say about me?"

He hesitated.

"Tell me, Kit."

"She said that if she were in love with a man and he wanted her to go, she would think the world well lost. That a woman's life was her own to live and that no one had a right to stand in the way of it."

"What did you say to that?"

"I told her she didn't know what she was talking about. That she had never had any more sense of responsibility than a cat with a family of grown-up kittens. And she flung back at me that I lived my own life."

"What did she mean?"

"Oh, it's an old story. . . . When my father was alive, I loved him, Jack . . . but he dominated me. He dominated my mother . . . that's the reason I won't impose my will on you. You shall do freely the things you want to do. We men are arbitrary creatures. We want to feel that we are right and to have our womenfolk feel it. Yet even as a boy I knew it was often my mother and not my father who was right, and she knew it, but she acquiesced that she might preserve the serenity of the household. For he loved her, and he was never harsh, only masterful. Too masterful by far. And one day I decided to go to Boston, and get a place in my uncle's warehouse. I told my mother I was going, and my reasons, and she agreed that I was right. There was no actual break with my father, but from that time on I was my own man. When he died, I went back and lived in Salem with my mother, but I still had my offices in Boston."

"I know now what Sue meant. She said you didn't care for the old house, and that if you said you did, you were sentimentalizing."

He laughed, "The Gilmans didn't know why I left, and I think they always blamed me. Sue especially resented it. We had been such pals, and she missed her playmate."

Jacqueline broke off a bit of macaroon, crumbled it on her plate, and asked a question. "Kit, why isn't Sue married?"

He laughed again, "Give her time, my dear."

"No. . . . I don't mean that. . . . I mean, she's so attractive, and yet there doesn't seem to be anybody."

Alarm Bells Tolling!

"In love with her? Oh, well, she'll come to it like the rest of you." He dropped then the subject of Sue to talk of the old house in Salem. "I have cared more for it since I have thought of you in it, Jack."

She told him of the friendly spirits, but she did not tell him all her dreams. Time enough for that when they were married.

Joel, when they saw him later, was still spurred by a determination to go to work. "My old firm has offered me a berth. Of course I'm a bit hampered by nerves and all that, but I'll snap out of it."

There was, too, it seemed some money in bonds, kept untouched through all the stringent days for the sake of Mary and the children — "if anything happened." But now Joel would use it to bring Mary home. "She can't stay in the hospital away from us all, and besides it eats up our income. We'll take on old Hannah for full time, and that will leave Jack free to look after Mary."

Free to look after Mary! And when she was looking after Mary, who would look after little Joel? And Yolanda? A black wave of fear threatened to engulf Jacqueline, but she breasted it and smiled. "We'll manage somehow, Joel."

"I always said you were a good sport, old girl."

But being called a "good sport" is poor consolation, when in the darkness of the night one lies awake and faces the future, and sees no glimmering beyond the growing up of a little girl, with eight years between. Could she keep on being a good sport until Yolanda should take her place? Jacqueline, on that night after seeing Joel, asked herself the question and dared not answer it. In search of sleep she turned on her restless pillow. At last she got up and looked out of the window. Heavy clouds shut out the moon and the stars. A heavy night, and one that promised storm. Well, life was like that, and when the storms came, would they beat her down?

Kit had raged when they had left Joel. "Do you think I'm going to stand for it?"

"Mary has done so much for me, dearest."

"You've paid your debt."

Tears were near the surface. "I can't argue," she had said. "I only know."

Kit had brought her to North Station and had put her on the train. He was to go to New York that night, and come back for the week end. Three days in between! "I don't know how I shall live without you," he had said, ardently, her hand tight in his in the taxi. "But I'll call you up every day."

Yet when he was in India, he couldn't call her up . . . !

The next morning, she told old Hannah all about it. Yolanda was at school, the baby asleep after his bath. Hannah was cleaning the silver which was set out on the kitchen table. Mary had little silver worthy of notice, except a fat teaset that had poured tea in an English drawing-room six generations back.

"I think I am honest," Hannah had said, as Jacqueline came into the kitchen, "but if I ever steal anything it will be that teaset. It's what I call a comfortable teaset. I'll bet in the old days they served hearty things with it — muffins and cheese cakes and plum tarts. . . .

Alarm Bells Tolling!

I had an English grandmother, and she used to tell about it. . . ."

But for once Jacqueline was not interested in teasets. "Hannah," she said, "I had a dreadful night."

"Did you, honey lamb? Tell me about it."

Jacqueline curled herself up in the rocking chair. There were dark shadows under her eyes. "We saw Mary's doctor yesterday. He says she isn't going to get well."

Hannah dropped her hands heavily on the table, "Don't tell me that," she cried.

"I don't mean that she's going to — die . . ." Jacqueline elucidated, "only she'll always be ill — in bed — it's her spine."

Without moving, old Hannah listened, while Jacqueline added further details. "It will change all of our plans, of course," she said.

Something in her voice made the old woman ask, "You don't mean that you'll put off your wedding?"

"Yes. I can't leave Mary. . . ."

Hannah picked up her cloth and began rubbing the teapot. Out of a short silence, she said, "Will they bring Mrs. Hutchins home?"

"Yes, and Joel wants to know if you can give us full time, Hannah. Come here to the house and stay. We can give you a good room, and, with you to do the work, I can look after the children and my sister."

Hannah stopped rubbing. "You can do nothing of the kind."

"Why not?"

"You'll just kill yourself, Miss Jack."

"We can't afford nurses, Hannah."

Again silence, and then Hannah said, "I'll come. But you'd better go on and get married. You have a right to your own life."

"Everybody tells me that." Jacqueline sat up, a vivid and demanding figure. "But how can I? How can I?"

Old Hannah sat with the teapot suspended. "You can't, dear lamb. Some women could. But not you."

"I want to go with Kit," Jacqueline said, wildly, "I want to go. . . . I don't want to stay here. Oh, why is God so cruel, Hannah, to let such things happen? The war? And Little Patsy? And Joel's leg? And now, Mary! It is like something way back in the Bible — Job or Jeremiah. . . ."

It would have been funny if it hadn't been so tragic. Here was a slip of a child challenging the high gods! But old Hannah saw nothing funny in it. "God isn't cruel," she said. "It is men who are cruel. And Death isn't the worst. And we can't change things no matter how we cry out. And we can't whine. Miss Jack, if you've made up your mind to do it, don't go on being sorry for yourself."

"I know. . . . I'm not sorry for myself. But Kit . . . oh, Hannah, he's — unhappy."

Old Hannah laid down the teapot and her cleaning cloth, went over to the sink and washed her hands, then came back and gathered into her arms the child who was weeping so wildly. "Honey lamb, honey lamb," she said, and after that they rocked and rocked with

Alarm Bells Tolling!

only the sound of Jacqueline's lessening sobs in the silence.

"Prayer," said old Hannah at last, and apparently with irrelevance, "is something in the heart, and not always on your knees. Remember that, Miss Jack. You are doing what you set out to do for those you love. God knows that and will bring happiness to you in His own good time. And if it isn't the happiness you ask for now, it will be happiness just the same."

"I know. . . ."

But Jacqueline did not know. It was not until years had passed that she was to understand what old Hannah meant. "And the great thing, after all, isn't happiness. It's to do good and be good. That's old-fashioned enough, Miss Jack, but you'll find that it works out. It was what the knights in the old stories went forth to do — to fight evil and do good, and sometimes they died — fighting —"

There was a Spartan quality in the things the old woman said that acted like a tonic. "Dear Hannah," said Jacqueline, clinging, "dear Hannah."

III

Long distance talks from New York with Christopher. Special delivery letters. Telegrams. Boxes of candy. Boxes of flowers. Books.

Yolanda was thrilled and excited. "Is that what they do when they love you?" she demanded, when, in the midst of getting her ready for a children's party, there arrived a marvellous basket of sweets for her aunt.

Jacqueline, reading the card, said, " Yes."

" What makes them? "

" They want you to be happy."

" Are you happy, Aunt Jack? "

"Not so happy as I would be if Uncle Kit wasn't going away."

"I thought you were going with him, Aunt Jack."

" Not until mother is — better — darling."

She went on brushing Yolanda's hair. The child had been told that her mother was coming home and would have to stay in bed, but she had been given no hint of the dreadful future. She accepted her mother's invalidism and the fact of Aunt Jack's not going to India philosophically. "Oh, well, when mother is better, Uncle Kit can come back, and you'll live happily ever after."

Fairy tales! How often Jacqueline had told them to Yolanda — " And the prince and princess lived happily ever after! "

Well, life wasn't like that. Nobody was really happy! Always she had looked at the world through rose-colored glasses. Making the best of things! And there was no best. Kit was going away, going away, going away — no golden bells rang now in her heart . . . only alarm bells — tolling!

" You're pulling my hair," Yolanda protested. " I wish mother would let me have it cut."

"Perhaps she will when she comes, darling."

Alarm Bells Tolling!

"May I have four pieces of candy to take to my friends?"

"More than four if you wish."

"No, I want one for my very best friend, and one for the next, and one for the next," Yolanda's voice trailed off into silence, as she bent over the basket.

Having made her selection, she straightened up. "I think Uncle Kit is perfectly adorable. When I grow up I am going to marry a man just like him."

Jacqueline kissed her, "There aren't any men just like him, darling."

"Well, I'm going to pray every night that God will send me one."

A little later, Jacqueline watching Yolanda from the window reflected that in these days her own prayers had been somewhat neglected. That is, formal prayers. But in her heart she had prayed that strength might come.

And now, suddenly, seeing the child go happily along the snowy street, there stirred in Jacqueline a sense of the meaning of it all. Here was Yolanda growing up—needing a mother. A need greater than Kit's or her own. This was the answer for which she had prayed. The reason for self-sacrifice. And not only the reason but the justification. And with this reason and justification came a sureness of purpose. The thing must be done, and if it must be done, why not do it gloriously? There should be no more tears for Kit, for herself. They had still two months together. They would live them at topnotch. And have faith in the future.

So, true to that sanguine self, which wrung courage from defeat, she wrote that night to her lover, "Oh, Kit, let's be happy in the little time we have left. You said when you first heard the news about Mary that things would work out. Let us believe that they will. Let's believe that Mary will get better, or that Joel will get rich, or that your ship will come sailing in with a cargo of diamonds! Let's believe *anything* but that we must live apart. Sometimes I think that wishing brings things to pass. Let's bring them, dearest."

Kit, reading the letter at his Boston club where he arrived the day before New Year's, smiled over it. She was still putting-her-best-foot-forward, bless her. As for himself he had little hope. Human relationships were so complicated. Human sacrifices seemed at times so futile. Might not one eat, drink and be merry and let the rest go hang? He stood at the window and looked down on the old graveyard and the distinguished dead. They, too, had hoped and suffered, had lived out their lives, and now lay quietly at rest. Yet there must have been a meaning in it all, a Plan. Christopher believed in the meaning, in the Plan. The faith of his fathers was in him. He had held to it through all the horrors of war, he would hold to it now.

He called up Jacqueline. "I'm coming down to answer your letter."

"Did you like it?"

"I'll tell you when I see you. . . ."

"Tell me now!"

"Not at long distance," she caught the note of emo-

Alarm Bells Tolling!

tion in his voice, and flung back. "Oh, Kit . . . hurry . . . !"

"I can't possibly make it until after dinner. But we'll see the old year out together."

"The Gilmans want us over for a midnight supper. They are having a lot of people in."

"My dear child — must we go?"

"I'm afraid so. They are really having it for you."

"Can't you call it off? I'm no returned hero to be trotted out."

"I knew you'd hate it. But Sue has set her heart on it."

"I see. Oh, well, I suppose we're in for it."

"It's going to be rather a grand party, Kit, and I've nothing in the world to wear."

"Tell me your size, and I'll bring you something."

"Kit, dear, I *couldn't.*"

"Why not? If I had my way I'd wrap you in gossamer and gold."

"I know. Well, there's my old blue taffeta. . . ."

"You look like an angel in it. . . ."

IV

So she wore the blue taffeta, and Kit brought her a knot of pink roses tied with silver ribbon, and as she came into the great drawing-room at the Gilmans and as he saw her moving about among the other women, he thought how delicate she seemed and fine among all the gorgeous glittering ladies.

For Sue wore white, silver-spangled, and Paula was in green with the family emeralds set in a pendant which hung from a long gold chain, and studded the golden band about her hair, and a lot of the other women had diamonds dripping all over them, but Jacqueline wore only the ring her lover had given her, and the bracelet he had brought overseas.

He wanted her to meet everybody. There were all his old friends, and some day she would take her place among them. But she had insisted that the engagement should not be announced. " People talk such a lot. And it's nobody's business but ours, darling."

" I know. But I want to shout it to the world."

The midnight supper was a wonderful affair. Everyone sat down at the long table which was set with all the tinkling, twinkling glass and silver which had graced the boards of bygone Gilmans. There were red roses in the tall epergnes, and red candles in the tall holders. The food was delectable, creamed oysters in pastry cases, chicken salad and crab salad in mounds on platters, boned turkey in aspic, lobster Newberg in chafing dishes, ice-cream in meringue shells. There were things to drink brought up from a pre-war cellar, and Mrs. Gilman at one end of the table in mauve velvet and diamonds, and Miss Phoebe at the other in gray velvet and pearls looked out over all of it and assured themselves that nothing was lacking in all the old elegances and the old abundances which had belonged to the past.

Alarm Bells Tolling! 99

When the bells rang the new year in, a song was sung, a toast was drunk, and Kit was called upon to say something to his friends.

He rose, and stood for a moment smiling at them as they applauded. Then he raised his head and spoke, and Jacqueline, listening, was amazingly aware that here was a Kit she had not known — a Kit at his ease in this brilliant assemblage, a man of the world, a wit. She had thought of him simply as her Kit, brave, strong, splendid. And in the war as a man among men. She had not thought of him with this social background, with people like these for his friends. None of them could point to a more distinguished ancestry than her own, but where her forbears had known plain living and high thinking, in the families of those about this table had been money for generations, ease of pocket-book, social intercourse of a kind which demands large means and the freedom of action which comes with affluence.

And when she was his wife, these would be her friends, and she must take her place among them. She must shine as Kit shone. She must wear glittering gowns like Paula, and Kit would have the family jewels set for her. She began to feel frightened. Would she measure up? Could she?

Then, suddenly, there swept over her the memory of Kit's financial limitations. He would be poor for a long time. And she was glad of it. She would grow with Kit's fortunes, and perhaps by the time he had what he wanted in worldly goods, she would learn to be all he needed in a wife. He had told her that his own father's fortune had been swept away when New England's railroads went to pieces. She had been sorry then, but she wasn't sorry now. She and Kit would work together. There would be no hint of the beggar maid in their bargain.

When Kit sat down, Paula, who sat near Jacqueline, leaned across the man next to her and said, "Aren't you proud of him?"

Jacqueline's breath was quick. "He's wonderful—"

Paula nodded and settled back in her seat. She talked to the man beside her, but her mind was not on him. It was on Sue who sat on the other side of the table. Sue, who, in her white and silver, had listened, still as a statue, while Kit spoke, her heart in her eyes. "Oh, she's mad to show it that way," Paula raged, inwardly, "she ought to have more pride." Yet no one else seemed to notice. "It's because I care so much for her," Paula reassured herself.

When they rose from the table, Paula said to Jacqueline, "Is Kit staying over tomorrow?"

"No, he goes back to Boston, then on again to New York."

"Then why not ride with me in the afternoon? I'll drive over and get you. Sue is going up to town, and I'll give you a breath of fresh air if you'll let me be her substitute."

"I'd love it."

Paula smiled and went on to other guests. Moving among them in her green gown, her russet hair banded with emeralds, she gave an effect of almost youthful

Alarm Bells Tolling!

beauty, so that people noticed it and spoke of it: "She's holding her own."

And Paula heard them saying that, and hated it!

The fun, after supper, grew fast and furious. Women wearing paper caps and men blowing horns danced in the wide hall where the rugs had been taken up. Paula, with a crowd about her, was serving punch. Sue, also the center of a crowd, had avid eyes for Kit. She saw him join Jacqueline, but she did not hear what he said.

"Let's get out of this, Jack. I've had enough."

"Kit, you're wonderful."

He looked down at her, "I'm not fond of the limelight," he said, abruptly, "we'll say 'good-bye' to everybody and get away."

But saying "good-bye" was not so easy as it sounded. People caught at Kit here and there, so that even when Jacqueline, wrapped in her shabby squirrel coat, stood waiting for her lover, he was held by one and another of the now thoroughly exhilarated guests.

At last he was free, and as he swept her with him out into the night, a fine snow blew in their faces. They went down the walk, but, instead of helping her into the car which had brought them over and which stood waiting, he turned towards his own old house, and opened the gate. "Let's run in here, Jack, for a moment. I have the key."

Then, as the big door swung back, he leaned down and lifted Jacqueline in his arms, "I'll carry you over the threshold — darling —" he whispered.

Her heart was beating wildly. So quickly had it all

been done that there had been no time to protest. Nor would she have protested if she had had the time. He had closed the door behind him and they stood in the deep darkness together. "We're under my own roof tree, dearest, and it's New Year's morning."

"It isn't my own roof yet, Kit."

"But it will be some day, no doubt of that dearest," he still had her in his arms. "Jack, don't think I've lost my mind to bring you here in this mad fashion. But when you sat at the table it was to you I spoke — so quiet and lovely. But I didn't want your quietness and loveliness there — in all that glare. I didn't want to welcome the New Year in with that howling crowd. I wanted you here — here. I wanted to welcome the New Year with you — in our own house, Jack — on our knees!"

Oh, friendly spirits draw near to them! Youth and ecstasy! But more than that, ecstasy mingled with exaltation. Youth consecrate to an ideal. All about them were beating golden wings. Never again, perhaps, would they know such a moment. But it was enough that they had known it!

V

All the next morning, Jacqueline went about the house, singing. Kit had gone to New York again, and it would be a week before she would see him. But she did not need to see him. They were together in spirit. They would always be together. The exaltation of the night before had not left her.

Alarm Bells Tolling!

Paula, arriving in the afternoon in her little car, said, "Sue went in to Boston on the train with Kit. The rest of us stayed in bed until noon."

"I slept four hours."

"You ought to be napping that minute instead of riding with me. But then, you don't need a beauty sleep." Paula smiled as she flung out the bit of flattery. She was weighing the happiness in the sapphire eyes, the radiance which seemed to wrap the child in a shining mantle. It seemed a pity to spoil it — but then there had been Sue the night before, stripping off her white and silver gown, and coming into Paula's room as the dawn broke, clad in a flaming robe that matched her hair, so that as she sat on Paula's bed, with her knees drawn up under her chin, she was like a figure carved in copper.

"Aunt Paula, what spoiled your romance?"

"Pride."

"Do you mind telling me about it?"

"I have never told anyone."

"I know — but we Gilmans are unlucky in love. There must be a reason."

Paula, propped up on her pillows, looking her age and more than her age, with her head tied up in a green silk handkerchief and an embroidered Japanese coat about her shoulders, said, "We try to dominate — and strong men want to rule."

"Oh, but that's archaic."

"No. Men and women haven't changed much since the world began." Paula chose another cigarette from a silver case set with jade. "You know, of course, that I went to visit Billy Walton's people and came back with the engagement broken. Well, I wanted to be queen on my throne and Billy wanted to be king. And one day when I was there he asked me while we were all at table to wear a certain dress to a dance that night. There was no reason why I shouldn't wear it, but I didn't. I came down in something else. Everybody knew he had asked me, and he was hurt. It was a silly thing to quarrel about, but we quarrelled. I wanted to show my power, and I wouldn't say I was sorry. Then, suddenly, in the very midst of our argument, I was aware I had gone too far. I was frightened, but I wouldn't back down. I broke the engagement before he could do it," she blew smoke rings into the air. "Pride, you see, Sue, and I've suffered for it."

"But I've never been proud with — Kit — " Sue stopped there, and gave Paula a startled glance.

"Oh, don't mind me," Paula said, "I've known how you felt for a long time."

"It's been since I was a little girl," Sue told her in a tense voice. "I can't remember when I didn't care for Kit."

"And how did you show him?" Paula demanded. "By trying to beat him in everything when you were a child, and by taunting him with lack of courage when he was too polite to be rude. . . ."

"I know," Sue said miserably, "and I do it now. Just the other day I told him he wasn't red-blooded — "

There was a moment's silence, out of which Paula

Alarm Bells Tolling!

remarked, "Things work out. Life may bring you more than you are looking for, Sue."

"How can it, without making Jacqueline unhappy?"

"She might as well be unhappy as you."

"But I wouldn't steal her happiness. I'm too sporting for that, Paula, even if I could do it."

After Sue left her, Paula lay thinking about it. Sue would never take what she might have. Some one else would have to turn the trick for her.

And now riding beside Jacqueline in her little car, Paula said again to herself that it seemed a pity. Why couldn't everybody be happy? Perhaps they would. Kit wasn't the only man in the world.

The snow of the night before had piled up in drifts, and made the going a bit difficult, but the sky was clear and the air like wine. Paula drove Jacqueline to an austere little tea-room on the North Shore which was open in winter for those who thought it worth while to motor out and enjoy its reticences.

For this tea-room gave no thought to the demands of hearty appetites. The tea was pale, but hot and strong. There was thin bread and butter. There were thin, crisp cookies. There were delicate glasses of currants put up in honey. The toast was small and square and melted in your mouth. As for the rest, the room in which the tea was served had gray rugs on well-scrubbed boards, there was yellow paint, and a clear crackling fire. There were no pseudo-antiques, or gift-shop accessories. They were waited on by a tall thin woman with gray hair. She wore a fresh gingham dress and a white apron, and was as restful as her surroundings.

"Like it?" Paula asked Jacqueline.

"I love it."

"You won't have things like this in India." Paula said it with an effect of carelessness. She had ordered their tea, and was seated opposite Jacqueline at a little table by the window, which looked out on a snowy street beyond which was a view of the sea, ultramarine under the afternoon sky.

"But I'm not going to India," Jacqueline said. "Didn't Sue tell you?"

"Yes. She thought you were very foolish. But I'm not sure. It might be a great adventure, and it might not."

"Going with Kit would be."

"Perhaps. One never can tell. And anyhow, since you're not going now, you'll both of you have time to know your own minds."

Jacqueline laughed, "I think we know them now."

"Not as you will when you are separated. Long distance makes things seem different. As I understand it there's to be no engagement."

"Not an announced one."

Paula hesitated, then said, frankly, "My dear, I think you're making a great mistake to tie yourself up to any engagement. It isn't fair to you. Suppose you should change . . . ?"

"But I shan't change."

Paula screwed her cigarette down into a little dish, "You don't know what may happen. And besides — it isn't fair — to Kit."

Alarm Bells Tolling!

Dead silence, out of which Jacqueline demanded: "What do you mean, that it isn't fair to Kit?"

"Oh, a man is different from a woman. He can't live on letters and dreams. Kit will want a home, a wife. Yet if you have his promise, how can he break it? He will feel bound — in honor."

"Kit won't want to break it."

Paula shrugged her shoulders. "You know him best, of course. And I'm sorry I said so much. It really isn't my affair, is it? But I like you both. . . ." Tea had been brought, and she began to pour. "Isn't everything perfect?" she said, as her eyes swept the tray. "I hope you have brought your appetite with you, Jacqueline."

But Jacqueline ate little. A shadow had fallen across her radiance. Paula saw it but steeled her heart. The child might as well face it now as later. Men wanted reality, not illusion. And Kit Howland was no different from the rest of them.

CHAPTER FIVE

The Impregnable Tower

I

JOEL was home again, and the whole house was in a state of flux. Nothing was as it had been. Joel, having a masterful trend of mind and having so lately commanded men, brought military tactics into domestic matters. Jacqueline found herself constantly with pencil and paper in her hands, making lists of this or that. Menus. Orders for Hannah. Things to be moved upstairs. Things to be moved down. Joel had a passion for tabulation. All the old easy-going methods which had contented Jacqueline and Hannah were abolished. Housekeeping, Joel contended, was an exact science. Half the labor might be saved by adopting a systematic schedule.

"I hope you don't mind, Hannah," Jacqueline said to the old woman, one morning when Joel had left them with orders for the day.

"Not me, my dear. He'll get over it."

"I'm not sure that he will, Hannah."

"Then we'll put up with it and not worry, my lamb."

They all worked like mad to get the big front room

The Impregnable Tower

ready for Mary. Everything was in rose color. "She'll need it, my poor girl," Joel had said to Jacqueline, as they had looked over the samples of chintzes for the chair covers and over-curtains.

That was the lovely thing about Joel. His tenderness for Mary. Wonderful! He spared no expense, and Jacqueline was at times apprehensive. "Ought we to spend so much, Joel?"

"We must. For her. And I'm not worried about the future. I've a brain if I haven't two legs."

His courage was amazing. Not once since his breakdown in the surgeon's room had Jacqueline heard a whimper. It was as if Mary's weakness had flung a challenge to his strength. And he had taken on family cares as he had never done in the old days. Baby Joey, he decided, was to sleep in the little room next to his father's. "You'll have enough of him, Jack, during the day."

Yolanda and her father got along well together. Except for one thing. She refused as she refused with everyone to surrender her will to his. He might use military tactics with the rest of the world, but not with his small daughter. "I don't see why you told me to do that, Daddy," she would say, when he issued certain commands.

"It is enough that I have told you."

"It isn't enough, of course, Daddy, but I'll do it," and so judicial was her tone, so utterly divorced from impertinence, that Joel was at a loss how to meet the situation.

"What would you do with her?" he asked his sister-in-law.

"There isn't anything to do," Jacqueline told him, "Yolanda is Yolanda."

As for herself, Jacqueline avoided issues. Joel was not her husband. Yolanda was not her child. She had already been made aware in the days since Joel's return from the hospital that her position in the house was not authoritative. She had the responsibilities, but not the perquisites. She did everything that Mary had done, but it was Joel who decided things. She wished sometimes that she were older and wiser. "He treats me as if I were a child. . . ."

Yet he had his moments of confidence and consultation, when he would sit on the other side of the fire and discuss ways and means, and listen to her small advices as if he meant to follow them.

But he never did follow them, and she wondered sometimes if it would always go on like this — or if some day she would rise up and demand the just dues of her efforts and intelligence.

She dared not speak to Kit of her problems. He was impatient enough as it was of the situation. He had been away for two weeks, and in two weeks more he would be sailing. Jacqueline pushed the thought of that parting from her. She felt she could not let him go. She couldn't. . . .

He had written to her of certain matters of business. "Some of it has to do with you, my darling. I've made my will, and you're to have the old house if anything happens to me."

The Impregnable Tower

She had written back, "Kit, if anything happens to you, I shan't want the house. There won't be anything left to live for."

On the night of Kit's return to Boston, he came down and dined with them. Joel was delighted, and did most of the talking. "You must see all we've done for Mary," he told their guest, as he carved the roast. "After dinner I'll take you up and show you."

Jacqueline had put on the blue taffeta, and her bronze hair shone under the candles. To her lover she seemed very beautiful. But Joel was blind to her beauty. Jack was a good little thing and all that, but he missed Mary's golden loveliness and tall grace.

After dinner, Joel took Christopher up to Mary's room. He showed him the rose-chintz chairs and the over-curtains. "Everything is ready for my poor girl when she comes home."

Then all at once, his composure broke, and he stood leaning against the head of the bed, his shoulders heaving. And Christopher flung an arm about those heaving shoulders. "It's hard lines, old man, but you'll — carry on."

With his arm still about Joel's shoulders, he said that he'd like to send up some roses — pink roses, to put in Mary's room when she arrived, and there was a silver bowl in the house in Salem, he'd get Hannah to polish it, and there was a seascape done by one of the nineteenth century Dutch painters — with the sky in a sunset glory — perhaps it could hang opposite Mary's bed, and cheer her up a bit. . . .

And as Kit talked, Joel got himself in hand. "I haven't let any of them see me like this," he apologized, "it is hard enough for Jack as it is."

Kit had no words for that. No one knew as well as he how hard it was for the woman he loved. She did not have to tell him. Coming back after two weeks, he had seen it in her changed looks — in the whiteness of her cheeks, the violet shadows under her eyes. "It will be easier for her, when I am gone," he told himself, "she dreads the parting."

He followed Joel into the hall, and waited a moment while his host went to peep at small Joey, to be sure he was sleeping. And so it happened, that he found himself standing on the threshold of Jacqueline's room, which was at the head of the stairway, with the door open.

He knew at once that it was her room, because his picture in the silver and ivory frame which he had given her was on the dresser. Except for that frame there was nothing in the room of any value. The colors were blue and white, and there was a virginal effect of neatness and order. Her little blue dressing gown hung over a chair, with her blue bedroom slippers on the rug beneath. There was no view of the sea, no elegance of draperies and furnishing such as invested Mary's room. Yet here, in these plain surroundings, the love of his life would live until she could let him come for her.

His thoughts travelled fast to the room that he would give her. There should be panelled walls with rose garlands, silken hangings, silver and crystal bottles and bowls for her perfumes and powders, brushes and mirrors backed by old ivory, like that of the frame.

When they went downstairs and found her alone in the firelighted room, Kit put his arm about her as they stood together. "You've got to be wonderfully good to this girl, Joel, or I shall carry her off."

Joel had lighted his pipe and with his back to the fire was beaming on the pair of them. "You'll have to lend her to us for a little while, . . . And you needn't think we don't appreciate what you're both doing. We shall owe Jack a debt we can never pay."

"You've paid it already, a thousand times, in the things you and Mary have done for me," Jack said, and began, suddenly to cry, with her face against Kit's coat.

Yolanda coming in from the kitchen, presently, saw nothing amiss, for Jacqueline had regained her self-control, and the three of them were talking quietly. Yolanda sat down on a footstool and listened. The talk was of war and she was much interested. "Hannah says there's never going to be another war," she vouchsafed, when a slight pause gave her a chance for a word.

"Hannah knows, of course," her father told her, smiling.

"Well, she says it won't be because the world is any better, but because we've got more sense," Yolanda, in red, with a bobbing red hair-ribbon, danced on her toes across the hearth-rug. "Daddy, do you remember the day you went away?" she began to sing, lustily, stepping in time to the tune.

> "This is the way we march to war,
> March to war,
> March to war.
> This is the way we march to war,
> All on a Monday morning—"

The three of them stared at her, at the little red flame of a child, light-heartedly resurrecting memories that should have been buried deep. They were seeing beyond her, seeing the years between, the fears, the frightfulness . . . incredible years now that one looked back on them. The two men sat rigid, their faces stern.

"*This is the way we march to war . . . march to war. . . .*" sang Yolanda blithely.

Joel said, sharply, "For Heaven's sake, Yolanda. . . !"

She stopped at once, "Don't you like it, Daddy?"

"We're done with all that. Let's forget it."

"How can we forget it when we can't?" Yolanda demanded.

Joel laughed harshly. "She's right. It's burned into our souls. Is it any wonder, Kit, that men, remembering it all, go mad?"

"There are things," said Kit, steadily, "that I want to remember. That right or wrong, we did the best we could. I think we were right. I should think so again.

The Impregnable Tower 115

I shall always believe that death is not as bad as dishonor. I shall always believe that no nation has a right to run rough-shod over the rest of the world."

They argued it after that, Joel caustic, savage, Kit with his steadfast air of finding a reason for it all. "Looking back, we can see our mistakes. But at the moment? What would you have had us do? Stay out? When a fire starts in our neighbor's barn, must we let it burn? Or lend a hand?"

Yolanda having started all this, again sat at Jacqueline's feet and listened. And when there was a pause, she said, "Well, God could have stopped it and he didn't."

Jacqueline remembering the astounding episode of the fighting dogs and the dipper, interposed hastily, "It isn't for us to question that, darling."

"Why not question it?" Joel demanded. "He could have stopped it, why didn't he?"

The bitter words struck them all into silence. Then Kit said, "He neither started it nor stopped it. Man must bear the punishment of his own passions. And out of it all, old orders have passed away. Peoples are free who were in bondage. Emperors and kings have lost their crowns. This is the good that was born of evil."

Joel, standing now on the hearth-rug, looked down at him. "I can't see the good. I shall never see it. I see only my broken life — and Mary's."

Then, meeting the startled glance of his small daughter, he caught himself up. "I'm talking a lot of rot. Don't listen to me, sweetheart. We'll go upstairs and I'll tell you a story. And don't remember a thing I've been saying. Now and then I like to be a big bear and growl."

She trotted along beside him. "Will you tell me about the big bear, Daddy?"

Their voices receded, and Kit and Jacqueline were left alone.

"Poor Joel—" Jacqueline said.

"Not so poor, with a child like that," Kit said, unexpectedly, "and a son to bear his name, and a wife by his side."

The breath seemed to leave Jacqueline's body as Paula's words swept back upon her—"*He'll want a wife . . . a home. . . !*"

"Oh, Kit, Kit, it isn't being fair to you."

He had been staring into the fire, but now he lifted his head quickly and looked at her, "What isn't being fair to me?"

"Tieing you to me in this way."

"What way?" he reached out his hand and drew her towards him.

"Oh, being engaged with no idea when we can be married."

She was beside him now on the old sofa, her head against his shoulder. He turned a little so that he could see her eyes, "Who has been telling you things like that?"

"Paula Gilman."

"Paula? What has she got to do with it?"

The Impregnable Tower

"She said I had no right to keep you from marrying —somebody else. That you'd want a home."

"Not without you in it."

"And you'd want a wife."

"I want no other wife but you. Jacqueline, do you think I would listen if you told me you wouldn't marry me? I'd simply keep on asking . . . until the end. . . ."

He whispered the last words as he held her close. Happiness burned deep in her blue eyes. His protestations did not seem to her extravagant. At eighteen one looks upon love as eternal, on constancy as the attribute of all honest men. One has all the poets to prove it, and all the great old lovers—Dante, and Aucassin and Abelard. . . . Women like Paula might not know these things. Poor women who had lost their lovers!

II

The next day, Jacqueline went to Kit's office to meet his uncle, Timothy Howland. "I want you to know him before I go," Kit had told her, "then if anything happens. . . ."

"Nothing is going to happen, Kit. . . ."

Well, anyhow, there she was, meeting old Timothy, who was a fresh-faced bachelor of seventy, with a thatch of curls like Kit's, but silvered at the temples and thin on top. He laughed, too, with his eyes like Kit, but he lacked Kit's tallness and lean grace.

He breezed into the room where the lovers were

waiting, and kissed Jacqueline on the cheek. "Welcome to the Howland clan, my dear. Kit has told me a lot about you. But he hasn't told me enough."

Kit, sitting on the arm of Jacqueline's chair, said, "I wanted you to see for yourself."

Old Timothy rang for his man and ordered tea. "It's a habit I brought with me from the East. I've had my man, Alexander, since he was a young chap. He's in his forties now — Scotch and faithful. I'm going to bequeath him to Kit some day."

Alec brought the tea and Jacqueline poured. "Kit says you aren't going out with him to India," old Timothy remarked as he took his cup. "It's a great mistake, my dear. If I were in his place I'd carry you off. . . ."

"No, you wouldn't," said Christopher, "not if you knew her."

"As bad as that?" old Timothy demanded. "Well, if business were what it used to be, I'd keep you here, Kit. But one of us must go."

And Jacqueline said with earnestness, "Even if he stayed, I couldn't marry him. . . ."

Old Timothy made a shrewd estimate. "It's these little wisps of women who are as strong as rocks. But who'd believe it with those blue eyes . . . ?"

When they had finished their tea, they went down to the docks to see the ship on which Kit would sail. It was a dingy cargo steamer, but it had comfortable cabins, and Kit's quarters were roomy. "Better come with me, Jack," he said, as he showed her about.

The Impregnable Tower

"Don't tempt me—" she smiled at him, "oh, Kit, distance isn't going to make any difference. Not when we care so much."

He let it go at that. He knew the loneliness he was facing. The loneliness he had felt in France. But there, at least, had been hope of a kind. And now there seemed no hope.

But Jacqueline put aside today the thought of separation and all it meant. She loved being on the lumbering old steamer with the harbor shining under the winter sun, and with the gulls sweeping down from the blue, and with Kit and his uncle so happy to have her there, and making her feel a person of importance, an honored guest, an adventuring comrade.

And Joel didn't make her feel any of these things. The moment she got back to the house she would cease to be a Personage. She would be again trying to fit herself to Joel's pattern. She would be anxious, almost obsequious. She was aware of the weakness of her attitude, but she couldn't help it. She collapsed utterly in an atmosphere of criticism, as she expanded in one of approbation and adoration.

Old Timothy came up with a parrot which one of the crew had brought—a blossom-headed parakeet, blue-green, with touches of vermillion, a purple face and black beard. It talked in a strange language, with now and then an English word or phrase. It's name was Simon—Simple Simon.

"It belonged to an English officer," old Timothy elucidated, "he died, and this man got it."

The parrot, navigating obliquely with beak and claws across the cage, cocked a mournful eye at Jacqueline, and murmured . . . "Simple Simon . . . went . . . a-fishing. . . ."

"Oh, Kit, he's adorable. . . ."

"He's yours if you want him," old Timothy said.

"Really. Oh, I'd love it —" It seemed to Jacqueline as if the parrot brought to her something of the enchantment of the country from which he came. If he were hers, he might be a link, as it were, between herself and her lover.

Then she remembered, "I'll have to ask Joel."

Kit's face darkened, "Why should you ask anybody?"

"It's his house."

Kit showed himself high-handed. The parrot was hers. He would bring it up when he came.

They lingered for a long time on the boat, watching the sun set over the water, and Jacqueline missed her train and had to wait for another one.

She was late for dinner, and found Joel in a state of irritation. "Everything has been ready for a half hour, Jack."

"Why didn't you sit down, Joel?"

"Because we expected you every minute. We thought of course you'd get the earlier train."

Jacqueline did not answer. A wave of indignation swept over her. Fresh from the homage of Kit and his uncle, and liking the pedestal on which they had put her, she was in no mood for Joel's high-handedness.

The Impregnable Tower

"You might as well sit down," she said, "I've got to change my dress and fix the baby's food. I am sorry I was late, but I couldn't help it."

Upstairs she was deliberate in her movements. And when she returned to the kitchen she gave no hint of hurry. She measured Joey's food in leisurely fashion and waited for the water to boil.

Old Hannah who was going back and forth to the dining-room, said, "Your dinner will be cold, my dearie."

"I don't want any dinner, Hannah."

Old Hannah stopped and stared, "Aren't you well, my lamb?"

"I had tea with Mr. Christopher."

"There's a beefsteak pie and a salad."

"I know, Hannah, and I know they're delicious, but I'm not hungry."

Old Hannah glanced at her. Something had come over Miss Jack. In the dining-room Mr. Joel was glowering. Serve him right, if she'd show a bit of spunk! And she was showing it. Old Hannah sailed in now with the salad. And sailed out again with the beefsteak pie. "Where's Miss Jack?" Joel asked her.

"She says she doesn't want any dinner."

"Nonsense. She can't go without food."

"Yes, sir."

Joel got up and laid down his napkin — then strode to the kitchen. "Look here, Jack, you can't starve yourself in this way."

"I'm not starving myself."

"Then why don't you come and eat?"

"I'll come — presently."

She was stirring hot water into Joey's food. Her hand did not shake, and she preserved outwardly an appearance of serenity. She felt that here was a crisis. She was not going to be at Joel's beck and call, and he might as well know it now as ever. If he didn't like it, he could — to use an inelegant phrase — lump it. She went on stirring Joey's food.

And then, just as she thought herself in an impregnable tower of independence Joel battered it down with the only weapon against which she had no defence.

"Oh, look here, Jack, I'm so darned lonesome."

"Oh, Joel . . ." all her defences were down, and she knew it. She couldn't stand it to see that look on his face . . . Joel, who had lost his leg, and who had, in a sense, lost Mary! "I'll be there in a minute." She turned Joey's food over to old Hannah and went in and ate salad, and thought of all the gay things she could tell Joel to cheer him — of old Timothy's office, and the little jade god he had given her; and of the cargo steamer, and the foreign crew, and the Simple Simon parrot. . . .

"He's mine, Joel. Kit's going to bring him up."

"My dear child, what will we do with a parrot?"

She grasped desperately at an answer which would satisfy him. "He might amuse Mary."

His face cleared, "Perhaps he would — poor girl. We can try it anyhow."

The Impregnable Tower

So that was that, and Jacqueline wrote to old Timothy that night. "Thank you so much for my heavenly afternoon and for the darling parrot. I am so glad you are Kit's uncle. When he's away, may I come and see you sometimes, and will you come up now and then and dine with us? The little goddess you gave me has a shelf of her own in my room. I hope she doesn't miss her temple bells—perhaps some day I shall take her back to them."

III

The next day Mary was brought home in a great motor ambulance. She was carried upstairs by Joel and the doctor who had come with her. A nurse was with her also, and was to stay until Jacqueline learned the routine of Mary's day.

The nurse braided Mary's hair and put on one of the pale pink jackets, and when Joel and Jacqueline came in to see her, they found the invalid looking more than ever like an Arthurian lady, with her golden braids framing her face and measuring their length on the coverlet, and with the rose of the jacket giving color to her cheeks.

"It's so good to be home again," she said, and how was she to know that she was to lie there in that bed until the gold in her braids had turned to gray and until one rose jacket had been succeeded by another and another and another throughout the weary years? For the surgeon had advised that she should not be told of the hopelessness of her case. "She will adjust herself to it day by day. To tell her now would be unnecessarily cruel."

Yolanda was delighted to have her mother home. "Did you know Aunt Jack has a parrot?"

"My darling—no—"

"Yes. Uncle Kit's going to bring it down. And it's name is Simple Simon."

Joel, standing by the bed, elucidated, "Of course if it worries you, dear, Jack's perfectly willing to get rid of it. . . ."

Thus from the beginning was established the fiction that Jacqueline's happiness was founded on doing what Mary wanted. Set herself as she would against it, she found herself being submerged by the personality of this new Mary who was in bed and an invalid. Mary, shorn of physical strength, refused to relinquish her place as mistress of the house. "I'm not an imbecile if I am on my back," she had said on the day the nurse had left. And she at once began to plan menus, check up expenses, give orders to old Hannah, "It keeps my mind off my troubles, Jack."

So it came about that Mary settled everything from pies to puddings, from veal cutlets to vacuum cleaners.

"Hannah had better go over Joel's room this morning, Jack."

"Could it wait until tomorrow, Mary? Hannah has a busy day in the kitchen."

"Why is she having a busy day in the kitchen?"

"Joel asked for a pumpkin pie, and I thought while she was about it she might do some other baking."

The Impregnable Tower

"I'll plan all that, Jack, if you'll let me." This was a new Mary, indeed, with her petulances— "She can make the pie and do Joel's room and let the other baking go—"

"But Mary—"

And Mary had stopped her with "Oh, if I were only on my feet—" and how could Jacqueline tell her then, that she wanted to go to Boston to lunch with Kit, and couldn't if old Hannah's day was filled with household duties so that she couldn't take care of Joey.

It wasn't, Jacqueline told herself that Mary was selfish. It was simply that she did not realize the increased labors her illness imposed upon her sister and the old servant. There was her own special diet, her morning bath, the freshening up of everything about her, so that when Joel came in, her room would be perfumed and rosy. Then there was little Joey who must be crisp and curled and cooing when he was taken in twice a day to see his mother.

"Isn't he adorable, Jack?"

"He's his Auntie Jack's own darling." And Jacqueline meant it. Small Joey was the joy of her days. Her only problems with him were his food and drink. Everybody else bossed her, and she didn't see how she could help it, for there was always Joel's leg to think about, and Mary's back, and Yolanda was Yolanda!

It seemed as if everybody in the world came to see Mary, and among the rest were all those women with whom she had worked in War days. They were, Jacqueline felt, different. The exaltation which had upheld them during that time of trial, no longer lighted them. Their husbands were back and their sons, stripped of illusion. Or if their husbands and sons slept in France, the glamour of grief was gone. There seemed little now of distinction in being a war widow or a gold star mother.

Most of these women now played bridge or golf, or took trips around the world. Or if they were too poor for that, they worked in their homes or in offices, and there was a general atmosphere of restlessness and discontent. The God who had been real to them during the war seemed to have receded, so that he again sat up among the clouds. A good many of the women went to church and said their prayers. But none of them seemed to serve at sacred altars, or be dedicated to any cause.

Jacqueline spoke to Sue about it. And Sue said, "You can't expect a thing like that to last."

"I did expect it."

"Oh, you. . . ." Sue was scornful. "You have never lived in a real world, Jack. You see things as you want them to be. And as for the war, we know now that we were emotionally swayed. That all our talk of holding high the torch was simply talk — and that the vision of Christ in Flanders was the hallucination of neurotics."

Jacqueline glowed with sudden fire. "I hate to hear you say things like that, Sue. And it isn't true. Christ was there for those who — died."

Sue shrugged her shoulders, "Illusion."

"No," Jacqueline said, "it was not illusion. The

The Impregnable Tower 127

spirit is as real as the body. And the world knew it for a little while, because it faced Death. . . . And death is not the end of — life. . . ."

Sue shrugged her shoulders, "Have it your way," she said, "but you're going to be hurt some day — dreadfully."

Sue was having dinner with them that night. There would be four of them, Joel and Kit, Sue and Jacqueline. Yolanda was not to be at the dinner table. Mary had settled that. "Hannah can wait more easily on the four of you. And besides Yolanda has a way of wanting to hold the center of the stage. She can come up here and have a tray with me."

Yolanda, outwardly accepting the situation, protested later to Jacqueline, "I can always eat with Mother and I like to be with Uncle Kit and Sue."

"I know, darling, but Mother has planned it."

"Why don't you plan things, Auntie Jack?"

Why indeed?

Mary had showed much interest in the small dinner party. The menu she presented to Jacqueline was perfect, but beyond Hannah's limitations. "I had thought of something simpler," Jacqueline told her sister. "Two courses. Hannah finds it hard to cook and serve, too. She suggested one of her beefsteak pies and a salad; Joel could serve the pie, and I'd mix the salad, and we could have fruit and cheese and coffee at the end."

"Heavens, Jack, what would Sue Gilman think of us?"

"I don't care what she thinks. She knows we can't attempt to compete with the perfection of their cuisine and service."

"Even if we can't, we're not quite — barbarians. . . ."

Jacqueline was silent. How unlike Mary it all was, this bitterness — ! She set herself to see what she could do, and the result was a modification of Mary's menu. It was still, however, too elaborate. And the final outcome would, Jacqueline felt, be failure. Hannah was not at home in the dining-room. Her domain was the kitchen. She was dubious when the details of the dinner were explained to her. But she would have walked over hot plowshares for Jacqueline. "I'll do my best, Miss Jack."

Whatever the difficulties in the kitchen, however, the table looked lovely, and Jacqueline had a new blue dress — sheer and flowing with touches of silver. She had spent all of her tiny balance in the bank to get it. These were Kit's last days — after that, what matter what she wore?

Sue in a gorgeous brocade of white with roses, and whose hair blazed more than ever, got along famously with Joel. It seemed, indeed, to Jack that she had never seen Joel so gay and gallant. It was, indeed, a very gay party. Sue was in wild spirits, and as the meal progressed flirted openly with Joel. Jacqueline was not sure that she liked it. Of course it meant nothing. People did things like that in these days. Whether they were married or not. Yet she had a tug of the heart as she thought of Mary. Of Mary lying straight and still on her narrow bed, who had once been the life of the party.

She pushed the thought away, however, and was, presently, laughing with the rest of them. Kit was at his best and matched Joel's stories with his own. Sue, unlike most women was an excellent *raconteur,* and Jacqueline, listening, marvelled that it was she and not Sue whom Kit had chosen. . . .

Yet she had no sense of jealousy. Kit was there beside her, completely her own. Now and then under the table he caught her little hand in his strong clasp, and his smile as he looked down at her was one of utter content.

She came out of her haze of happiness, to find that things were going wrong with the dinner. Hannah was slow with the serving and clumsy, and Joel was obviously getting impatient. "I knew it," Jacqueline told herself, desperately, "if only Mary hadn't insisted on five courses."

She tried to console herself with the thought that the cooking was delicious. But the chicken grew cold on their plates before the vegetables were passed, and the climax came when Hannah disappeared and was gone interminably. Jacqueline rang the bell and rang it again, and got no response.

She tried to laugh it off. "Hannah must be asleep."

Joel's face darkened. She knew he was thinking that if Mary had been there all this would not have happened. "I should rather think she's dead," he said, with a touch of irritation.

Hannah came at last with her fluted cap over one eye, and with small Joey in her arms. "I'm sorry, Miss Jack, but he's crying his head off."

Jacqueline rose in her seat, "I'll take him, Hannah. You go on and serve the dinner."

The baby came to her rapturously, drying his tears at once at the sight of the shining candles and all the smiling people.

But Joel was not smiling. "Give him to me," he said, masterfully.

"He's happy here, Joel," Jacqueline drew the child closer, "he loves the lights."

Joel's voice was sharp, "He's spoiled to death. He needs a bit of discipline."

Jacqueline thought nervously that this was no place to begin it. If only Joel would talk to Sue and Kit. . . .

But Joel wouldn't. "Give him to me," he said again. So small Joey went to his father, and from that time on things were dreadful. For Joel, intent on discipline, held the child in an iron grip, and Joey, sensing a hostile atmosphere, howled to the heavens, and in the midst of it all, Hannah brought in the salad and passed the cream cheese and Bar-le-duc, and her old hands trembled.

And the sight of those trembling old hands gave Jacqueline courage. "Take the baby upstairs, Hannah," she said, quietly, "we'll do the rest of the serving ourselves. . . ."

"Jack!" Joel protested.

But Jacqueline was laughing, carrying it off with a high hand. "Kit will help me," she said, "he can play butler and I'll play cook, and you and Sue can see how well we do it."

The next few moments were uproarious as Kit sailed out with the salad plates, with his nose in the air, and Jacqueline in one of old Hannah's fluted caps crumbed the table.

Sue played up to it, and so, after a startled moment, did Joel. And Kit played, too, but when he and Jacqueline were at last safely out in the kitchen, he shut the door behind him.

"If you think I'm going to let all this go on . . . !"

"All what?"

"This bulldozing—Joel's insufferable."

"Hush, Kit—not so loud."

"Do you think I care if he hears me? What does he think you are? A lackey?"

"Kit, help me through with it," her cheeks were flushed, Hannah's cap almost covered her ears, the blue dress floated and flowed about her. "Help me through with this dinner. Make it a joke, and we'll talk about it afterwards."

He towered above her, "I'd like to beat Joel up."

"Kit, you *couldn't*. You've got two legs, and he . . . hasn't."

He began to laugh, suddenly, "Jack . . . was there ever such a child . . . such a darling . . . !"

They went in presently with the dessert. The game went on, and at last Kit carried the tray with the coffee service into the living-room, and their labors were ended.

Kit was to take Sue home. "I hate it," he had said

to Jacqueline, frankly, "for I'll lose the evening with you."

"We'll have a week of tomorrows, Kit."

"What's a week in a desert of months ahead?"

They played bridge until it was time for Sue to go home. Joel had recovered his equanimity, and was again gay and gallant. He had Jacqueline for a partner during the first rubber. Young as she was, she played an excellent game. Sue couldn't hold a candle to her, and even Joel condescended to compliment her. "That redouble of yours was masterly, Jack. I wish you'd look at our score."

She was proud of the score, but she hated to beat Kit. It was much nicer when she had Kit for a partner, and they could stand or fall together. It was wonderful how well things went for them. And when Kit kissed her, "Good-night" in the hall, while Joel and Sue added up the score, and whispered, "You're as lovely as you look, my angel," she had a singing sense of triumph.

And when Kit had gone with Sue, she came back into the living-room and faced Joel, "I'm sorry about the dinner."

"Hannah made a mess of things."

"Hannah couldn't help it. I told Mary we could have two courses, and Hannah would be equal to that. But she insisted on five."

"Mary planned it?"

"Yes. She plans everything. And you and I must let her. She has so little in her life, poor dear. But I'm not going to take the blame for her mistakes, Joel."

The Impregnable Tower

She was standing on the hearth rug with her blue dress flowing about her, and suddenly, he was aware of her beauty — the flame in her cheeks, the deep azure of her eyes, the delicacy and whiteness of her skin, the glory of her bronze locks. "I am not going to take the blame of Mary's mistakes," she repeated, "I'm here because you need me, and Mary, and the children, and I'll do my best. But I'm not a doormat."

"My dear girl," Joel stammered.

She smiled at him, "So that's that," she said, serenely, and left him staring. She was amazed at her own daring. But the thought of Kit had sustained her. She was his goddess on a pedestal, his angel in blue! And who was Joel that she should be afraid of him?

CHAPTER SIX

"*My Heart Is Like a Singing Bird*"

I

WHEN Sue and Kit arrived at the house in Salem, they found Paula waiting up for them. She had a book and a cigarette, and sat under a pink lamp which shed over her a gracious light.

"Better late than never," she said, as the two young people came in.

Sue dropped her sable fur on a chair, and sat down at the piano, her back to the keys. "Shall we tell you all about it, Paula?"

Kit still stood. "I'm sorry. But I'm going over next door. There are some papers I want to take in with me to Boston tomorrow morning."

"It will be freezing, Kit. You'd better stay here."

"There's wood in the library, I can get a blaze in a second. And there are a lot of things in my desk I must look over."

Sue turned to the piano and began to play softly. Paula said, "We have seen so little of you, Kit."

Sue flung over her shoulder, "Why complain, Paula? We'd better be thankful for crumbs from the king's table."

"My Heart Is Like a Singing Bird" 135

Kit, unaware of the forces warring about him, laughed lazily, "You'll be glad to be rid of me. A man in love isn't the best company. But you've been no end good to me."

"We've been good to ourselves," Paula said, smiling, and Sue whirled around and demanded, "What did you expect? That we'd show you the door? Don't our years of friendship count for anything?"

Paula's heart almost missed a beat. Would Kit see what she saw in Sue's eyes? And if he did, what then?

But Kit saw nothing. He wished only that Sue and Paula wouldn't be so insistent. He wanted to be alone with his thoughts of Jacqueline.

He said "Good-night," presently, and left them, and when he had gone, Sue rose and stood by the fire. "He doesn't know we're on earth, Paula. And in a week he's going away."

Paula with her eyes on the fire, said, "Sue, have you ever let him see how much you — care — ?"

The room was dead still for a moment, then Sue said, "Paula, how could I? He loves — Jacqueline."

"I know. . . . But she's hurting him. Sending him away — unhappy. If that is love, well, let her think it. He'll grow tired. Turn to someone else."

She stopped, and there was a long silence, and when they spoke again it was of other things, until Sue yawned, and said, "I'm sleepy," and went upstairs.

Paula, left alone, smoked a last cigarette by the dying fire. Everything was, it seemed to Paula, dying. Her sisters were old. It was only a question of time with them. Her own beauty had a blight on it, the spring and summer of her life had passed, winter was upon her.

But Sue was young, her beauty unblemished. Might she not claim of life all that it had to give? Why let one's pride, one's sense of personal dignity stand in the way of happiness?

Sue upstairs, still dressed and prone on her bed, was asking herself the same questions. Paula's words had shaken her, "Have you ever let him see that you — care?" Well, what if she did let him see? What good would it do? And she would have forfeited that which meant much to her — her right to be wooed whole-heartedly by a man who loved her. Should she, then, do the wooing. . . ? She hated the thought of it.

Yet — it was pride which had brought Paula to lonely spinsterhood. And Jacqueline was making Kit unhappy. Might not these things weigh in balance against those reticences that the world called womanly?

She rose and looked out of the window. A faint light in the library next door showed where Kit was still at work. She could see the shadow of his head against the curtain.

A half hour later, Kit, very busy, became aware of sounds in the house. It seemed to him that somewhere a door had opened and shut. He listened and half rose from his seat. Then again there was silence, except for the weak whisper of the wind as it swept around the corner.

He turned once more to his desk. He had found

the papers he sought, and he had found something else. A little book which his father had sent to his mother, long ago when he was at sea. At the time of her death, Kit had tucked it away in his desk, after glancing through it. But now he was giving it more than a glance. In the light of his own love affair, the words which his father had penned seemed to flame with celestial fires. There was a verse here, a verse there — from the Bible, Shakespeare, Keats, Shelley — written in fine and perfect penmanship, and the book was bound in hand-tooled leather. He turned down the corners of certain pages, marking them for Jacqueline — "*Shall I compare thee to a summer's day. . . .*" "*She walks in beauty. . . .*" *She is coming, my own, my sweet. . . .*"

And there was the one of Christina Rosetti. He read and re-read it!

"My heart is like a singing bird
   Whose nest is in a watered shoot;
My heart is like an apple tree,
   Whose boughs are bent with thickest fruit;
My heart is like a rainbow shell
   That paddles in a halcyon sea,
My heart is gladder than all these,
   Because my love is come to me."

Taste in poetry had changed since his father had copied that. Yet to Kit there was something strong and sustaining in that simile: "*My heart is like an apple tree . . . . whose boughs are bent with thickest fruit....*" He leaned back in his chair, smiling. His love for Jacqueline was a golden orchard, hung with shining globes....

Again a door seemed to open and shut. Again the slight sound made echoes amid the silences of the house. This time he went out into the hall and listened.

Standing there in the great hall, encompassed about with dense blackness, he felt it not unlikely that the sound was of ghostly origin. For the house was full of ghosts for him. The ghost of his father — bluff and hearty, domineering, stumping up and down the stairs; the ghost of his mother, tall and slender, with all the elegance of her trains slipping behind her; the ghost of a little brother who had died in his childhood, and who flitted about in bobbing curls and black velvet; the ghost of the old butler, his face black, his wool white, his brass buttons gleaming!

A line of gold shone now beneath the dining-room door, and all at once it opened, and standing in a square of yellow light, he saw Sue Gilman.

She was carrying a small tray in one hand and a candlestick in the other. The flame of the candle turned her red hair into a blazing nimbus. She still wore her dinner dress of rose brocade, and over it the sable coat. There was the sparkle of buckles on her silver slippers as she came on noiselessly across the carpet.

The light of her candle illumined him, and as she saw him, she laughed. "Kit, you idiot, to stay over here and freeze. I've brought you some coffee."

"My Heart Is Like a Singing Bird" 139

Her words were light, casual, and how could he know that she was trembling with more than cold. "Come in to the fire," he said, "this is awfully good of you — but you shouldn't have done it."

She preceded him into the library and set the tray on the table. There were cups on it and a plate covered with a napkin. "I made some sandwiches, and there's a thermos jug of coffee in the dining-room. Will you go and get it? There was more than I could carry."

"I thought I heard some one in the back of the house," he said, as he returned with the coffee, "but I wasn't sure."

"I made two trips," she told him.

"Why didn't you let me help you?"

"I wanted to have it all ready before you knew. And I had to wait until every-one in the house was asleep."

She was pouring coffee, and did not look at him. "I wanted to wait," she repeated, "because I thought it would be nice to have a bit of time to ourselves over here ... and they're such old tabbies ... they wouldn't have thought it proper."

Kit selected a sandwich, "It's a rather late day to worry about the proprieties with us, isn't it?"

"With you and me? Yes. We never thought of chaperones in the old days."

"I'll say we didn't," he went on eating sandwiches.

"They were nice old days," she said, presently, "do you remember," she went down on her knees before the fireplace, "you put our initials here on the wood-work — with a heart around them?" She settled back on her heels and looked up at him, "I was twelve and you were fifteen . . . such a silly pair of youngsters, Kit."

The ruddy light of the fire shone upon her. Against the rich shadows of the room, she was like a gorgeous portrait. And still kneeling there, she said, "I wish we were back in the old silly days—before you knew Jacqueline."

He had a startled sense of something impending. But he told himself he was mistaken. "Why before I knew Jacqueline?"

"Because you were happy then—and she is making you unhappy, and I can't bear it . . . ," her upturned face showed tears upon her cheeks.

He said, uneasily, "I'm all right. Don't let it worry you, old girl."

"But it does worry me, Kit. You don't know what's ahead of you. The loneliness, the uncertain years. If she loved you, why doesn't she go out with you to India? Tell me that, Kit, why doesn't she go?"

There was a touch of sternness in his voice, "You know why. Mary's illness."

"But if Jacqueline were not here, Joel would work things out. And why should Joel be made comfortable at your expense? Oh, if she cared, Kit, as some women care, she'd go, she'd go. . . ."

The thing that had impended had come! He knew now what he had not known before. It was in Sue's voice. It was in her wet eyes as she looked up at him.

He chose not to see what was in the eyes, nor hear

what was in the voice. He reached out his hand for the little book which he had laid aside when she came. "Let me read you something, Sue. It is a verse my father copied long ago for my mother. I have marked it for Jacqueline."

He began to read:

"My heart is like a singing bird,
  Whose nest is in a watered shoot,
My heart is like an apple tree,
  Whose boughs are bent with thickest fruit. . . ."

"My love for Jacqueline is like that," he said, when he had finished, "and so is hers for me. . . ."

There was a long silence, then Sue got up from the hearth and drew her sable wrap about her. "Perhaps I shouldn't have . . . protested. Perhaps it is all . . . none of my business. . . . But I thought our long . . . friendship . . . made it . . . possible. . . ."

He had risen, too, and laid his hand on her shoulder. "It has been a good friendship," he said, heartily, and smiled down at her. "And now I am going to take you out of this freezing house. Even the fire doesn't seem to warm it."

He carried a candle with him to the door, then extinguished it, set it on the hall table, and joined her beneath the stars. The air was very still and clear. The sound of their footsteps was audible on the frozen sidewalk.

Paula, who had not slept, lifted her head from the

pillow. Then she rose, and standing by the window, drew the curtain aside a little so that she might see. The light from the street lamp showed Sue walking beside Christopher. Paula's heart gave a great leap. "She's been over there with him in the old house." She wondered what Sue had said to him.

She lay awake for a long time . . . wondering. . . .

II

On the day before Kit's departure, Jacqueline waked very early in the morning. She had slept little, and now as she watched the dawn come in, she told herself that in another day he would be gone. She wondered how she was going to stand it.

Yet she had sent her lover away to war with brave words, her head high—drums beating, flags flying! But this was different. He had been torn from her then by his country's call—*I would not love thee, dear, so much, loved I not honor more!* But this time by her own act she was breaking his heart—and her own—.

She thought of what it would be if, even now, she should change her mind and go with him. What a glorious rushing-about there would be. . . ! A quick train up to town . . . a whirlwind descent upon the shops . . . another quick train back again . . . a hurried heaping into new trunks of new and lovely raiment; a simple wedding service beside Mary's bed; a swift motor trip to Boston and to the docks! And

"My Heart Is Like a Singing Bird"

then the boat! Kit's comfortable quarters made ready for two, her own feminine belongings lying about, the boat getting under way, the throb of its engines, the beat of wind and water, herself safe and happy with Kit—forever. . . . !

She began to cry wildly, with her arm over her eyes. Then as the dawn whitened the road, she rose and looked out of the window. A blanket of fog lay over the town. Away off somewhere, she could hear the boom of the sea—the sea that would carry Kit away. . . .

The air was freezing. She got back into bed and lay there, spent and despairing. The advancing light showed the white jade goddess on a shelf. "She's a heathen goddess," old Timothy had told her, "but I like her looks, and she's said to watch over sailors in their ships."

Men who go down to sea. . . ! The phrase beat against Jacqueline's brain. *Men who go down to sea. . . !* "Don't let Kit go," she found herself saying to the goddess on the shelf, "don't, don't. . . ."

She was sobbing again, and presently she was aware of what seemed an echo to her sobbing. She listened, and was out of bed in a moment. Small Joey was awake, and Joel did not hear him.

The baby's crib was in Joel's den, which adjoined his bedroom. Jacqueline stole in on noiseless feet, and gathered the weeping child in her arms. Then she sped back with him to her own bed.

He stopped crying at once, and curled up beside her

like a kitten. He murmured soft nothings with his lips against her cheek. His hand beat on her throat. "Mum . . . mum, Mummy," he gurgled.

Jacqueline had tried to teach him to call his mother, "Mummy," but here he was saying it to the aunt who nightly crooned to him and cradled him in her arms, and who meant to him all that Mary had meant in the days before she had been tied to her bed.

"Mum . . . mum, Mummy," murmured small Joey, and Jacqueline who had prayed a moment before frantically to the jade goddess, held the child close. She kissed his little hand. With the baby beside her, she was eased a bit from wild rebellion.

And then, another voice from the threshold, "Aunt Jack, may I come in?"

It was Yolanda, who charging across the carpet said, "Is there room on the other side of you?"

"Room for everybody, darling. But shut the door so you won't wake Daddy."

Yolanda did as she was told, and, first discarding her red dressing gown and red slippers, climbed up. Then, plunging beneath the warm covers, she embraced her aunt. "I've got something to tell you."

"What is it?"

"Mother's going to give you a party."

Jacqueline, lying straight and still between the two rapturous and wriggling youngsters, stiffened. "A party?"

"Yes. Tonight in her room. It's going to be a surprise. She hasn't told anybody but Daddy and Hannah."

"My Heart Is Like a Singing Bird" 145

"You shouldn't have told me, Yolanda."

"Why shouldn't I?"

"Because it isn't playing the game to tell other people's secrets."

Yolanda raised herself on her elbow and looked into her aunt's eyes, "Didn't you want to know?"

"Well . . . yes. . . ."

Yolanda dropped back on her pillow. "I told Kit, too, and he said, 'Gosh.'"

It was Jacqueline's turn to look, "When did you tell him?"

"Last night when he came to take you to town, and you kept him waiting."

Jacqueline reflected that in their long evening together, Kit had not said a word about the party. She knew he must have loathed the thought of it. On their last night together. But he wouldn't, of course, criticise Mary. He was tender of her helplessness.

Yolanda, having shot her bolt, was demanding, "Tell us a story, Aunt Jack."

"What story?"

"About when Daddy went to war, and Patsy and I danced."

"My dear, I should think you'd hate to hear about it."

"I don't. I like to think of Daddy when he had his other leg, and Patsy was so pretty."

Jacqueline, going on with the story, told herself that Yolanda *was* different. The child didn't shrink from memories. She didn't shrink from *anything*. . . .

She stopped her recital of harrowing details to ask, "Who are asked to the party, Yolanda?"

"Sue Gilman and a lot of others. Mother's going to have her bed made up as a divan, so it will look like India. Sue's coming over to help Hannah this afternoon when you go to Salem."

"I see." Jacqueline made a quick finish of her story. "You must get up now and dress, Yolanda."

"I don't want to get up."

"We have to do a lot of things, we don't like to do."

Yolanda, sliding out of bed and flinging on the red dressing-gown, proclaimed, "When I grow up, I'm going to do as I please."

"No one can do that, Yolanda."

"I can," said Yolanda, securely, as she went away.

III

Jacqueline, going into Mary's room to get her ready for Joel's "good morning," found her sister shining with cheerfulness. The reason was, of course, easy to guess. And when Mary said, "I'm going to have Sue Gilman over this afternoon, when Kit takes you to Salem," Jacqueline braced herself for the ordeal.

"Mary," she said, flushing a little, "you mustn't plan anything tonight for Kit and me."

Mary demanded sharply, "Who told you I was planning?"

Jacqueline tried to take it lightly, "A little bird."

"Yolanda, of course."

"Please don't ask me, or blame anyone. But this is our last night — together, Mary."

"My Heart Is Like a Singing Bird" 147

"I know. But it isn't as if Kit were going away forever. You mustn't make such a tragedy of it, Jack. He'll be coming back when I am better."

"Yes." To Jacqueline braiding the invalid's bright hair, it seemed horrible that Mary should talk in that hopeful way. When there was no hope.

Mary went on. "It isn't as if you weren't so young, Jack. Much too young to take on the responsibilities of marriage. You'll be all the better wife for waiting. . . ."

Jacqueline went to Mary's dresser and rummaged among the ribbons in a drawer. She wanted to cry out, "What are the responsibilities of marriage as against those you are imposing upon me?" But all she said was "Anyhow I'd rather not have the party."

"I think you are very foolish," Mary said, with a touch of severity. "It was Sue Gilman who suggested it. She thought Kit would like it. Having all his friends about him, and a gay, good time — not tears. Sue's very sensible."

Jacqueline turned and looked at her, "Do you think that Sue Gilman . . . do you think that if Sue were engaged to Kit, and he was going away, she'd want a gay party?"

"Jacqueline!"

"Do you think you would, if it were — Joel?"

Mary hesitated, then she said, "That's different. And anyhow I wouldn't make a tragedy of it."

"No. . . ." Jacqueline was wrapping about Mary's head the wide pink ribbon which covered her hair in the morning. "Let life be rose-colored! Laugh and the world laughs with you, and things like that, Mary! Let's tie our emotions up in pink ribbons... !"

Her voice was hysterical. Mary caught her hand and held it, "Jack, what's the matter with you?"

Jacqueline was very white. "I ... don't see how I can let him go, Mary. I ... love him ..." she fell on her knees beside the bed. ...

Then, through a haze, she heard Mary saying, *"If only I could get up ... if only I could get up."*

Jacqueline's arms went about her, "Darling Mary ... darling...."

"Oh, Jack, I want you to be happy...."

"I know...."

"But I can't let you go, dearest. Not yet, Jack, not yet... !"

When at last Jacqueline went downstairs, she passed the cage of Simple Simon, the parrot old Timothy had given her. He chuckled as she came up, and she stood looking at him. "Do you like your cage, Simon?" she whispered, "do you like it? We are two of a kind, Simon. Two of a kind. Shut up in our cages!"

IV

In the hours that followed, Jacqueline forgot everything but Kit. She forgot Mary, she forgot Joel, she forgot Sue Gilman, and all their demands and difficulties. She thought only of her lover.

She motored with him that afternoon to the old

"*My Heart Is Like a Singing Bird*" 149

house in Salem. "It will be yours some day, Jack. Whether I live or die, it shall be yours. . . ."

He built a fire in the library, put her in the big chair on the hearth, and wrapped her in a fine old India shawl which had belonged to his mother, and his mother's mother. Then he opened his desk, took out a blue velvet box, and showed her a necklace and brooch and earrings of seed pearls. "My father gave them to my mother on her wedding day." He made her bend her head, while he looped the earrings over her little ears with a fine silk thread. He clasped the necklace about her throat and pinned the shawl with a brooch. "I shall like to think of you sitting by my fire wrapped in my mother's shawl and wearing her pearls. . . ."

He lay on the rug at her feet, with his rough curls under her hand. "It will be like this," he said, "when I bring you here — a bride." He turned and kissed her hand and held it over his eyes, and his eyes were wet.

She bent down to him, "Dearest. . . ."

Before they went away, he gave her the little book with the verses which his father had copied for his mother. He sat again at her feet and read them to her and when he had finished, he put the little book in her hands: "If the time ever comes, Jack, when you don't want me . . . send this back. . . ."

"Kit . . . that time will never come. . . ."

They went next door later and had tea with the Gilmans. "We're coming down to the boat tomorrow," Sue said, as she moved about restlessly, we're going to give you a great send-off, Kit."

"The more the merrier," Kit said with his lips, but his eyes denied it.

Sue was aware of the look in his eyes, as was Paula, and when Kit and Jacqueline had gone, Paula said, "Perhaps it would be better if we didn't go to town."

"Why not, Paula?"

"One can press a thing too far."

"I'm not pressing anything," Sue flung out, "what makes you say things like that, Paula?"

And at that very moment, Kit was saying, "Why can't people leave us alone, Jack? I want no one but you when I say 'good-bye.'"

Their real parting was on the bluff. It was late that night when they climbed the hill. A wild March wind was blowing and the sea was rough. "If this keeps up we'll have some weather tomorrow," Kit said, as they stood looking out over the tossing waters.

Jacqueline clung to him, "This time tomorrow you'll be miles away from me. . . . Kit, how am I going to bear it?"

He held her close and after a while he said, "Do you remember, Jack, when I was overseas? You called and I answered? I shall answer again . . . when you call."

The next day when Jacqueline went down to the docks with Joel and old Timothy to see Kit off, the wind was still blowing, but the sun was shining. The cargo boat was fresh with paint, and the foreign crew was gay with the thought of going. Kit, with all his laughing friends about him, laughed with the rest. But when he had Jacqueline for a moment alone with

"My Heart Is Like a Singing Bird"

him in his cabin, he kissed her and put her from him, "Dear love — don't make it too hard for me."

Later, she too, among all the people, laughed and was gay. But when the boat left the pier, and she watched the waters widen, and Kit, waving his hand, was just a black spot against the sunshine, she was aware all at once of the blankness of the heavens, of the barren years ahead of her!

And then, at last, she told herself the truth. *Kit was gone, and her youth had gone with him!*

CHAPTER SEVEN

Five Years

I

FIVE years of Kit in India! Five years of Yolanda growing up! Five years of Mary flat on her back in bed. Five years of Joel fighting for his life financially. Five years in which small Joey left babyhood behind and arrived at rampageous boyhood.

Five years, too, of women having their hair bobbed, and of shamelessly shortening their dresses. Five years of after-the-war adjustment. Five years of prosperity! Of Prohibition! Of bootlegging! Five years in which Jacqueline moved about in a maze of duties, from which she emerged competent, but dimmed and dulled by the process.

She knew that she was dimmed and dulled. She no longer flamed and thrilled at every slight adventure. In a world of bobbed-haired women, she still braided her tresses. Her dresses covered her knees, and they were, as a rule, of serviceable colors. Once when reading again Quality Street, she had sighed a bit over Barrie's heroine, whose lover came back to find her in spectacles and cap!

Five Years 153

Kit had sailed home each year during the five to ask her to marry him. He had not found her in spectacles and cap, but on his last trip he had noticed the dimming and dulling. "What are they doing to you?" he had demanded.

She had tried to make light of it. "Nothing. And I am really just as nice as ever, Kit."

"You're nicer . . . but . . . I hate that dress, Jack."

It had been the best she could do. Joel was so fiendishly hard up, with all the doctor's bills for Mary. So Jacqueline had worn a black lace of Mary's made over, and even Kit's flowers had not brightened it into becomingness.

The next day Kit had taken her to town and had bought her a dress — a rosy thing of tulle with floating ribbons, and that night they had gone to a dance at the Yacht Club, and she had felt young again and pretty.

Mary hadn't quite approved of Kit's getting the dress for her. "In my day, men didn't buy clothes for the women they were going to marry."

"Your day is my day, too, Mary. But Kit wanted me this way — so I let him do it. . . ."

Joel, too, had disapproved. "You'd better let me buy your things, Jack."

But Jacqueline, high-hearted and happy, had touched her rosy ruffles with light finger-tips, and had parried, "Why worry, Joel? On an average I am really a very proper person."

When Kit had gone back to India, the rosy gown had

become a symbol of that short time of happiness with her lover Jacqueline had worn it until it was hopelessly out of date, and always with a memory of her first joy in it, and of Kit's masculine appreciation of her surrender to his masterfulness.

"There's so little you will let me do for you, Jack."

"Some day, you'll do everything."

"I wonder if that day will ever come."

"Of course," she had smiled up at him, and had tucked her hand into his, and the salesman had brought back the parcel, and Kit had gone off with it under his arm, and they had been whirled away in a taxi for lunch at the Club.

But the night before he left, Kit had said again, "I wonder if that time will ever come," and there had been discouragement in his bearing, and weariness in his voice.

"Things *must* work out soon," Jacqueline had said. But Kit had not answered her, and had sat staring into the fire. And this time, after his return to India, his letters changed. They were no less loving, but it was a love which had settled down to wait. He ceased urging. And in a way she missed it.

The letters came once a week and were made up of daily bulletins jotted down wherever he might be. And so she came to know his life as if it were her own. She lived, indeed, two lives, in one of which she was Mary's proxy in all home matters. The other, in which she followed Kit about in a land of peacocks and ivory, of snow-tipped mountains and dense forests, of tropic

Five Years

heat and lush gardens, of smart English officers and their smarter wives, of that older civilization of opulence and intrigue, and Arabian Nights' adventures.

She developed a technique in her own letters which kept them from monotony. There was, really, she told herself, nothing to write. One couldn't emphasize forever the fact that Joel was still kind but critical, that Mary's growing patience and sweetness made her more than ever heart-breaking; that small Joey was a handful but a darling, and that Yolanda in her confident and challenging youth ruled the household.

Yet as these things were her only news, she set herself to illumine the pages she sent to Kit with quaint and subtle humor. No matter how tragic the day, she managed to make the account of it amusing. And gradually she came to see the life about her as she wrote of it to Kit, and was saved from bitterness by her own whimsical viewpoint, and by the insistence with which she held to it.

And now at the end of five years, she sat one August afternoon on the front porch which looked out over the harbor. There were snapdragons in boxes on the rail, and their great masses of bloom were blown about by the wind, so that they were like pink plumes waving. Simple Simon in his cage in the corner made a spot of gorgeous color against the background of azure sky and sea. It seemed to Jacqueline that it was on such beauty that her soul was fed. In the midst of the dullest task, she could look out across the garden to the ever-changing sea and draw a quick breath of delight.

At the moment she was mending stockings. And she hated it. Not many women mended stockings in these days — but one couldn't be always buying. As she bent to her task, her bronze locks, neatly braided, shone in the sunlight. She wore a fresh frock of blue linen. She was young and sweet, but she felt a thousand years old. Her mind was on the dinner. There was fish again and Joel was not fond of it. But it was cheap, so they had it. But Joel was never quite the same on fish-dinner nights. He was apt to be — "carping." That was what Jacqueline had called it in a letter to Kit. But she had made a joke of it and a play on words, and had drawn a series of funny illustrations in which a huge carp with Joel's face was weeping as he read a sign, "Fish-dinners!"

Jacqueline hated having always to think about food. She hated it as much as she hated mending stockings. Yet she knew that in itself she did not dislike domesticity. It was only that, of late, all these things had seemed so futile. She had felt herself narrowing to the limits of a little life. She had so few outlets. Joel had his daily contacts in town, and Yolanda those of her school, but Jacqueline saw few people except those who came to call on Mary.

Yolanda's school had been one of the things which had increased their budget. Mary had wanted her daughter sent to an exclusive place in Salem. It was expensive, "But she'll make her friends there," Mary had insisted.

Joel had agreed, "It isn't as if we had a dozen daughters. And we must give her the best."

Five Years 157

Giving Yolanda the best meant that Jacqueline must pare household expenses to the extreme limit. Yet she too had felt that Mary was right. Yolanda must have the best. And perhaps the gracious heads of the school might find some way to curb the child's galloping spirit. "She's running away with all of us." Jacqueline would tell herself now and then, when Yolanda, keen of mind and eloquent of tongue, would force her reluctant family to her way of thinking.

"I think you are very silly," she had told her aunt, one day after Kit's departure, "not to marry Uncle Kit. Why don't you do it?"

"Oh, I'm needed here, Yolanda."

"You think you are. But why should you worry about us? It's your own life, isn't it?"

"Yes. But there's your mother — and Joey."

Yolanda had considered that. Then she had said, "Mother ought to have a good nurse."

"Your Dad can't afford it."

"He thinks he can't."

"Yolanda, you know how hard it has been for him since the war."

"Yes. But that doesn't mean you're to carry him on your shoulders for the rest of his days. Gracious Peter, Aunt Jack, if I had a man like Kit in love with me, I'd run a mile to meet him."

The child when she said it, had been sitting with her aunt on the bluff which overlooked the sea. She had worn a sweater and skirt of soft dull blue, and her bobbed hair had made a close gold cap for her head. Yolanda at fifteen was taking on some of her mother's loveliness. She had the same golden beauty and grace of line. If she was still somewhat awkward, she made up for it in a flame-like quality of spirit, which her mother lacked, but which Jacqueline possessed in full measure.

It was this flame-like beauty which had lighted her when she said, "If I had a man like Kit to love me, I'd run a mile . . . to meet him."

Jacqueline, her braided hair soberly banded about her head, her slender figure clad in a drab sweater, had felt all at once a twinge of envy. Yolanda's youth! Yolanda's courage! "If I ran away with Kit, what then?" she had demanded.

"Oh, my soul, Aunt Jack, do I have to tell you? If I ran away, I'd forget there was anybody in the world but myself and him — and be happy."

"Happiness isn't won that way, Yolanda."

"Isn't it? Have you ever tried any way but your own, Aunt Jack?"

She flung the challenge at her aunt's feet, and Jacqueline flung back a startled, "No."

"Well, then — " triumphantly.

"I've done the best I know — " Jacqueline had said forlornly, and suddenly Yolanda's arms had been about her, "You darling old thing. I'd hate having you go."

"Would you really, Yolanda?"

Yolanda had given her a big hug. "You're too nice to be true. But nobody else in the family knows it."

Their eyes had met, and Jacqueline had been all at once aware that Yolanda was at last grown up. The child was a woman. The thought had given her a sense of security. Here was young Yolanda, clear-eyed, understanding. Her challenging youth seemed to take on an unexpected value. Her strength might be a shield and buckler to them both.

The wind had come up and was blowing about them — the wild wind that Jacqueline loved. Jacqueline had raised her voice to speak above it. "Darling, it has been a great help to have you say all this."

With her cold cheek pressed affectionately against her aunt's, Yolanda said, "I'm going to tell Dad what I think of him. . . ."

"About what?"

"You."

"Oh, don't, Yolanda."

"I shall. He's so obsessed by the thought of Mother that he can't see anything else. He puts things over on you, Aunt Jack. We all put things over, but he's the worst of the lot."

Nothing that Jacqueline could say would deter Yolanda from her purpose, and that night Joel, voicing a small complaint about the roast, was stopped by Yolanda's cool voice, "Don't make Aunt Jack the goat, Daddy."

Joel had looked up startled, "What do you mean, Yolanda? I don't like your language."

Yolanda met the issue squarely, "I had to say it that way to make you listen. We're all getting so that if the furnace doesn't work or the ice-cream doesn't freeze, or the morning paper doesn't come, we blame it on Aunt Jack. And it's not a sporting proposition."

Deep red had come into Joel's cheeks, and Jacqueline

had feared an explosion. Joel's nerves were not of the best in these days. For a moment he had gone on with his carving and had said nothing. Then he had laid down his knife. "Do we — bulldoze you, Jacqueline?"

And suddenly she had found herself saying, "It's like this, Joel. I sail the boat. But I'm not the captain!"

Joel had flung back his head and had stared at her, while Yolanda shrieked with laughter, "Oh, you darling, *darling*."

And all at once, Jacqueline had heard them all laughing, Yolanda's staccato shrieks, Joel's bass, small Joey's piping treble. "We're a darned poor crew," Joel was saying, "but after this we're going to do better."

In some ways things had been better. But human nature is human nature, and the Hutchins family was not ripe for sainthood. But they had all scrambled along throughout the years without great friction, and had it not been for that constant ache at her heart for Kit, Jacqueline might have been happy.

II

The telephone rang, and Jacqueline went in to answer it. It was Mrs. Gilman speaking, "We've had a marvellous letter from Sue."

"Really?"

"Yes. I'd like to have you read it. Can't you come over and take tea with us tomorrow? Or shall I send the letter to you?"

"I'll come. . . ."

Jacqueline hung up the receiver and went back to the porch. Standing by Simon's cage, she ruffled the feathers of his neck thoughtfully. Her mind was on Sue and Sue's letter. For Sue was in India. She and Paula had at last sailed around the world, and Kit had spoken in a recent letter of their anticipated arrival. "It will be good to see some one from home. Yet in a way it will open my wounds, Jack. I sometimes think it is better to have no reminders of you, dearest. I live along fairly well between letters, shutting away the thought of what might be if I had you here. . . ."

That letter had not sounded like Kit. Never before had he spoken of "wounds" and of "reminders." He had seemed content with her letters and his hope for the future. Yet Paula had said these things would not satisfy a man forever — men want more than — dreams. . . ."

Now and then she had begged Kit to come back — to be near her. Old Timothy Howland had said that it was possible. "There's a place for him in the office. Business is much better."

But Kit had not been willing to come. "I'm not sure I can make you understand, my darling, that it is easier to be at long distance. When you say you'll marry me, I'll give you a honeymoon of romance and adventure and then we'll come back to Boston."

And now it was Sue who was having the adventure . . . if not the romance! Jacqueline voiced her own restlessness, her own longing, as she spoke to the parrot.

"Oh, Simon, Simon, if only we could flap our wings and fly away!"

She had developed a habit of confiding in Simon. They were great cronies, and his weird, murmuring voice would take on soft notes of comforting as she stood by his cage. It was as if his yearning for the freedom he had lost and her yearning for her freedom she had never found had brought them together.

She went back to her work. And as she wove her needle back and forth in one of Joel's golf stockings, she was thinking busily of some of the things Sue had said to her on the eve of departure. "I feel as if I were running away from my old self, Jack. As if I should find a new self—out there."

"I hope it will be as nice as the Sue I know," Jack had told her, smiling.

"I show my best to you, Jack...." Sue had said, with her eyes on the floor, "I hope I shall always show it." And after that, she had gone away, and Jacqueline had wondered just what she had meant, and why she had said it.

Simon was screaming a welcome, as small Joey came up on the porch. Joey had hair like his mother's and Yolanda's. But he was more cherubic than Yolanda. He had no angles. He was all soft plumpness and dimples and smiles. His nose had little golden freckles and at the moment his flushed face was beaded with perspiration.

He flung himself down on the step, "Gee, I'm thirsty!"

"Hannah has some lemonade in the kitchen."

He rushed in and came back with a tray on which was set two frosted glasses. "One for you, too, Aunt Jack."

She smiled at him as she took it, "I didn't know I wanted it, but I do."

He sat down at her feet. "'Landa's in swimming."

"I told her she could go."

"She'd have gone if you hadn't told her."

Jacqueline knew that he spoke the truth. She gave Yolanda permission to do things, lest she risk disobedience. Yet Yolanda rarely asked to do that which got her into trouble. Her courage and caution and common-sense, combined to make her independence less alarming than it might otherwise have been.

Joey's voice had an injured note, "You didn't say I could go."

"Darling, you stayed in too long yesterday, and your ear hurt last night."

Joey considered that. "Doesn't 'Landa ever stay in too long?"

"Not often. But then she's older. . . ."

"When I get old can I do the things I want to do?"

"Not if they hurt you — or other people."

"I wouldn't want to hurt anybody," Joey said, earnestly, "I wouldn't want to hurt anybody. . . . Not even the teeniest, tiniest kitten."

He was adorable as he said it. His little freckled nose was wrinkled, his blue eyes were clear and confiding. She went and sat on the step beside him.

Joey was so very much her own because he was like her. He had the same sensitiveness, the same fear of giving pain to others. "Of course you wouldn't hurt the teeniest, tiniest kitten," she said, and took his hand in hers and patted it.

He drew closer and tucked his hand in the hollow of her arm, "Tell me a story."

She told him of How the Sea came to be Salt. Joey never wanted stories of the war as did Yolanda. He even balked at "Fee-Fi-Fo-Fum" and the "blood of an English-*mun*," in which Yolanda's soul delighted. "I don't want to hear," he would say, sturdily, when Yolanda pressed her gruesome reminiscences upon him. He was a child of peace, as Yolanda was a child of war. Yet Jacqueline knew that it was he who would suffer, as she herself had suffered, as all those suffered who took unto themselves the pains of others.

As she sat there on the step, however, with small Joey held close while she told him his story, Jacqueline was very near happiness. And she looked childish and charming, as the wind blew soft tendrils of hair about her face, and the declining sun drew broad bars of gold across her blue linen.

It was thus that Joel saw her as he came up the walk. He often came home to find her sitting there on the steps with small Joey. At first it had given him a bit of shock to see her in Mary's place. But the years had softened the first agony of his wife's illness, and he had been glad of Jack's welcome and of her presence on the porch.

Five Years

Now and then, however, he had wondered, that small Joey did not sit upstairs. Mary was so gentle with her children, so eager for their confidence, and how could Joel know that small Joey would say, when his aunt urged him to go to his mother, "I'd rather be with you, Aunt Jack. Mummy's sick, and it makes me — sorry. . . ."

Yet Yolanda would sail into her mother's room, bringing her youth and freshness, giving an account of a lively and interesting day, and doing it all with such an air of enjoyment that Mary was carried away from an atmosphere of invalidism into one of activity and energy.

"Mary gets a lot more from Yolanda than she gets from the rest of us." Jacqueline told herself. "We sympathise too much, and she needs stimulation."

III

Joel sat down on the step. In his somewhat shabby summer clothes he lacked the smartness which had been his when he returned from France. He looked tired and depressed. "Broiling in town," he said, wiping his forehead.

Jacqueline knew that it was more than the heat which weighed on his spirits. Business had not been good. He had spoken of it a few nights before. Jacqueline had been so sorry for him then. She was sorry for him now.

"Why don't you go down for a swim before dinner," she suggested.

"'Landa's swimming," Joey complained, "but Aunt Jack won't let me."

"It's his ear," Jacqueline elucidated, "but if you are going in, Joel, you can see that he gets out before he is chilled."

Joey flung himself upon her, "May I really, Aunt Jack?"

She kissed him, "Of course you may, with Daddy."

"You come too."

The idea appealed to her. The air was sultry and the thought of the deep still waters refreshing. As she hesitated, Joel said, "Come on in, Jack, you need it as much as we do."

As she went up to her room a few minutes later to change, she heard Joel talking to Mary. There was no sign of weariness in his voice. He was gay and laughing. "You won't mind, old darling, if I leave you for a moment for a dip? The heat has been deadly." Down the long hall she could see him sitting by the bed. He had lifted Mary's hand to his lips — "How sweet and cool you look, my precious. . . ."

Joel was always like that — bringing his best to Mary. Jacqueline prayed that he might always bring his best. Every fresh evidence of his devotion was balm to her fears. She knew she should not be afraid, but there was so much skepticism in the world about the happiness of marriage — the books, the plays, everything emphasised the fact that men grew tired of old wives and wanted new ones. That men wanted youth and beauty, comrades along the way. And here was Mary and her dim room. There swept back upon Jacqueline now and then the thought of that night when Sue had dined with them on the eve of Kit's departure. Joel had played the gallant and Sue had played up to him. Since then there had been other moments of gallantry; other charming women. But there had been nothing serious in Joel's small philanderings, and Jacqueline had told herself that there was no cause for her alarms. It was only that she was so jealous of Mary's happiness. And it was this fear and jealousy which had spurred her to greater endeavors in making the home what Mary would have made of it. Men were, after all, somewhat held by creature comforts. If Joel missed nothing in the domestic atmosphere, he might be content. So she had fought throughout the years for Mary, setting herself against the forces of unrest which might have made Joel seek livelier company.

When the three of them came down to the float at the foot of the hill, they found Yolanda sitting on it and talking to Stuart Carleton. Stuart's family had a home on the Neck. It was a great estate, kept in order by a large staff of servants. Stuart was an only son, a good-looking lad of eighteen, with a strong body which showed to good effect in his black and orange tunic, and a frank smile which lighted his features as he greeted Joel and Jacqueline.

Yolanda in a sea-blue bathing suit with her head tied up in a red handkerchief was having her own way with Stuart as she had it with every one else. "Stuart wants me to go to a clambake on the Neck. Tonight. Tell him I can't Aunt Jacqueline."

"Of course you can't," Jacqueline said, "you're too young for grown-up parties."

"I knew she'd find a reason," Yolanda surveyed Stuart from under long lashes, "I couldn't think of one. . . ."

"She's dying to go," Stuart told them. "But she won't because I ask it."

"You flatter yourself. . . !" Yolanda at fifteen! As accomplished in the art of coquetry as a lady of some old court!

"I'd ask somebody else," Stuart informed his listeners, "if I didn't know it was just what she wanted. I'd be bored stiff with any other girl, and that's what she's hoping."

Yolanda fluttered her fingers in the air in a mocking gesture, "Bright lad. . . !" She turned a somersault and flung herself from the float into the deep water.

Stuart was after her in a moment. And Joel and Jacqueline sitting on the float heard the shrieks of laughter with which Yolanda greeted his approach.

But Joel was not laughing. "Would you think," he demanded, "that she was Mary's daughter?"

"Times have changed, Joel."

"But would Mary ever — could you have played the game as — expertly? Even now. At your age? You couldn't. And Yolanda's nothing but a child."

"Yolanda has always known what she wanted—and gone after it. . . ."

"Do you mean that she wants—that youngster? Great guns, Jack. It hasn't been any time since she played with dolls."

"I'm not so sure that Yolanda ever played with dolls. Not as Mary and I played with them. They were our babies. They were puppets for Yolanda's show. . . ."

Joel turned and looked at her. "Just what do you mean by that?"

"Oh, Yolanda's world is a stage." She laughed, "I'm not criticising her, Joel. But she plans her effects. Most of the girls of today do that. They are conscious of their power. Mary and I were not."

"Mary wants to send Yolanda to a boarding school in Washington," Joel said, his eyes still on the fleeing pair. "I think this settles it. I'm not going to have my daughter mixed up in a boy and girl affair. Even if the boy is Stuart Carleton."

"Boarding school will be frightfully expensive."

Joel squared his shoulders. "I'll make ends meet somehow. It isn't as if Yolanda had her mother, Jack. If Mary were on her feet, she might hold her back a bit. . . ."

Had anybody ever held Yolanda back?

Jacqueline felt it was useless to argue. And she would be glad to have Yolanda off her hands. Even if the child's going made her own future more uncertain. With Yolanda away—there would be less chance than ever of leaving Mary. . . .

As she swam off through the bright and bouyant waters, she had a sense of the futility of fighting fate . . . if only she might drift and drift across this shining sea, until she came at last to the shores of India. . . !

IV

Jacqueline went over the next day to the Gilmans to hear Sue's letter. Mrs. Gilman and Phoebe were having tea in the garden, which was at the back of the house and ran down to a thin stream of water which had once been a wide river, up which had sailed the ships of some Gilman ancestor who had docked at his own pier, and had entertained his crew in the kitchen.

The garden was gorgeous with late bloom — solid masses of pink and white phlox rose up tall behind the tea-table. Mrs. Gilman and Phoebe were in basket chairs. They wore thin dresses, such as they had always worn in summer, and beads and chains were about their necks. Their white heads were curled and carefully coiffed. Although their gowns were of modern cut, they retained in their figures and bearing something of the stiff and formal aspect of the nineties.

They welcomed Jacqueline with enthusiasm. "We have missed you, my dear, of late."

"I should have come long ago," Jacqueline said, "but I've had a thousand things to do. And just now Hannah and I are putting up pickled peaches. We have a dozen stone jars of them."

Five Years 171

"We buy ours in Boston," Miss Phoebe said, "it's less work."

Jacqueline laughed, "But more money. We have to look to our pennies."

She leaned back in her chair and smiled at them. Her sheer dimity frock was flowered with pale yellow, and her wide hat had a flat bow of yellow ribbon. The dress was cheap and she had made it herself, but it gave an effect of elegance.

"Shall I read the letter to you?" Mrs. Gilman asked, "Sue's writing is rather difficult—and there's a volume."

"I'll listen," Jacqueline took off her hat and dropped it on the grass beside her, "and I'll drink two cups of tea while you're reading, and eat a lot of Miss Phoebe's cakes." Her voice was light and lazy. She looked like a lady quite at ease with the world. Yet she was dreading to hear what Sue might say. She began to understand what Kit had meant when he had talked of "wounds" and "reminders."

Sue's style was characteristic. She wrote as she talked. "Everybody wants to know why we came to India in the hot season. But it is heavenly up here in the hills, and we aren't submerged by tourists. Kit is with us, of course. He had a chance for a holiday, and took it at this time. Paula is in her element. We've met all the officers in the world, and you know what a hit she makes with them. And she got a lot of gowns in Tokio."

"I bought some new gowns also. But I'm not wearing many of them. Kit doesn't care a lot for parties, and we spend most of our time on horseback. . . . I'm sending you some pictures. We've been to oceans of old temples, and often we go off for a day with a sandwich or two in Kit's pocket, and a handful of nuts and chocolate. One day I rode an elephant, and we went through a forest—it was like something out of the Jungle Book—and Kit quoted Kipling. . . ."

Jacqueline's hand on her teacup was steady. But her blood was racing. So Sue was seeing the temples. . . . Sue was riding into the deep forest. . . . Kit was quoting Kipling—to Sue!

"Kit is no end popular. . . ." Mrs. Gilman's voice went on, "but he doesn't go about much. . . . Everybody out here knows he's engaged. He doesn't make a secret of it. People thought at first that I was the girl, and we made a great joke of it . . . some of them still insist that we are holding something out on them. But Kit says he doesn't mind their teasing if I don't. He has a picture of Jack on the table in his sitting-room. He says that he who runs may read; that anybody would know that I'm not the lady of the picture."

"But you tell Jack that if she doesn't come out pretty soon that somebody will snap Kit up. I may even do it myself. I give her fair warning. A man like Kit deserves something better than these lonely years in a foreign country. Of course I don't mean all that. Jack's a darling, but she isn't giving Kit a square deal . . . and she'd know it if she could see him."

Again Jacqueline's blood was racing! So Sue was giving her warning . . . Sue!

Five Years

Mrs. Gilman laid down the letter. Her voice seemed to come from a thousand miles away. "Sue will have her joke. You mustn't mind what she says, Jacqueline. She and Kit have always been such good friends. . . ."

Miss Phoebe pouring more tea for her sister, said, "It was more than that for a time. They had quite a little romance before Kit left college."

Mrs. Gilman stopped her, "They were nothing but children, Phoebe."

"Yes," Miss Phoebe pursued her theme relentlessly, "but he carved their initials by the side of his fireplace. . . ."

Mrs. Gilman again interposed. "You'll be making Jacqueline jealous, Phoebe."

Jacqueline smiled and shook her head, "How old were these children?" she asked, and helped herself to a slice of lemon.

"She was twelve and he was fifteen."

Fifteen! Yolanda was fifteen. Jacqueline's mind flashed back to that mad chase in the water. Boys and girls grow up so soon. She had been only two years older than Yolanda when Kit had met her . . . but then there had been the war and she had grown old all at once.

She jabbed her lemon slice with her spoon. "He really should have married Sue," her light laugh seemed to dismiss it as casual, "perhaps he would, if he hadn't met me — at a dance. . . ."

Mrs. Gilman folded up the letter, "He's proved that you're the one he wants — or he wouldn't have waited so long, my dear. . . ."

Miss Phoebe, forthright and frank, remarked, "Men don't wait forever."

Her words rang in Jacqueline's ears, as still with that effect of a lady at her ease, she looked at the photographs Sue had sent—*"Men don't wait forever.... men don't wait forever...!"*

She didn't want to look at the pictures. To see Sue and Kit together. But what could she do with Mrs. Gilman and Miss Phoebe expecting it. So there they were.... Sue in white—an arresting and graceful figure—and Kit. *Oh, my wonderful, wonderful Kit...!*

Sue had been photographed on horseback, on the steps of the temples, under great trees, riding the elephant, and always Kit was with her—tall, sitting his horse like a Centaur, his hand on the bridle of Sue's mount, towering a bit above Sue as she sat on the temple steps ... his arm above her head against a tree trunk where the picture had been snapped in a sunlighted space in the forest....

No wonder people had thought they were engaged or married. The way Sue looked up at him.... *But, Kit, oh, my Kit, you aren't looking down at her as if you were engaged or married? You are saving that for me ... when I come?*

Yet again came the knell of Miss Phoebe's words, "*Men don't wait forever...!*" She wanted to shout to the world, "My Kit will wait—forever...."

She was glad when at last she got away without having showed a sign of her seething emotions. As she turned at the gate and waved "Good-bye" she seemed

Five Years 175

to the two older women as cool and calm as the waters of the quiet stream which flowed at the foot of the garden. But she was not calm. She was faint and dizzy with her effort at self-control. Her temples throbbed. She felt that she could not face the people on the street. She had the keys of the Howland home in her handbag. She ran up the steps, opened the door and let herself in, then stood in the hall, trembling.

And now no friendly ghosts were there to greet her. All the dead and gone Howland's were silent, as if they were hiding something from her. She and Kit had wound the old clock before he went away, and it had been her joy to keep it going, so that it might greet her like something alive when she came in. But today it did not greet her. Its pendulum, swinging back and forth, sang a sinister song, "*Sue — Kit! Sue — Kit! Tick — tock! Tick — tock!*"

She went into the library and let in the light. Then she got down on her knees before the fireplace. It was some time before she found what she sought, but at last she came upon the carving — Sue's and Kit's initials intertwined and enclosed in a fat heart with a little flame at the top.

So Kit had cut into the wood that heart with its flame! And he had not told her. It seemed to her that she could stand it better if he had spoken of it . . . had laughed about it . . . lightly! But he had not laughed. Perhaps it had gone too deep with him; perhaps when he had carved that flaming heart, Sue's bright head had been against his shoulder!

Still kneeling, Jacqueline stared into the black and

empty fireplace. Tears began to drip. She wiped them away. She must not cry. Presently she would have to meet the glare of sunshine outside and people staring. She rose and went into the hall. There was light from the transom to show her reflection in the mirror above the table. She took from her bag a tiny puff and freshened her face with powder. The mirror gave back a charming vision in wide hat and flowered frock. Kit liked her in things like that — sheer and colorful. Oh, why had she said "like?" He *loved* her.

CHAPTER EIGHT

Life and Little Things

I

JACQUELINE, riding home in the trolley, had a sense of something impending. The day was hot and still, and black clouds were piling up in the west. There would be rain and wind, she heard one of her fellow passengers saying, and cared not a bit. The more the elements raged, the more fitting it would be to her mood. She had been shaken to the depths by the events of the afternoon. She felt dazed and numb. She wanted to get home — to think it all out — to regain if she might some measure of serenity.

When she reached her corner and the car stopped, the rain was coming down in torrents. She had no umbrella, and she walked straight through the drenching storm to her own front porch. The yellow-flowered frock was bedraggled, and the wide hat was limp, but the ruin of her crisp apparel brought no sense of distress. What was one frock, more or less, or one wide hat, when weighed in the balance with the Gilmans' soul-shaking revelations. . . ?

She went through the hall and opened the kitchen

door. Old Hannah looked up from the roast she was basting, and saw the drenched and dripping figure. "My lamb," she cried, "you'll take your death!"

"I'm not cold, Hannah . . . but my head aches. . . ." It seemed to Jacqueline that the kitchen with its bright pots and pans, its glowing range, its geranium in the window, the old woman in her blue dress, was whirling about her in a mad dance. . . ! She caught at the door-post, and Hannah dropped the spoon and hurried towards her. With the old woman's arms about her, Jacqueline said, "Do you think it would be dreadful if I didn't come down — to dinner?"

"Not dreadful at all, my dearie. You run right up and get into dry things. And I'll bring you a hot drink."

So Jacqueline climbed the stairs, thankful that neither Yolanda nor small Joey was about, and got into bed and lying cool and comfortable among her pillows, looked at her room as if it were a strange place.

For hitherto, it had been — sanctuary. To it she had withdrawn when the world outside had seemed unbearable, and there had been Kit smiling at her from his ivory frame, and the white jade goddess, and Kit's letters in the lacquered box, and after an hour spent with her treasures, she had gone forth ready to meet anything, girded, as it were, by the armor of Kit's constancy and devotion.

But now . . . Kit's smile hurt! *Did you smile like that — at Sue?* The jade goddess seemed cold and unresponsive . . . and she dared not open the lacquered box!

She felt that she might sleep if only things wouldn't beat so in her brain. She moved restlessly to get rid of the sound, but could not—"*Tick-tock—Kit-Sue . . . Tick-tock. . . .*"

Old Hannah brought up a pot of tea. "I don't want it, Hannah."

"You need it, my lamb," and the old woman sat beside her until she had drunk two cups.

Old Hannah knew that her darling had been crying. But she said not a word. Before she went down she drew the curtains, so that the room was dark, and she kissed Jacqueline on the cheek.

And after old Hannah had gone, the clock still beat in Jacqueline's brain—"*Tick-tock. . . .*"

She heard Joel's voice when he came from his train, and presently he tapped at her door. "Sorry to know you're not up to things, old girl."

"I'm all right, Joel. A bit of a headache. Don't worry."

And after that came Yolanda, tip-toeing in. "Asleep, Aunt Jack?"

"Not yet," Jacqueline was glad of the dim light. Yolanda's young eyes were sharp.

"Anything I can do?"

"Not a thing, darling."

"Aunt Jack, may I talk to you for a minute?"

A muffled, "Yes."

"What do you think—? I'm going with Stuart to the clambake!"

A moment's silence, then, "Does your father know?"

"Yes. Stuart came over with a note from his mother.

She'll call for me in her car. I told Stuart I was going because I adored — his mother."

"That wasn't very nice for Stuart, was it?"

"It doesn't pay to be nice to men."

"Yolanda, *darling*...! I hate to have you sound so sophisticated."

Yolanda laughed, "Oh, well, one gets a lot from books."

A thousand years old, this young Yolanda? Jacqueline had no weapons with which to meet such worldliness.

She said from her pillow, "I hope you'll have a good time."

"It will be gorgeous, Aunt Jack."

Yolanda went away ... and the beat began again in Jacqueline's brain — *Kit and Sue ... Kit and Sue ... tick-tock ... tick-tock...!*

Small Joey crept in to say "Good-night." He stood by the bed and patted her cheek. "Will you be well in the morning, Aunt Jack?"

"Of course, darling. I'm not really sick — just tired."

"Aunt Jack, I've got a little kitten."

"Really, darling?"

"Yes. I brought it up to show you. Mother says I can keep it."

It was too dark for her to see it, but she put out her hand and Joey guided it to the warm furry body. She could feel the whirr of the little creature's ecstatic purring, as her fingers brushed its throat. "How wonderful that you can have it, Joey."

"Mother wouldn't ever let me keep one before. She doesn't like cats."

"But we do, don't we, Joey?"

"Yes. Mrs. Carleton brought this when she came for Yolanda in her car.

In the dark, Jacqueline smiled. Mary had let Joey have the kitten because Mrs. Carleton had brought it. Mary adored the fact that people on the Neck were making much of Yolanda.

Joey went away with his kitten, and after a time Jacqueline got up and sat by the open window. The rain had stopped, and the moon, rising over the tops of the houses, showed roofs and gables, thin as cardboard against the pale sky. The windows across the way were brimming with yellow light which spilled over in a shining stream to the sidewalk. Gradually the lights went out. She heard Joel's voice as he read aloud to Mary. Then came his step on the stairs. He would go out on the porch to smoke his last cigar and to wait for Yolanda.

A half hour later, the big car slid up, and Jacqueline leaned out in the darkness to listen. She heard Stuart and Yolanda laughing; Mrs. Carleton speaking to Joel in her charming voice; Stuart saying, "I'll see you tomorrow, 'Landa," and Yolanda answering, "I'll be dead to the world after the lobsters n'everything . . . but you can call me up"; Joel and Yolanda talking together on the porch; the rustle of Yolanda's dress as she passed the door — then silence.

And in that silence Jacqueline dressed and went

downstairs. As she climbed the hill she told herself, tumultuously, that she couldn't stand that beat in her brain a moment longer. She felt that if she could only go up to the bluff, she would meet Kit as she had so often met him, and her doubts would die. She would tell him, there on the bluff, that he meant more to her than all the world ... more than Joel or Mary, or Yolanda, or small Joey; that she was going to leave them all — "forsaking all others, Kit," and go out with him to India. For her there were only two people in the universe — herself and Kit. She would tell him that...! As for Sue, hadn't Kit himself said that all the Gilmans were "hard and handsome?" He had said it of Sue as well as the others.

She had reached the bluff and stood on its edge. The moonlight was flooding the world. There was no sound but the lip-lipping of the waves on the rocks below. Jacqueline missed the wild wind, which had so often borne her messages across the sea. She had a message now, *"Kit, I'm coming!"*

She flung the words forth and waited for a response. But none came. For the first time in all the years, Kit did not answer her!

She put her hands to her mouth, trumpet-wise, "Kit — my darling...." But the gold of the moonlight seemed to build up a bright wall about her, against which her voice struck and splintered into a thousand echoing murmers. She felt impotent and insignificant in the vast golden space.

Oh, well, she would come again when the wild wind

Life and Little Things

blew. It would wrap her about as Kit's arms had enfolded her. Then it would go shrieking across the sea with her message, and Kit would hear, and she would see him as she had so often seen him, coming down to the shining strand!

II

The next morning brought Kit's weekly letter. There was a lot of mail, but Jacqueline, seeing Kit's bold script and familiar blue envelope, seized upon it, and went out on the porch where she might be free from interruption. Simon in his cage gave her a noisy welcome. Joey's small kitten, a smoky puff-ball, danced in the sunlight. Simon screamed when he saw the kitten, then settled down to a gentle scolding.

Jacqueline's hands trembled as she tore open the blue envelope. She had a sense of foreboding, as if in some way this letter would be different. Yet as she read, her fears vanished. Kit begged her to come out to him. At once. "Jack, I must have you. This can't keep on — forever."

He said little of Sue. She was there and he had been around with her, but he gave no details of their adventures. People had entertained them a lot, and Paula was having the time of her life with plenty of new clothes and plenty of new officers. "She's a great old girl, when you come to think of it."

But Jacqueline was not interested in Paula. She dwelt on the part of Kit's letter which had to do with her own coming. Of course she would go. Hadn't she told him last night, out there on the bluff? And wasn't this his blessed answer? Oh, Kit, Kit, my darling...."

The kitten danced towards her sideways. Jacqueline caught it up in her arms. She felt that she loved every living thing. *Kit ... Kit ...!*

Simon screamed again when he saw her with the kitten. "Oh, Simon, Simon," Jacqueline told him, "I'm going to fly away. And I'll take you with me, and I'll set you free somewhere in a great deep forest...."

She saw the forest, and Kit there beside her. Perhaps they would ride an elephant, with Simon's cage set up in front of them ... and there would be a still green light, and Kit would open the cage, and set Simon on a branch of a great tree, and there would be all of Simon's red and blue and purple in the dim, still place.... And Kit's arm would be about her. And she, too, would be free. Free in her happiness, with Kit ... her husband...!

She would go up right now, and tell Mary. And Mary would understand. Mary who loved Joel. She would say to Mary, "Kit can't wait any longer. I must go to him now. Or not go to him at all."

She had made up her mind to that. Kit must not be tied. If she would marry him, he must be free. Sue had said it, and she could see that the Gilmans thought it.

As she began idly to separate her mail, she saw that

Life and Little Things

there was a letter from Paula Gilman. Jacqueline recognized at once the thin angular script which had been the style taught in fashionable schools in Paula's time.

Jacqueline sat down again, and read the letter through, and when she had read it, the world crashed about her. For Paula had not minced words. "I might as well tell you the truth, Jacqueline. It is as plain as the nose on your face that Kit and Sue are in love with each other. He'd be telling her so in a minute if he dared. But there's his promise to you, and you know his chivalry. He wouldn't make you unhappy for the world. Yet why should Sue be unhappy? Or, for that matter, why should Kit? I know I am taking a lot on myself to be writing you this. But why not? I told you long ago, you were making a mistake to tie Kit down, and I am more than ever convinced that I told you the truth. Kit is losing the best years of his life waiting for you. . . . And you should see him and Sue together."

"And you made your choice, Jacqueline. Deep in your heart you cared more for your family, than for your lover. It was their happiness against his, and you let him be unhappy. Forgive my frankness, but, my dear, I am a woman of the world, and I know men. They are not as constant as women. Kit has been a marvel. I'll say that for him. But he has been punished enough."

Oh, Paula was outrageous. . . ! *Outrageous!* Jacqueline crushed the letter in her tight fist. Her cheeks were blazing, her slight body shaking. Simon screamed and the kitten danced. But she saw neither of them. She saw only a spectral, Stygian space, with Paula's angular letters stalking. . . .

In this mood she dared not face Mary. And presently Yolanda would be coming down . . . and there was Hannah . . . and small Joey . . . she must hide from them all.

She ran upstairs, got into her bathing tunic and beach coat and ran down again. There was no one on the float when she reached it, or to see her as she gave herself up to the rocking waves. There was an incoming tide and enough wind to roughen the waters. She swam far out, then turned on her back and drifted with the tide. The sea was green and the sky a faint chrysoprase. Encompassed about by sea and sky she seemed suspended in a translucence which belonged to no material world but was, rather, that of some supernal sphere, uninhabited, except by herself and the gulls above her.

She had forgotten to put on her rubber cap, and the salt water soaked into her braids. But she had no thought of anything but Kit's letter, and Paula's. Kit had said he wanted her. Paula had said he did not. But might there not be a hidden meaning in Kit's letter which Paula had revealed? He had said, "This can't keep on. . . ." Was he giving her a last chance? Had he meant if she refused to come, to let her go — forever?

Oh, why had Paula written? Jacqueline saw suddenly the russet hair, the carefully made-up face. All Paula's kindness that day in the tea-room had been false kindness. Even then she had wanted Kit for Sue. Her smile had been baleful. She had been like a witch in one of Joey's fairy tales.

She floated on and on. She was aware, as in a dream, that Yolanda in an inadequate negligee was waving from her window to Stuart Carleton whose speed boat had just come pip-popping up to the float. Her voice carried clearly, "I'll be down in a moment."

Neither of them had seen Jacqueline. She knew she ought to go in. That Mary would be waiting. She knew, too, that she should be giving Hannah her orders. Joel would come home that night hot and hungry. There ought to be something cool for dinner ... chilled cucumbers cut up with little onions, cold salmon with mayonnaise and capers, iced tea, a melon....

She found herself laughing hysterically. Oh, what kind of woman was she who could think of capers and salmon—onions—in the midst of her life's tragedy? But then, it had always been like that—little things— Joel's dinners, and Mary's morning bath, Joey's small tempers, and Yolanda's cocksureness. She had never been able to shake herself free from the burden of the commonplace. She had been held and bound by them, when, waiting to her hand as it were, had been the big emotions—the things of which Kit had written in the little book....

"My heart is like an apple-tree,
  Whose boughs are bent with richest fruit...."

And she had sacrificed the big things — the rich things, for dry-as-dust-duty. Well, she wouldn't any more. She would take what was her own — *my heart is like an apple-tree* — what did she care for Paula's angular tirade? Or Sue's scoldings?

She swam back to the float, and climbed the hill to the house. As she went through the lower hall, she heard old Hannah in the kitchen, singing. Yolanda in a bright red beach coat passed her like a flash, "I'm going for a swim with Stuart." Small Joey was in the garden, with his kitten, and Simon screamed on the porch.

Jacqueline when she went at last into her sister's room, wore her blue bath robe and had her hair down to dry. "Sorry to be so late, Mary, but I had a swim."

"And you got your hair wet. You should have worn a cap."

"I forgot it," Jacqueline handed the mail to Mary, then sat down by the open window, lifting her long locks fan-wise to catch the breeze.

Mary looked over her letters. "Did you get anything, Jack?"

"One — from Kit."

"Sue still out there?"

"Yes." But Jacqueline did not want to talk of Sue. "I got caught in the rain when I came home from the Gilmans. I had to run for my life through the rain, and my dress is a ruin. And my hat...."

Mary laid down her letters. A shadow had fallen across her face and she said, listlessly, "Have a good tea?"

"Yes. There were the little cakes that Kit likes . . . and a lot of things . . . it was too hot . . . to eat much . . ." she stopped for a moment and went on. . . . "They are buying their pickled peaches in Boston, Mary . . . its expensive but easier, Miss Phoebe says . . . . Mrs. Gilman is reading Pickwick Papers and Miss Phoebe, Martin Chuzzlewit . . . they always read Dickens in summer . . ." another pause, then "they read me a letter from Sue. . . ."

Mary was not listening. She looked up from the rings which she was turning thoughtfully on her thin fingers, and said, with a touch of vehemence, "Sue Gilman's a cat!"

Jacqueline stared at her, startled, "Mary!"

"Oh, I mean it. She has always had an eye on Kit."

"Mary, don't. . . ." Jacqueline's voice was sharp. It seemed to her dreadful that Mary should be putting crudely into words, the thought which she had been trying to deny to her own consciousness.

"Don't, Mary," she repeated, "Sue is my — good friend."

"No woman is another woman's friend when there's a man in the case," Mary said, inexorably, "and we might as well speak the truth about it. You needn't think, Jack, that because I am up here in bed, I haven't known what was going on about me. Sue comes and talks to me and makes eyes at Joel. And now that she's in India, she is probably making eyes at Kit."

Jacqueline had a shuddering sense of the awfulness of the things Mary was saying. They seemed to drag them both down to dark levels of suspicion and jealousy. And then, poignantly, came sweeping over her the memory of that day during the War, of the children's party, and of herself and Yolanda holding their hands high above the heads of the singing children. . . .

"London Bridge is falling down,
Falling down, falling down,
London Bridge is falling down. . . . "

And she had felt that more than London Bridge was falling. The world was falling when women lost faith in the men who loved them.

And she had said to Mary, "When the time comes that I can't believe in Christopher — I won't believe in — God."

And now she was going out to him not because of her faith and trust, but because she was afraid of Sue. She wasn't going because he had asked it, as he had asked through all the years, or because she could be better spared here. She was needed as much as ever. Perhaps more. Yet she was going — because Sue was there — and might — get him. . . !

That was the vulgar truth of it, stripped of all glamour. She was flying to her lover, not in the free upper air of unquestioning devotion. She was beating through the storm on anxious wings, hoping to find a haven. What was it Paula had said? That she could depend on his chivalry, but not his constancy?

Life and Little Things

As she sat there in the bower of her bronze hair, thinking it out, Mary, watching her, said to herself, "If Kit could only see her like this. . . . She's lovely."

And, suddenly, Jacqueline looked up at her and said, "Mary, I'm not going to marry him."

Mary gasped, "My darling, why. . . ?"

"Because I trust him so much . . . that I can set him free. I know what everyone is saying . . . that he's tied . . . that if he were . . . rid of me . . . he'd marry—Sue. Well, I don't believe it. I believe he'll care forever . . . as I shall care. But I shall send back his ring . . ." her voice wavered, stopped.

"Jacqueline, don't do any thing so idiotic."

"Yes," she came over and stood by the bed. "I've let everybody treat me like a child, Mary. But I'm not a child. And I've got my pride. If Kit chooses to wait . . . he can love me in his heart, as I love him . . . distance will make no difference. . . . You see how I—trust him—Mary. . . ."

She was white and shaking. Mary held out a hand to her. "My darling, marry him now. . . ."

"No."

"Why not?"

"I've told you."

"Is it because you think—we need you? I'll be better soon. . . ."

Jacqueline did not answer, and Mary looking up saw something in her sister's wan gaze had made her cry out—"Jack, is it because I'm not—going to get well?"

It was the first time in all the years that she had asked

that question of Jacqueline and she had never asked it
of Joel. "I think she's afraid, poor darling," Joel had
told Jacqueline, "she'd rather not know."

But now she was asking. Jacqueline dropped to her
knees beside the bed, "Dearest, dear, things will work
out for all of us."

But Mary clutched at her shoulders, "Jack, look at
me — is it because you knew . . . that you have stayed
. . . all these years?"

"I wanted to stay, Mary."

"Do you think I would have let you, if I'd known?
Why, you're sacrificing your whole life. And it's bad
enough for me . . ." she flung out her hands. "Oh,
when you were talking about running home in the
rain, I thought I'd give the whole world if only I could
run like that. I wouldn't have cared if my dress was
ruined and my hat. I wouldn't have cared for anything, if I could have felt the rain beating and my feet
flying, and my body coming — alive. . . ."

She was sobbing wildly. Jacqueline set herself to
soothe her. "Doctors don't really know."

"Jack," she could hardly catch the whispered words,
"Jack, I've heard if — one has faith. . . ."

"Darling. . . ."

"Oh, God . . . make me well. . . ."

Jacqueline shrank from the sound of that whispering
voice. And in that moment her own bitterness was
blotted out by the awful shadow of Mary's misery —
*I wouldn't have cared what happened, Jack. . . . I'd
give the world if I could feel my feet flying . . . and
my body . . . coming alive. . . !*

CHAPTER NINE

The King of France

I

PAULA watched Sue and Kit as they rode away.

"Such a pair. Such a pair," she exulted.

They walked their horses down the hill through a huddle of houses. The morning sun was hot and gold, and the goldness had painted Sue's skin until her blue eyes looked out deeper and warmer because of the sunburn, and her hair was ablaze under her white helmet.

"Such a pair," Paula said again in her heart, and turned back to her shadowed room and sat down to read her letters. There was one from Phoebe which told about Jacqueline's afternoon in the garden. "She was very pretty and young in her flowered gown. We read her Sue's letter . . . and showed her the pictures. . . ."

Paula read that again — "She was very pretty — and *young.*"

Paula hated the thought of Jacqueline's youth. There was something so obvious about it, and enviable. One looked at Sue and felt that her beauty might fade, as Paula's had faded. But Jacqueline's youth had an undying quality. "She'll be young for a thousand years — her spirit will go on through the ages, questing, eager...." Paula found herself prophesying, and hated herself for the prophecy.

She tore up Phoebe's letter with quick nervous fingers, "I must be losing my mind to think of her like that. She'll grow old like the rest of us, and have false teeth, and spectacles and ear trumpets." Yet even as she said it, she knew it was untrue. Jacqueline had a child-like faith in things. And people who believed in life never grew old. Paula had an uneasy memory of Jacqueline's eyes when the two of them had had tea together that afternoon on the North Shore. She had an uneasy memory, too, of her letter.

Well, there were seas between New England and India! And the thing she had planned then had come to pass. Kit was falling in love with Sue!

Anybody with half an eye could see it! And nothing else really mattered. Sue would be happy. And the Gilman pride would be saved. For Paula had put herself vicariously in Sue's place. If Sue should be scorned, that scorn would sear Paula like a hot iron. Jacqueline's happiness counted but little as set against the happiness of the pair of them.

She went back to her letters. Why worry? She would write and read and lunch at her leisure. And Kit and Sue would be back for tea. She hoped when they came that Sue would have something to tell her. Every day she had hoped . . . but she could wait.

Sue, riding beside Kit in the shimmering heat, told

The King of France

herself that she, too, could wait. Kit had been so *perfect*. No woman could expect more than he had given of comradeship, confidence. He had even talked to her of Jacqueline. "She is such a little thing, Sue. She doesn't realize that she is robbing us both of the years we ought to have. I might take her . . . but I won't have her unless she comes willingly. . . ."

He had talked like that when Sue first came. But of late he had been silent. Sue wondered if it was because Jacqueline had ceased to occupy the foreground of his thoughts. "It's good to have you here, Sue," he had said more than once.

They were off for the day now. Sandwiches and tea things were tucked in Kit's saddle bag. Their goal was the wide forest which was spread now like a blue sheet below them. There had been other days in the forest — and Sue had wished those days would never end. They were like, she told herself, something in her old French fairy book, where the lovers in an enchanted forest lived on forever.

Yet she and Kit were not lovers. Or were they? Was not this wish of his to be off for the day together, evidence enough? He had called her up early that morning, "I've got to talk to you, Sue," he had said, "how about a ride? We'll find shade somewhere under the trees."

She loved riding beside him. He was so straight and good-looking. Other women in the little colony envied her. Some of them had been a bit feline about it. Had hinted that she was poaching on Jacqueline's preserves. Thank Heaven, she had managed to keep her temper. What did she care? If only Kit loved her!

She turned to look up at him, and found him staring ahead sternly. He had had little to say since they started. She had tried to make conversation and had failed. Well, Kit was the soul of honor. He would not easily be off with the old and on with the new. It would be only in some great moment of emotion that he would show what he felt. She had thought a lot about it. She did not feel herself disloyal to Jacqueline. Friendship had, of course, its claims, but love broke all rules, and she knew herself deeply, desperately in love with Kit.

"A penny for your thoughts," she found herself saying, bromidically.

He flashed a smile at her.

"Not pleasant enough to share. I'm afraid I'm not being very sociable. But you're such a good fellow, you put up with my grouches."

She wanted to cry out, "I'll put up with everything." But she did not. She talked of little things. The dance the night before — a junior officer had made love to her, "Such a boy, Kit. I am ages too old for him."

He glanced down at her, "You don't look too old for anybody."

She knew that she did not — in her white, with all that sunburn, and with happiness in her heart. It simply stripped her of age, and made her a little girl again.

She laughed, and went back to her officer, "He was

The King of France

great fun. He called me a golden goddess, and said that my skin was sun-ripened, and that it was an inspiration that I had chosen a gold gown. He said it set me apart from all the others."

"It did set you apart," Kit said, "not many women are brave enough to match their gowns to their complexions."

She nodded, "I sacrificed my pink and white for the gold effect. . . ."

"You always had pink cheeks. What a ripping little girl you were, Sue."

She laughed again—and then was silent. And so they entered the wood.

It was an unreal world to which they had come, a world of ebony shadows superimposed on patches of emerald and orange, and then as they went further into the forest, a world of clear, sea-green light, as if they were fathoms down in mid-ocean, with all about them the stillness of unplumbed depths.

Kit chose for their resting-place a space between two trees. Sue took off her hat, and sat with her back against the trunk of an age-old deodar. "Oh, Kit," she said, with a catch of her breath, "how far we are from Salem. . . . I feel as if . . . I had been born again . . . as if I could do and say things that no Gilman had ever done before—"

She said it lightly, smiling, but she meant it. What mattered those old inhibitions. She and Kit were here, in this mystical lovely land. Somewhere, miles away was an old town on a rocky coast, where the wild wind blew, and where a girl waited. But the girl was just a shadow among shadows. She had no place here beneath these strange trees, under these strange skies. These skies, these trees, belonged to Kit, to Sue, and to no others.

She lay, lazily watching Kit make the tea. He did it deftly, boiling the water over a little can of solid alcohol, tending the blue flame, setting out the sandwiches and fruit on delicate paper doilies.

Sue ate with an appetite. "Kit. Why aren't you eating?"

"I'm not hungry."

He peeled a peach for her, "You see, I remember. You always hated the feel of the fur."

"We have so much to remember, Kit."

"Yes . . . ." he shelved that. "These peaches came from Dickey's hot house. He sent them to you. You've made a great hit with everybody, Sue."

Dickey was a certain plutocratic Colonel, who spent a small fortune on horticultural experiments. He was fat and red-faced. Sue smiled as she flickered her juice-stained fingers, "Finger-bowl, Kit?"

He poured ice-water from the thermos into a paper cup and presented it. Sue's hands were lovely — gold like the sun-dyed rest of her, the fine skin unwrinkled, the nails rosy.

But it was not Sue's hands which Kit saw as he held the cup, but other hands, small and white and weighted with a sapphire ring, and seeing that hand, he tossed the cup away and spoke impetuously.

"I've had a letter from Jacqueline."

Sue, drying her slim fingers, said "Oh," uncertainly.

"That's why I brought you here — to talk about it. . . ."

"Yes?"

"I've got to talk to somebody."

"Of course."

He sat at her feet, his knees hunched up, his arms around them, "I might as well tell you — she's broken our engagement."

It seemed to Sue at that moment as if the clear air about them splintered suddenly into sharp bits. It was like glass breaking, a crash in your head and a frightened feeling. Then out of the fright leaped a keen, tall flame and by its light she saw her future and Kit's. Jacqueline has given him up! For what reason Sue cared not. She knew only that Kit was free. . . !

"Tell me about it," she said, and her breath came quickly.

"There isn't much to tell. She sent back a little book I had given her . . . and wrote a few lines — releasing me. She gave two reasons. One, that as Mary will never be well, it isn't fair to bind me. And the other that she can't stand the strain of having me in her life without any prospect of marriage. From all I can make out she — wants — to forget me — Sue."

He said it simply, but suddenly Sue began to be afraid. Afraid of something in his voice which was like that of a man tortured and not daring to cry out. Afraid of his eyes, meeting hers now, haggardly.

"You care so much, Kit?"

"Why shouldn't I care? I've loved her all these years. I've waited.... She's as much a part of me as — my right hand —" He held the hand out, flexing the fingers, "If my hand were chopped off, I'd — bleed...."

She had never seen him like this ... hopeless and unhappy. She knew now that he had been upheld through all the years by his faith in the future. And the years ahead were blank.

She leaned forward and laid her hand on his. "Perhaps Jacqueline knows what is best, Kit. She is so devoted to them all. Perhaps she isn't made to feel as you and I feel — that love — dares everything...."

"What do I care how she's made? She's little and sweet — and mine...."

He said it savagely, biting the words off.

Sue drew her hand away, letting it fall heavily in her lap. "But she shouldn't have kept you — dangling —"

His head went back with a jerk. "Don't blame her. I wouldn't have her different."

So that was that! And Sue had thought that he loved her. Fool that she was! Her mind went back tumultuously. Was it for this that she and Paula had circled the globe, always with that unconfessed purpose of pushing Jacqueline out of Kit's heart?

And was this her punishment? She had come out today with such high hopes. She had thought to tell Kit that her holiday was ended, that she must go home.

The King of France

She had felt that the news would move him, and that under these great trees, he would ask her to stay. That under these trees, too, he might speak to her of all she meant to him.

And she meant nothing!

In halting words Kit was rehearsing the story of his years of devotion. "I thought if I waited...! Sue, I couldn't tell you all this if you weren't her friend and mine."

She listened until she could stand it no longer. Her hands shook as she reached for her hat and pulled it low over her eyes. "Kit, I'm sorry, but I'm afraid we must be going."

He turned his wrist to look at his watch. "Great guns, it is after four. And an hour's riding to get back." He jumped to his feet. "I've been running on unpardonably about myself. I hope I haven't bored you."

"You never bore me. It has been wonderful being out here with you, Kit. I hate to think that when we leave, you'll be alone. Unhappy."

"Leave?" sharply, "you're not going?"

"Oh, well, we can't stay on forever."

"But I'll miss you a lot, old girl."

"Will you?"

"Of course...." He hesitated, "Why can't you stick around a bit?"

"Do you really want me, Kit?"

"I always want you," he smiled at her and held out his hands to help her up. She lifted her head and looked at him. Any other man seeing that look would have taken her in his arms. But Kit was blind — and his arms were for Jacqueline.

II

Back in the bungalow, Paula had written letters, lunched, and was now waiting to serve tea to the lovers when they came. Cool, in pale green organdie she sat on the porch and watched for them. At last she saw them coming, walking their horses up the hill as they had walked them down. The phrase brought to her mind somewhat whimsically an old nursery rhyme, *"The King of France . . . and forty thousand men . . . rode up a hill . . . and then rode down again."* It had always seemed to Paula the extreme expression of futility. She wondered why she thought of it now. Perhaps because all her life she had been riding up hills and riding down, hoping to find something at the top of the hill, finding nothing and returning as she came. Perhaps the trouble had been that she would not take what she could get. Other women compromised. She would not. She would have what she wanted or go without. And Sue was like that. Having set her mind on Kit, she would have no other.

She waved to Sue and Sue waved back. She called, "You're late," and Kit answered, "We went a long way."

The horses stopped.

"You must be tired. I'll have tea for you in a moment."

The King of France

Kit dismounted. "Sorry, but I'll have to run along. It isn't often that I take a day like this. And I wouldn't for anybody but Sue."

He helped Sue down, and she stood there with her hat pulled over her eyes. And suddenly Paula was aware that something was wrong. Dreadfully wrong. Paula could not have told how she knew, for there was Sue all white and gold as when she had ridden that morning down the hill, but the glory which had shone about her then was gone.

Kit mounting again, said, "I'll see you tonight?" and Sue said, "Yes." Then caught herself up. "I forgot, I've promised Colonel Dickey."

"Promised him what?"

"That I'll let him show me his rhododendrons by moonlight."

"Tomorrow then? And thank you for everything, old girl."

Sue knew what he meant by that. He was thanking her for listening while he talked about Jacqueline, and for staying on, so that he might pour his troubles in her ears. . . !

She turned and went up the steps. Paula said: "Aren't you going to have tea?"

"Yes, but I want to get into something cooler. I'll be down in a moment."

When she came she wore a negligee of sheer white, tied with pale blue ribbons. She threw herself on a couch among the cushions. "I'm dead," and shut her eyes.

Paula poured the tea in silence. Cream and no sugar for Sue. "Here's your cup."

Sue opened her eyes, "Jacqueline's broken her engagement."

"Broken it?"

"Yes."

"My dear, I congratulate you."

"Congratulate me, why? Because now I can take what another woman won't have?"

Paula stared at her, "But I thought. . . ?"

"Oh, I know," Sue sat up, all her sheer white flowing about her, "you thought I'd take him at any price. Well, I won't — not if I died for it."

Paula, knowing the world, and knowing men and women, told herself, "He hasn't asked her. He hasn't asked her . . ." and again the rhyme which had been in her mind as she watched Sue and Kit ride up the hill, recurred to her. . . . "*The King of France . . . rode up . . . and then rode down again. . . !*"

Had it all been as futile as that — this day in the forest? She refused to believe it. Busy among her tea-things, she said, with outward serenity, "You're very foolish."

Sue, having set down her cup, was once more among her cushions, "No," she said in a muffled voice, "I'm not foolish. I know myself. And I'd hate being second-best."

Paula glanced at the white figure with the blaze of bright hair, the face hidden. Some one else would have to play Sue's cards for her. "You run on upstairs," she advised, "and take a nap before dinner. But I don't see what you want with old Dickey and his rhododendrons."

Sue rolled over and looked at her. "He thinks he's in love with me, he's asked me to marry him. And that young Olcott proposed to me last night. I'm being very popular, Paula."

But her laugh was mirthless. She went upstairs and to bed, and lay there wondering if she could stand the strain of it much longer. She had almost broken down that afternoon in the forest. She had wanted to tell Kit that she cared — cared desperately. It had been at that very last moment, when he had helped her up, and had stood above her, smiling.

Perhaps it would be best, after all, to go home. To the old house in Salem. It seemed to her that the sight of the portraits on the wall, and of her mother and Aunt Phoebe, marcelled and in gray satin, would stiffen her backbone. A place like this was made for romance, and all she had was old Dickey, and that silly sap of an Olcott!

Downstairs, Paula sat at her desk. Through the wide window, she could see the emerald twilight, with the stars glimmering through. With her chin on her hand she was pondering the situation. The thing she had played for had come to pass. Her letter to Jacqueline had brought results. If only Sue's pride didn't spoil things. Oh, well, there were still other moves in the game. . . .

She drew a sheet of paper towards her and began to

write. "Jacqueline has broken her engagement, and Sue and I shall stay a little longer. And when we come home we may bring Kit with us. Stranger things have happened, Phoebe, and between the two of us, old girl, Kit loves Sue. . . ."

There was more of it, and when she had finished and sealed her letter, Paula again sat with her chin in her hand. The pale green of her dress melted into the green of the twilight until she was lost in the dark gloom of the shadows, but still she sat there, thinking it out.

CHAPTER TEN

O Happy Wind!

I

IT WAS Yolanda who first learned that Jacqueline had broken with her lover. It was three weeks after the thing had happened, and Yolanda was in a mad whirl of getting ready to go to school in Washington. Some of the sewing had to be done at home, and Jacqueline was helping.

And one day she took some bits of flesh-colored crepe and went out on the front porch and sat for a long time whipping lace on all the edges. The seamstress upstairs was making a brown velveteen dress for Yolanda, and between fittings, Yolanda wrapped in a new dressing gown of amber-colored corduroy came down to talk to her aunt.

"I think I've done exactly the right thing to have all my clothes in shades of brown and yellow. With my hair—"

"It's economical at any rate," Jacqueline agreed, "all your shoes and things match."

"Um...." Yolanda murmured, leaning back in her low chair. Then, after a moment, "Aunt Jack, where's your sapphire ring?"

"I'm not wearing it."

"Why not?"

"I'm not going to marry Kit."

"You mean you're not going to marry him now?"

"I mean that our engagement is definitely broken. . . ." Jacqueline's needle stopped for a moment as she looked up and met Yolanda's eyes.

"Aunt Jack, you don't mean that you did it?"

"Yes."

"But why?"

"My dear, it isn't fair to tie a man to an uncertainty. I mustn't ask him to waste his life — waiting."

"But what of your life?" Yolanda demanded fiercely. She stood up, wrapping the amber gown about her, so that she was like a slim young aspen in the autumn sunlight. "Oh, Aunt Jack, if I wasn't such a pig, I'd stay home and be an angel in the house. But I'm not made of that sort of stuff. I couldn't. Aunt Jack. I just — couldn't."

"There's no reason why you should."

"Yes. You did it —. But the girls of your day were different. Why when you were fifteen you were a baby in pinafores compared to me. And . . . you didn't want to grab everything from life as we do. Stuart says that's the gorgeous thing about me. That I take and don't give. He says it sort of sets me apart. . . ."

"Apart from what, darling?"

"Oh, the other girls. Stuart says I am the last thing in self-expression. That I belong to the splendid women of the Middle Ages. That I'm a sort of throwback."

Jacqueline, helpless before this catalogue of charms, was aware even in the midst of her amusement that Stuart's estimate had in it elements of truth. Yolanda needed only a ruff and a lot of rubies to look the part of a lady of that ruthless age, when beauty ruled, and the moralities had but little to do with the romantic program. She was glad, however, that Yolanda's self-absorption had switched her from the subject of Jacqueline's own love affair. Indeed, she seemed to have forgotten it entirely, "That was Stuart's word for me, Aunt Jack . . . 'gorgeous.'"

"The sooner you go to school the better, Yolanda."

"Why?"

"You're too young to have your head filled with things like that."

"I'm not too young for anything."

And indeed she did not seem it. When she went upstairs presently to be fitted, her voice floated down through the open windows. She was talking to Miss Drew, the seamstress. Her tone was decisive. "You'll have to rip that out, Miss Drew," Jacqueline heard her saying, "I don't like it."

Jacqueline remembered the days when she had not liked things but had worn them rather than hurt anybody's feelings. Had she been weak-minded then as she was weak-minded now? And was this thing called sacrifice what some of the modern psychologists analyzed as self-love of a sort? She wondered what people would think if she, too, should declare herself a throw-back to one of those "splendid women of the Middle Ages"? If she peeled off, as it were, her shell of austerity and took from life what she wanted? Perhaps, she too longed to go careless and free to her lover. Perhaps, she **too,** desired flame and fire and wild romance. She knew her own heart, oh, how well she knew it!

Yet she had been aware in the days since she had made her decision about Kit, that a kind of peace had come to her. She had closed a door, as it were, that she might not open, but as long as it remained shut, she could live serenely, steadfastly. Behind that door was the Kit who had gone to war—*this is the way we march to war ... march to war ... march to war. ...*

Behind the door was the Kit who had given her tenderness, constancy, everything that a man could give a woman. And if she had put it away, it had been because life could not be lived normally for either of them on this plane of intense need. For herself, she knew, it was best. She had hidden his picture, his letters, the gifts that he had bestowed upon her. She must have nothing to remind her, and having nothing she could go on.

II

She came out of her reverie to find Stuart Carleton ascending the steps. He greeted her, then demanded, "Where's Yolanda?"

O Happy Wind!

"Being tried on upstairs."

"Can't she come down?"

"I'm not sure. . . ."

A voice from above cut the air, "Of course I can come. 'Lo, Stuart."

Color had flooded the boy's cheeks at the sound of the unseen voice. He called back, "Hurry," and sat down to wait. But Yolanda did not keep him waiting long. She came almost at once, still clothed in the amber-colored gown, which she had sashed with a length of gold ribbon, caught up from Miss Drew's sewing table.

"Pardon, my costume," Yolanda said, airily, "it won't shock you, Stuart. But I'm not so sure of Aunt Jack. She and mother burn fires on the altar of formality."

Jacqueline laughed, "My dear, what would you do if we didn't?"

"Light my own fires. . . ." Yolanda said, then forgot her aunt, forgot everything but her own young eagerness to snatch from the moment everything that was in it. With the radio turned on, she and Stuart were presently swaying to the rhythm of a fox trot. And they talked incessantly, the murmur of their voices mingling with the music. The lamps were lighted and twilight and lamplight filled the room with rose and amethyst. So had youth danced since the beginning of time, so would it dance through all the endless ages. Jacqueline sat with her hands folded quietly in her lap and thought about it.

As the clock chimed, she warned her niece, "You know what your Dad will say if he comes home and doesn't find you dressed for dinner."

Yolanda stopped, and still encircled by Stuart's arms, turned and looked at her aunt. "Stuart says I ought always to wear amber."

Stuart emphasized, "It makes her — gorgeous."

That seemed to be their word for the moment, "gorgeous." Well, the child was gorgeous. And frank and fine. Yet a little bit drunk — with freedom. "I'll give you five minutes," Jacqueline capitulated, and again they swayed and stepped to the music.

Small Joey came in before the five minutes were up, "Let's you and I dance, Aunt Jack."

It was not the first time he and his aunt had danced together and they did it well. Yolanda and Stuart coming to a stop stood staring, for this Jacqueline of the dance was not the Jacqueline who had sewed on the porch a sedate seam. Her cheeks were flushed, her hair ruffled, her eyes like stars. She was little and lithe, and graceful. She had, indeed, a grace which Yolanda lacked, a vividness which surpassed that of her niece, so that Stuart watching, said, "She's a peach. And as young as they make 'em."

"I've never seen her like this," Yolanda told him, "Stuart, she's beautiful."

"Not as beautiful as you," he said, loyally, "Gee, I'm going to miss you, old girl."

"Of course you'll miss me," Yolanda told him, sparkling. "But it will be a good miss. . . ."

"In what way?"

"You'll get your mind on your work . . . and I'll get mine on my work, and we'll both live happy ever after."

"Yolanda," her aunt was urging, "there's your father's train. . . ."

"Run away, little boy," Yolanda said, and Stuart caught up her hand, and drew her after him into the front hall, from which she presently came back, smiling and triumphant.

"He wanted to kiss me," she told her aunt as they went up the stairs together, "but I told him my code didn't include it. He'll probably kiss a lot of girls when he's at college, and I don't want to become one of the mob."

Jacqueline made no comment. Yet she hugged the thought to her heart that Yolanda was, after all, upholding the traditions of the family. She was not making herself cheap, and while she professed to scorn the prohibitions of her elders, she was, in her modern way, following in the footsteps of her aunt and of her mother, who had never given their favors freely.

It was late that night when Jacqueline went to bed, and she read for a long time, so that it was nearly one when she heard a sound at her door and looked up to see Yolanda standing tall and white on the threshold.

"May I come in, Aunt Jack?"

"Of course."

Yolanda sat on the foot of the bed, her knees hunched up, her arms about them. "I couldn't sleep."

"Why not?"

"Oh . . . going away . . . and all that. . . ."

"It will make a great change in your life, Yolanda."

"Three years—"

Silence. Then, "When the three years are over, I'm coming back and let you marry Kit."

"My darling girl."

"No, I'm not a darling girl. I shall hate being tied down. . . . But when I saw you dancing. . . . Why, Aunt Jack, you're *young* . . . and gee whiz, you've got to have your chance."

She laughed, and then broke down all at once into wild sobbing, "I don't know why I'm being—such a —fool. But I'm not really . . . a selfish pig, Aunt Jack . . . not really."

"My precious. . . ."

Yolanda came to the arms that received her, and wet cheek was pressed against wet cheek. "I never felt this way before," Yolanda sobbed, "I'm so—lonely . . . Aunt Jack. . . . I don't know what's the matter with me."

Jacqueline knew, but she said no word. Child and woman struggled in this young heart . . . little girlhood was being put definitely behind, young love was demanding, demanding, yet Yolanda did not know it yet, as love. . . . All the mother in Jacqueline rose to meet this need.

"My dear, school will be good for you. And the girls . . . you'll love it all after a little. . . ."

Yolanda burying her bright head in her aunt's neck, said, "But life won't ever be the same again."

"Perhaps it will be — lovelier."

Yolanda sat up and looked down at the face on the pillow, "It hasn't been lovely for you, Aunt Jack."

"In some ways it has. I've known the best thing in the world, Yolanda."

The young face hung breathless above her, "Even if you've lost it, Aunt Jack?"

"I haven't lost it. Nothing can take away the memory."

And now Yolanda burst out. "Oh, Aunt Jack, I think you're *beautiful*. . . ."

It was youth's tribute to high romance. It was, indeed, for the two of them, a high and solemn moment, when the child who was going forth to meet love, met at heart's level, the woman who was giving it up.

They talked long into the night, and at last when Yolanda fell asleep, her aunt's arm was about her, and her bright head was pillowed on Jacqueline's white shoulder.

III

In the days that followed, Jacqueline was very busy, getting Yolanda off to school, helping Hannah with the fall cleaning, finding a nurse for Mary.

For Joel's affairs were looking up. He was even thinking of buying a house. "The Benton house, Jack, on the bluff. With my added salary and the bonus they have given me, there's no reason why we should be so crowded."

Jacqueline was wistful. "I like it here, and we'd need more help in a big house, Joel."

"Well, with a nurse for Mary."

"Have you told her about the nurse, Joel?"

"Not yet."

"She won't want to have one."

"Why not?"

"She — oh, she doesn't want the idea of illness emphasized. She insists that the spirit is stronger than the body."

"Poor darling."

Poor darling, indeed! Poor Mary. Upheld by a hope which seemed hopeless. Jacqueline never entered the sick room in these days without being aware of the struggle within those walls. Mary persistently, doggedly, willing herself to be well, was a pathetic figure.

"If I buy the Benton house," Joel was saying, "Mary can have the suite that overlooks the water, and the nurse will be in the room next to her."

"We'd have to take on a second maid, Joel. Hannah isn't all that she used to be."

"I thought a nurse would be enough."

"If we stay here, yes," she set herself firmly to prove her point, "but in a big house, no. We simply couldn't manage it, Joel."

Joel was always glad to talk things over with Jacqueline. She was a restful little soul, he told himself. But he always resented any assumption on her part of authority. As now, when in her quiet way, she opposed his plan to move into more pretentious quarters.

O Happy Wind!

"We could entertain more," he argued, "have the Gilmans and a lot of others. And, by the way, Sue is coming back."

Jacqueline's heart seemed to stand still. In all the weeks of Kit's silence, she had avoided the Gilmans. She had meant to tell them of her broken engagement. She had wanted them to know that Kit was free. That he could have Sue if he wanted her. But she had put off the moment of her announcement. She had known that if the wound was opened she would suffer.

But now Sue was coming, and the thing must be faced.

She asked Joel, with stiff lips, "Who told you Sue was coming?"

"Her mother. I came out with her on the train."

"I thought Sue and Paula were going to stay until the winter season."

"Paula isn't well. The climate doesn't agree with her."

Jacqueline hardly heard what Joel was saying. Her breath came quick as she again asked a question. "Did she say anything — about Kit?"

"Yes. She seems to think he's coming — with Sue."

There was a roaring in Jacqueline's ears, and then great waves swept over her. . . .

She came back from those roaring depths, to find Joel bending above her, "Dear child . . . you fainted . . ." he was smoothing her hair, holding her up strongly with his right arm.

"How silly. . . ."

"Not silly at all. Haven't you been well, Jacqueline?"

"Oh . . . well enough. Maybe I'm over-tired, Joel."

She sat up, her cheeks white, her hair disordered. To Joel gazing at her with troubled eyes she seemed, in her black dress, very little and shrunken and old. He had a feeling that there was something very much the matter.

"You'd better go to bed," he said, gently.

"I'm all right," she rose and spoke without meeting his eyes. "I'm not going to marry Kit, Joel . . . I thought I'd . . . better . . . tell you."

Joel uttered a sharp exclamation, "What!"

"I'm not going to marry him. . . ."

Seeing her before him, so pale, so altogether insignificant, Joel made his own deductions. The thing was as plain as the nose on your face. Kit had grown tired of waiting. But then, what could you expect? A man was a man, and Sue Gilman was a ripping beauty. Joel remembered her as she had looked long ago in that rose brocade.

Being himself a man, Joel forgot that it was because of his lame leg and his wife and two children, that Jacqueline had lost her lover. "I'm sorry," he said, inadequately, "but if he could treat you like that, you're better off without him."

She saw what he thought — that Kit had thrown her over. Oh, well, why try to tell him? Should she say, "But he didn't throw me over. I did it myself."

O Happy Wind!

Joel wouldn't believe it. Or if he did, he would think Kit had learned to love Sue, and so Jacqueline had released him.

"He didn't treat me badly," she said, flushing, "I guess it just—had to be, Joel."

She started for the stairs and came back, "I forgot to tell you. The Gilmans have asked us to dine with them next Thursday. The note came this morning. They are having a famous author, and some young people up from town—" She went over to the desk, and found the note and read it. It was, Mrs. Gilman, confided, to be "quite a gay party for us old folks."

Joel grumbled, "I'm not keen about it. If Sue were there it would be different."

Jacqueline felt that if Sue were there it would be desperate!

"I suppose," Joel complained, "that it will mean our best bibs and tuckers?"

"I haven't any best bib and tucker."

"Get something," he reached for his wallet and opened it, "go to it, old girl."

She looked at the bills and protested, "It's too much, Joel."

"Not a bit," heartily, "you deserve it. What would we do without you, Jacqueline?"

She was glad to have the money. She would have hated to go shabby to the Gilmans. She would run up to town tomorrow and buy a dress. There were things to get for Yolanda and they could shop together. But she loathed the whole thing. Oh, if she might only fly away a thousand miles, or shut herself up in some hidden cell like a hermit!

She said "Good-night," presently, and went upstairs and to Mary's room. She stopped in the upper hall in front of a mirror and arranged her hair. And she saw herself in the glass as Joel had seen her, as little and shrunken and old.

And then she went in and saw Mary—pink and white and gold among her pillows. The room swam in golden light from a low lamp, and Mary transfigured by the light was young, younger than Jacqueline, almost as young as Yolanda. And Mary's gay voice was saying, "Jack, darling, did you see my roses? Joel brought them."

Mary's voice was always gay in these days. She kept it persistently to that note of lightness. She refused to admit into her room any note of tragedy. Since that night when she had known the doctor's verdict, she had held to the assumption that some day she would be well. "It will come if I think it," she said.

To Jacqueline, except for this artificial flow of spirits, Mary seemed no better. And she sometimes wished for the old Mary, the real Mary, who must be somewhere under this shell of persistent optimism. Yet had she herself not been like this in those days when Kit and Joel had gone to war? Had she not said "There is no evil" when she had known there was evil? And had it not been a sort of desperate courage which had made her do it? And the women who had had that kind of

O Happy Wind! 221

courage had helped their men. In a way, "thinking had made it come." Perhaps Mary was right, and there was health ahead of her. Jacqueline wished she had some of her former bouyancy. Perhaps Mary could help her.

She sat down by the bed and laid her hand over her sister's. "Mary," she said, "I'm not going to marry Kit. I've told him — it's all over. I'd rather not talk about it. Only, if he should marry Sue — I think — I'd die. . . ."

"Sue?" Mary demanded, sharply, "why should he marry Sue?"

"They are coming back — together. . . ."

Mary drew a sharp breath, "Didn't I tell you?"

"Yes. Mary it isn't Sue's fault. It isn't anybody's fault. It's just — Fate. . . ."

"No," Mary said, "it isn't Fate," she took Jacqueline's cold hands in her own, "it's because you haven't believed in Kit. . . ."

"I have believed in him. . . ."

"No. You've been thinking . . . Sue and Kit . . . Sue and Kit. . . ."

Jacqueline stared at her in amazement. "Mary, how did you know?"

"Because every woman knows — jealousy."

"Have you ever known it Mary. . . ?"

"Yes, since I haven't been able to be anything to Joel, I've been always — afraid. Until this came to me — that fear must not be a part of me lest I bring about that which I feared. . . ."

"I know," Jacqueline whispered, "and you think — I brought Sue to Kit?"

"I think you can have him back if you want him."

Jacqueline clung to the kind hands, "Perhaps it is — too late, Mary."

"It is never — too late," Mary's tone was feverish, "I tell myself that, over and over again, Jack, as I lie here. I tell myself it is never too late to — get well. . . ."

Their hands fell apart. Mary's mind was again on herself. Jacqueline had a sense of infinite loneliness. Was there no one on whose heart she could weep and who would understand?

When she left Mary, she passed small Joey's room and looked in. He was sound asleep in pink pajamas, and the dot of a kitten, lay in a fluff of bronze in the crook of his arm. There was always a faint night-light burning in the room. Joel had protested against it, but Jacqueline had known her Joey. "I'm not afraid of the dark, Aunt Jack. It's just that the blackness — smothers me." She felt that she understood Joey better than his mother, better than his father, better than anyone in the world. She knelt beside the bed, "My little boy," she whispered, and seemed to find in that possessive phrase, a certain solace.

IV

It was on the morning of the Gilman's dinner that Yolanda went away. Her departure was in the nature

of a triumphant ceremonial. She had staged it herself:
"Stuart is going to take me in his car to Boston."

"Alone?"

"Yes. Why not?"

"You know your father won't like it."

"Well, if you think we need a chaperone, Stuart can ask his mother."

"But Yolanda — you don't belong to the Carletons. And your Dad will want to see you off."

"He can meet us at South Station."

"But you really ought to give him some last moments alone with you, darling."

"Oh, listen, Aunt Jack, there won't be any last moments. I'm not dead or dying."

"You know how he hates to have Stuart in on everything."

"He'd better be glad Stuart wants to be in on things. The Carletons are such a gorgeous family. If I'm ever going to be married, I'd better keep an eye on Stuart."

Jacqueline's cheeks blazed, "Yolanda," she said, "I think you are positively — indecent —. No nice woman keeps an eye on a man."

"Well, you've kept your eye on Kit, Aunt Jack, for perfect ages. Of course you don't call it keeping your eye on him. But that's what it amounts to . . ." then as she saw dead whiteness of her aunt's countenance, she gave a little cry. "Oh, honey, I'm a *beast* — forgive me."

So during those last days they had alternated between

moods of high irritation and of affectionate demonstration. Both aunt and niece were on edge, but when the final hours came, Yolanda showed herself just a little girl, going away like other little girls, unhappily to school. She hung around her father's neck before he left on the early train, and begged him not to be late at South Station, "I'm sending everybody away, Daddy." And when Stuart arrived at ten, with his car heaped with florists' boxes, and boxes from a famous confectioner, and up-to-the-minute fiction in gay jackets, and with his mother serene and smiling in black and white tweed, there was no one waiting on the front porch but Jacqueline.

"Where's Yolanda?" he demanded.

"She'll be down in a moment."

But Yolanda did not come, and Stuart kept looking at his wrist watch, and Jacqueline at the foot of the stairs kept calling, "It's late, Yolanda, you'll miss your train."

And when there was no answer, Jacqueline ran distractedly up the stairs and in and out of the rooms, until she came finally to Mary's room. And there, on her knees beside the bed, was Yolanda, sobbing wildly. And Mary's thin hand was on her head.

And Jacqueline said, breathlessly from the threshold, "Precious child, you must be going. . . ."

Yolanda got up and wiped her eyes, and kissed her mother and kissed her aunt. "You've both been *angels*," she emphasized. Then she went into the hall and called down to the ramping Stuart, "Wait till I

O Happy Wind! 225

powder my nose," and in another moment she was gone. And something of youth and joy and radiance went out of the house with her.

Jacqueline, feeling lonely and longing for some heart to lean on, sought out old Hannah. The kitchen was warm and shining, and Hannah cutting up a pumpkin for pies, was part of a glowing color scheme in a stiffly starched apron of purple print.

Jacqueline sat down in the rocking chair in front of the stove, where all the kettles were boiling in a singing and bubbling ecstasy. "I'm glad you're making pies, Hannah."

"I thought maybe if I did, you'd eat a piece," the old woman told her. "You haven't got any more appetite than a bird."

"Oh, I eat enough," indifferently.

"No, you don't," Hannah wiped her hands on the roller towel and came and stood by the stove. "Aren't you well, my lamb?"

"Well, enough, Hannah."

"Then — you aren't happy, dearie?"

"Is anybody happy, Hannah?"

She wanted to talk about it, but she *couldn't*. She felt if she mentioned Kit's name she should die. For he hadn't written. Yet surely, if he were coming back with Sue, he would have said something. It seemed incredible that after all he and Jacqueline had been to each other, he should let her down like this. She told herself over and over again, that it was she who had shut the door of their future. But she was still his friend. He knew that . . . and it wasn't like Kit to hurt — anybody.

She sobbed a little, and Hannah stood beside her and patted her shoulder, "I'm such a baby, Hannah."

"It's best to cry it out, my lamb."

She wiped her eyes after a time, went upstairs to her room and threw herself on the bed. She knew she wasn't being a bit sporting. But there was the dinner that night at the Gilmans. How *could* she go and meet all of their eyes, and have them ask questions. . . ?

But she must go . . . and make the best of it. She rose and looked at herself in the mirror, leaning forward so that her white strained face almost touched the other white strained face in the glass. Then, suddenly, she smiled and the figure smiled. She rubbed her cheeks until the red came, she tilted her chin and swept her lashes up from her eyes in a flashing glance. . . .

She heard a slight noise, and turning, saw small Joey observing her with lively curiosity. "What are you doing, Aunt Jack?"

"Playing a game."

"What game?"

"The game of 'Putting your Best Foot Forward.'"

"Let me see how you do it."

"Well, I smile when I want to cry. And pretend that I'm cheerful when my heart is heavy. We all did it during the war, your mother and I and the men at the front, and the women who were left behind. We told each other nice things even when we knew they weren't true."

O Happy Wind!

"Were you all just lying to each other, Aunt Jack?"

"We didn't call it that, Joey. You see we couldn't have carried on, if we had told each other the truth."

He was uneasy. "I don't like to hear you talk about it. And there isn't any war now, Aunt Jack."

"No, but sometimes when life isn't easy, people go around smiling, and we call that — courage."

"Well, I don't want to be brave," small Joey decided, "I just want to be happy."

He began to walk about the room, restlessly, "I don't want anybody to fight," he said, "I don't want my kitten to fight, or Simon, or the boys at school. But they do. And I knocked one of them down today."

"Joey, you didn't."

"Yes, I did." Joey looked very masculine and complacent as he stood with his hands in his pockets, "I knocked him down and his nose bled."

"*Joey . . . !*"

"Well, I had to do it, Aunt Jack. He chased my kitten with his dog, and he wouldn't call the dog off. So I knocked him down and sat on him."

So this was her young pacificist! Faced with the problem of protecting the defenseless! And there would always be brutes in the world!

"I hope you'll do it again, Joey," she said, and hugged him.

Joey squirmed away from her embrace. "Well, I hated the blood," he said, "and I helped him wipe it off afterwards."

Her laugh now was genuine. No need to stand before a mirror and force a smile. "Oh, Joey, Joey," she said, "you're a darling." She held out her hand to him, "Let's go down and rescue Simon. I left him out on the porch to get the sun, and I hear him scolding the kitten."

They found the kitten surveying Simon with round and solemn gaze, and Simon maddened by such scrutiny, bobbing up and down, his wings trailing.

"Simon," Jacqueline said, "don't be so silly."

"He doesn't like to be looked at," Joey said, and picked up the kitten, "Aunt Jack, what shall I name it?"

She did not answer. The postman was coming up the walk. She ran down to meet him. "I'll get the mail," Joey said, but she raced ahead. . . . There might be something from Kit. Oh, if only she might have a line!

But she knew at a glance there was no letter. Kit always wrote on deep blue paper and his envelopes were big and square. She felt sick with disappointment, physically ill, yet she steadied her voice to exchange with the postman the daily commonplaces. Yes, there was wind in those clouds. Yes, it began to feel like winter. Yes, this crisp air was good for Mrs. Hutchins. . . .

The postman had a ruddy face and a plump figure. He was not young, and no one would for a moment have looked upon him as a messenger from the gods. Yet always after that, Jacqueline saw him as he had stood there, the red stain of the sunset back of him, bracing his body against the wind, as he dug in his bag for something he had forgotten.

O Happy Wind!

He found what he sought and handed it to her. "It's a parcel," he said, "from India."

He was not as has been said, a messenger from the gods, he simply served his government competently for inadequate pay. But to Jacqueline he was a Mercury, with winged sandals, a Hermes on a celestial errand. With the parcel in her hand she went flying, up the walk, passing Joey, passing the kitten, passing Simon, without a glance. Then, her feet scarcely touching the stairs, she gained her room, and shut the door and locked it.

v

That night Jacqueline and Joel found six other guests at the Gilmans — four men and two women. Two of the men were middle-aged and plutocratic, the other two were young, as were both of the women.

The man on Jacqueline's right, was slender and dark, and apparently, distinctly bored at having to talk to the small person in the silver gown. He gave a good deal of his attention, therefore, to the young woman on the other side of him, whose name was Margot and who was dressed in yellow. The young man's name was Bert. Both of the young people had other names, of course, but they seemed to need no surnames among their associates.

Jacqueline heard Bert saying to Margot, "I'll bet you don't dare smoke. Do you know you're in old Salem? They hanged witches for less."

"I'll dare do anything."

She looked it. She was of the restless, avid type, smooth as glass, hard as nails, brilliant as enamel. She talked for the benefit of the whole table. Told stories, calling on Bert to finish them for her. "I'm always forgetting the point."

The man on Jacqueline's left grew restless, and said, under cover of a storm of laughter that greeted one of Margot's sallies, "Do you know that starlings are a menace?"

Jacqueline lifted long lashes and stared at him, "Starlings?" she murmured.

His eyes, looking down into hers, had a twinkle behind the glasses. "Their chatter drowns the song of the more beautiful birds. . . ." Then turning a little so that his arm rested on the table. "You haven't said a half dozen words since we sat down."

The flattery was obvious. She smiled at him. "If you stick to that, you'll always have a flock of men about you."

"If I did, I shouldn't know what to do with them."

"So you're a one man woman? Well, you look happy."

"I am happy."

She said it so quietly, so confidently, that it was his turn to stare. "Why are you happy?"

"Because," and he could see the flutter of her pulse in her white throat, "because I had lost faith in a friend. And I've found it again."

They had forgotten the others at the table. "My dear child," he said, "to what Eden do you belong that

O Happy Wind!

you can shine like this because a man has kept faith with you?"

"How do you know it is a man?"

"How do I know that the pink in your cheeks is real and not rouge?"

They laughed together. "How wise you are," she said.

"If I am wise," he told her, "it is because I write books, and all of my heroines are like you. But I didn't believe there was a real woman such as you in the world."

"Tell me about — your books," breathlessly.

He told her, rather, what he thought about Salem. "I'm English, you know, and here in this old town I'm finding things that link me close to you Americans. But please don't make me talk about myself. You're much more interesting."

"Am I? Why?"

"Because I'm sure you have a romance up your sleeve — and I'd like to hear it."

"You mean — about myself?"

"Yes."

"There isn't so much . . ." she broke off, and lifted her hand, "Listen! Do you hear the wild wind blowing?"

Anyone could hear it — raging, roaring, coming down from the North! "Yes," he said, "and is that the beginning of your story?"

She nodded. "Some day . . . the wild wind will pick me up and set me down — in India!"

He was enchanted. "Go on," he urged. His eyes were appraising the delicate charm of her, the silvery frock, the brooch of turquoises set in old silver, the ringless hands. The child was choice — who would have dreamed of this among all these avid, eager women? "Go on, why India?"

"Because some day I am going to have a honeymoon out there, and ride an elephant."

"Such a mouse of a thing as you are — on an elephant! So the man's in India?"

She nodded.

"When is he coming back for you?"

"When I tell him."

"Don't keep him waiting too long."

"I have kept him waiting too long already."

She found herself telling him about it. Sketchily. That she couldn't get married because of the Family. There had been the war, she explained, and Joel's leg, and Mary's illness — one couldn't leave small Joey, just a baby, and Yolanda growing up and needing a mother.

"One might," he said, "but not you. I daresay that when you were a child you were always bringing up vast families of dolls, and breaking your heart every time one of them broke its head. . . ."

"Yes," she said, "it was like that . . ." her voice trailed off into silence, and it was several minutes before she spoke again. "We had been engaged over five years, and I thought I ought to give him his freedom, and I wrote him a letter . . . and then I was sorry I had written. And I thought he had taken me at my word, and it hurt. And this morning his letter came, and all the stars — sang."

He let his hand rest for a moment on her own, "Thank you for telling me."

"I've never talked to anyone like this in my life," she answered him. "But then, you are different. You're a wizard with a wand."

"It's because I understand," the brown eyes behind the glasses were warm with feeling, "I loved a woman once — and lost her. . . ."

Coffee was to be served in the drawing-room. Everyone was rising. Miss Phoebe moved towards Jacqueline. "We thought you might enjoy Bert Cummings, but our celebrity has monopolized you."

"He's a darling, Miss Phoebe."

"You ought to meet more men, Jacqueline. You are letting yourself grow stale, socially."

She went on to emphasize the eligibility of the celebrity. He was rich, of good family, unmarried. . . .

Jacqueline had a flaming sense that Miss Phoebe was trying to hand her over, as it were, to the celebrity, in order to clear the way for Kit and Sue. A week ago the thought would have stung her. But now she did not care. She had Kit's letter, that wonderful letter which had been a part of the parcel brought by the god-like postman.

Shut in her room she had read it. On her knees she had read it. So thankful, so happy, so adoring!

"My little child," Kit had said, "I haven't written

because for a time the whole thing seemed finished. But it is not finished. I have let the weeks pass, and not for one moment have I been separated from you, and I know now that I shall never be separated. And so I am sending the book back, with this letter in it. But I am not sending back the ring. You are mine always, Jacqueline, no matter what you say, but we need no outward symbol. Some day you will ask me to come to you, and I shall wait for that word. And in the meantime, if you wish that the world shall not know, we will hold the knowledge in our hearts. Even if you do not write, I shall understand — and wait. And I am ever your own,

Kit."

Every word of that letter was now a part of Jacqueline's consciousness, and so she could smile at Miss Phoebe and move on. But even as she smiled, she knew it wasn't going to be easy to forgive the Gilmans.

She drank her coffee sitting in a corner with the famous author beside her. Outside the wild wind blew—"*Oh, happy wind, tell Kit, I love him.*"

Margot sang for them, accompanied by Bert at the piano. The song was French and sophisticated. And the only thing that saved the situation was the fact that neither Mrs. Gilman nor Miss Phoebe knew the slang of the Paris streets.

The famous author said, impatiently, "Our drawing rooms are being turned into Music halls. Don't you sing, small silver bird?"

She shook her head, "My heart is singing."

O Happy Wind!

And presently she said, "Would you mind if I left you for a little minute?"

"I shall mind if you leave me at all."

She got out of the room unobtrusively, and made her way to the big front door. As she opened it the wind rushed in, and clutched at her silver draperies as she closed the door behind her.

It was a wonderful night, with scudding clouds, and a great moon, and Kit's big house like a shining palace under the sky. Jacqueline ran down the walk, and the famous author, following her, saw her, with silver draperies, flying through the night. And so he wrote about her in his book.

He had brought her wrap, and called to her, "Come back...."

"The wild wind called me." She turned and ran back to him. "I may never see you again," he said. "But to me you will be immortal. If it were not for that other man in India, I'd keep you with me — forever."

They went in together, and Mrs. Gilman who was showing her guests the latest pictures of Sue and Kit saw them coming. It would be wonderful, she told Miss Phoebe later, if Jacqueline could make a marriage like that. And Sue was the wife for Kit. And from Paula's letter, one might judge he knew it.

CHAPTER ELEVEN

Yolanda Takes the Center of the Stage

I

JOEY'S kitten had grown up! Yolanda's school days were over! And Kit was coming home!

It sounds very simple put into short sentences like that. But it had not been simple in the three years since Jacqueline talked to the celebrated author at the Gilman dinner. She had been happy then, and she had been happy since, but it was a happiness so near the edge of despair, that her heart seemed to stop beating when she thought of it.

For in all that time Kit had not written. Each Christmas he had sent her a gay and gorgeous box from India, packed with loveliness — sheer silken things, delicate embroideries, bits of beaten gold and silver set with uncut stones, porcelain, bronze and ivory — and in each box had been an envelope and with a sheet of paper on which was written a line in Kit's strong script — "My heart is like a singing bird . . ." and all the other lines he had marked for her so long ago in the little book.

She had hoped he might write a letter, and more

Yolanda Takes Center of Stage 237

than once she had put pen to paper to beg him for a word. But she had stopped there. Kit must be free. He must not feel himself tied. He had said he would wait until she called him back, but she had not called until two months ago when she had written that in October Yolanda would be home again, and small Joey would be sent to a prep school. And if he was still of the same mind. . . ?

The answer to that had been a cable. "I have never had but one mind about you. Letter follows."

There had been other letters, and now it was June, and tonight she was to meet Kit on the bluff where the wild wind blew.

No one knew he was back. Jacqueline felt that she and her lover must meet and talk before the world was told. She had questioned, "Suppose he should find me changed. . . ?" She had looked in her mirror and the mirror had said to her, "Perhaps when he sees you, he won't want you." And she had flung back at the mirror, "Love like ours is eternal. It has nothing to do with looks."

Yet even as she said it, she had wondered if the mirror might not be wise. Men were not like women. They wanted youth — and beauty — there was Joel, for example, whose eyes followed Mary's pretty night nurse, Miss Ogden. But Kit wasn't like that. Kit had an almost super-fastidiousness where women were concerned. "A man lacks taste who likes them all," he had said, "he looks only on the surface. The great lovers have been those men who have chosen once and have stayed steadfast. I know that modern psychology would make philanderers of us all, but we're not."

So all these years he had been — steadfast. "Kit, oh, my Kit," she was saying, as she stood looking out from the sunroom of the new house, watching for Stuart Carleton's yacht which was to sail in at six with Yolanda and her crowd.

The sunroom was very gorgeous. Joel's prosperity in the last three years had been amazing, and when he bought the new house he had insisted on new furnishings, and so set about the sun-room were lacquered tables in leaf green, and chairs in Chinese basket work, and the cushions were green and red and sea-blue, and the curtains matched them. And tonight the tables were laid for an informal supper with gay English porcelain which repeated the colors in the chintzes.

And in the midst of it all, Jacqueline moved about in her sober brown dress like a wren in a flower garden. Her hair was braided as she had worn it ten years ago. And brown was not becoming. She wondered why she had bought that dress. There was money enough now for anything she wanted, and Joel was generous. Perhaps it was because she had not cared how she looked, since Kit was not there to see.

Oh, well, there was another dress upstairs!

A voice from the threshold was saying, "I'm going now, Miss Griffith. I let Miss Ogden in. Mrs. Hutchins is sleeping. I am glad the house is quiet. The noise excites her."

It was the day nurse, Miss Meeker. Jacqueline was

aware that Miss Meeker did not approve of Yolanda and her crowd. They had made the day uproarious with their radio and their dancing. And the day was Sunday. Jacqueline didn't approve either of Sunday dancing. But then, what could one do? And Joel had said, "Just so you keep it from Mary."

Everything had been kept from Mary in these later years. She was no worse, but her nights were wakeful, and there were sometimes paroxysms of pain, and Joel had decided that two nurses were necessary. And he had liked the wide gesture with which he told Jacqueline, "You've done enough, old girl." He had also taken on a cook and a housemaid, and old Hannah, too rheumatic now for active service, had retired to her pleasant cottage near the Causeway, and came every week to do the mending.

"I am sorry about the noise," Jacqueline told Miss Meeker, "I'll speak to Yolanda. She would be sorry to disturb her mother."

Miss Meeker shrugged her white linen shoulders, "Young people are thoughtless."

They were thoughtless, Jacqueline had to admit that. And she had to admit, too, that Yolanda's presence in the house had not brought the rapturous results her aunt had anticipated. When Yolanda was at school, Jacqueline had written: "It will be a wonderful thing to have you here, darling. You can bring into your father's life all the youth and joy he has missed." And Yolanda had written back, "You pamper Dad too much. Gracious Peter, Aunt Jack, men have it all their own way anyhow. Let Dad find his own joy. And I'm no ministering child, but I'll do my best."

Miss Meeker had joined Jacqueline, and was looking out over the harbor. "They're coming now," she said, "isn't that Stuart Carleton's boat?"

It was a lovely boat with its great sails lifting it lightly over the water. And presently there stood on the pier a colorful crowd of young people, the late sun shining full upon them, so that the effect was that of a futuristic painting, flat and flaming against an ultramarine background.

"They are all coming up to supper," Jacqueline said.

"I hope they won't wake Mrs. Hutchins."

"I'll tell Yolanda," Jacqueline remarked.

She was at the door to meet them, and warned Yolanda, "Your mother is asleep."

"But Aunt Jack, this isn't mother's nap time."

"She couldn't sleep this morning."

"Our noise? Oh, well, don't worry. In a way she loves it."

Jacqueline knew that it was true. Mary delighted in the break in her monotonous routine. Yolanda's coming and going. Yolanda's clothes! Yolanda's lovers! "It's a new world," Mary would say to Jacqueline breathlessly.

Miss Meeker felt that the excitement was not good for Mary. Miss Ogden, the night nurse was not so sure. Joel and Jacqueline with their instinct of pro-

Yolanda Takes Center of Stage

tection were inclined to agree with Miss Meeker. Yet it would be marvellous, Jacqueline admitted, if Yolanda's presence should bring about a happier state of affairs in the sick-room.

"Is supper ready?" Yolanda was asking, "we're simply ravenous."

"Marta will bring it in at once."

"Tell her to hurry a bit, won't you? We're going to have another sail by moonlight. It will be a heavenly night on the water."

Marta was the housemaid. It was the cook's afternoon off, but she had made the sandwiches and had left them in the refrigerator, and there was cold lobster and mayonnaise, and crisp round pilot wafers, and pale dry ginger ale. And presently Jacqueline and Marta were rushing back and forth with the sandwiches piled high on silver plates, and the lobster pink and plentiful on a willow-pattern platter, and with cubes of ice in crystal bowls, and gold sealed bottles on a lacquer tray.

And all the while that her aunt went rushing back and forth, Yolanda danced with Stuart. And Jacqueline, hot and tired and in a sudden mood of rebellion, wondered why Yolanda was not rushing.

But Yolanda never rushed. It was not her technic to seem ever in a hurry. She took even her pleasures languidly, and the contrast between her vivid beauty and the effect of inertness seemed to constitute a charm in the eyes of the young men who followed after her.

The fact of Yolanda's beauty was inescapable. There had been the promise of it in earlier days, but now her coloring was more positive — the blue and gold and white of eyes and hair and skin. She was, indeed, Jacqueline often told herself the type of which Malory had written, and Chaucer. Had she let herself go, Yolanda would have shown the bouyant spirits of those women of an earlier age. But she did not let herself go, and the result was, perhaps, even more provocative.

To Jacqueline the poise and self-confidence of her niece seemed incredible. She had never been like that. She had never had the sense of rightness of her own point of view. She had simply muddled along trying to do the best she could for everybody. Perhaps Yolanda's way was better, to take all you could get and let the rest go.

And that, too, had been Sue's philosphy.

Poor Sue! Who had come back three years ago with her head in the air. And not once in all the years since then had she spoken of Kit to Jacqueline. Yet the Gilmans knew that the engagement was broken and that Jacqueline did not hear from Kit. Jacqueline felt they rather pitied her. Why, she did not know, unless Paula had given the impression that Kit had thrown Jacqueline over for love of Sue, and that Sue had then refused to marry him.

And now Sue took admiration where she could get it. Even Joel went over gladly to play bridge at the Gilmans. There was always a gay crowd, and Sue in

Yolanda Takes Center of Stage

the rustling taffeta gowns which she affected, of turquoise and apple-green and orange was a brilliant and arresting figure.

Joel was as devoted to Mary as ever, but who could blame him if now and then he wanted to get away from the silent house and his mouse of a sister-in-law, and be a part of a lively laughing company?

Jacqueline did not blame him. Yet she was always afraid. "What if he should find some one, some day, who would make him care less for Mary?" She had tried, however, to put the thought behind her. Joel was good-looking and attractive. But he would never, *never*, forget what Mary had been to him.

Jacqueline had hoped as she had said in her letter that when Yolanda came she would fill Joel's life for him. But water and oil do not mix, nor do those of Joel's generation and of Yolanda's. Yolanda and her crowd lived on a plane entirely separate from their elders. Joel admired his daughter immensely, but he was not at ease with her. "She's too modern for me, Jack," he had complained, "and as for those boys that hang about her...."

He hated the thought of lovers for Yolanda, "The child's too young."

But now as Jacqueline watched her dancing, Yolanda did not seem young. Not with that unselfconscious youth which had belonged to her aunt and her mother. All of the girls of Yolanda's set gave an effect of sophistication. Or, rather, of an almost uncanny sense of their powers. With their beautiful bobbed heads, their bare arms, their slim sport dresses, they were like nymphs in disguise, who having risen from the sea, might at any moment, strip off their human habiliments and return to their native element like the mermaid in the fairy story.

Yolanda, holding up her glass for Stuart to pour more ginger ale, called, "Why aren't you eating, Aunt Jack?"

"I'll have something later."

"Where's Dad?"

"He's having supper with the Gilmans. There are some people up from Boston."

"Good," Yolanda very definitely shelved Joel, drank her ginger ale, and again danced with Stuart. Stuart's interest in Yolanda seemed unabated, yet, of late, Jacqueline had noticed a difference in its quality. It was as if during his years at college, he had learned that a rich and attractive man might have his pick of the girls he gathered about him. Yolanda still held her head high and issued her commands. But Stuart yielded with an air of amusement rather than with the eagerness he had once displayed. He was listening now to all she said, and laughing. Yet when Yolanda a little later urged some plan for the evening of which he did not approve, Stuart said masterfully, "No," nor could she shake his decision.

Yolanda affected an attitude of good-humored acquiescense which Jacqueline was sure she did not feel. Three years ago, Yolanda would have stayed at home if Stuart had attempted to play the master. But tonight

Yolanda Takes Center of Stage

she did not stay. Before they left she asked the night-nurse who was passing through on her way to the kitchen, "Is Mums awake?"

"Yes."

"I'll run up and see her."

"Don't tell her you are going for a sail," Jacqueline advised.

"Why not?"

"Oh, she hates to have you out at night."

"Silly. Oh, she'll get used to it, Aunt Jack."

II

Upstairs, Jacqueline's dress lay on the bed. It was white — like a bride's, without sleeves and with a little coat. And there was a white fox fur, and a white felt hat. But she wouldn't wear the hat tonight for Kit would want to see her hair.

And he should see it as he had never seen it before. She had made up her mind to that as she had weighed and watched those young nymphs dancing. In her brown dress and her braids she had looked what she was — a woman of another generation. And they had treated her as if she were quite definitely old. Yet there were so few years between — .

And they had not been easy years. And they had tired her. There had been so much to think of . . . Mary's need, and Yolanda's, and small Joey's, and Joel's. Joel's money had helped but it had not lifted from her shoulders the responsibilities of vicarious motherhood, and of the distracting details of the house and home.

She let down her hair and brushed and combed it until it fell about her in shining beauty. Then she wound it close to her head, a part on one side, a wave over this ear, a wave over that — soft, deep, lovely waves that had never been touched by an iron. The effect was, she told herself, wonderful. Her hair might have been shingled, so flat and compact were the little rolls at the back. Then with pointed finger tip she touched this wave and that with fragrance, — a drop from a gold flask that Kit had sent and which imprisoned the scent of a thousand roses. It was so subtle that one was hardly aware of it, yet so fresh and sweet that it was like the breath from some magic garden.

She slipped the sleeveless frock over her head and went again to the mirror. She drew a quick breath as she saw her reflection. The years had dropped from her. She was the child Kit had known. The child Kit had loved. And she was going to meet him. . . .

And suddenly, all her little vanities seemed shallow. What would Kit care for shining hair and subtle perfumes? She was his and he was hers, and had been from the beginning! She went to the window and stood looking out. The sky was white with stars, and there was no moon. Somewhere under the high arch of heaven, Kit was coming to meet her. Even now, he might be at the trysting place, impatient, although it was yet a half hour from the appointed time.

She put on the little coat, and with the white fur in

Yolanda Takes Center of Stage 247

her hand went downstairs. The house was very still, and as she opened the door and followed the path through the garden, Joey's great cat rose and trailed after. She spoke to it softly, and it answered, and half way down the walk she met Joey.

She said, "Joey!" He stopped and said uncertainly, "Aunt Jack? What have you done to yourself? I didn't know you."

"It's my hair and my dress, Joey." The light from the street lamp was full upon her, and she could see him staring, "Do you like me?"

His arm went around her, "You're the darlingest ever! But why all this elegance?"

"It's a secret."

"I didn't know you had any secrets from me."

"I'll tell you — tomorrow."

"I want to know tonight."

She laughed, "I'm sorry."

"You won't?"

"No."

"Then may I go with you wherever you are going?"

"You may go as far as the corner."

At the corner he left her, bending to kiss her, for she was such a little thing, and he was tall for his age — tall and slender, with something of Yolanda's whiteness and goldness, but less obvious and spectacular. There was, indeed, a spiritual quality in Joey's looks, and Jacqueline often linked him in her mind with those boys of the poets — the Boy of Winander, Endymion and the rest. In spite of his youth, he showed a creative bent, and she had great hopes for him. She hated to have him sent away to school, yet knew it to be best. When she was gone, there would be no one for Joey — neither his mother, nor Yolanda, nor Joel. He loved them all, but was not linked to any of them by the ties of understanding which bound him to his aunt.

Yet, loving him as she did, Jacqueline forgot him as she went up the hill — for ahead of her on the high bluff was Kit, her lover, and for the moment there was no one else who mattered in the whole wide world.

III

She saw him at last, standing under the white stars, and she heard herself crying, "Kit, Kit, is it really you?" Then she was in his arms, and all the rest was a whirling ecstasy.

And after a while, she said, "Oh, Kit, to think you waited."

He drew her closer, "It was worth it."

"Was it, darling. . . ?"

"Yes — to have you now — like this. . . ."

She clung to him, "I wanted you so much."

"I know."

She was shaken by a storm of feeling. His strength was hers, his adoration. Never again would she be alone, afraid of life, unhappy, "It is heavenly to have you, Kit."

He led her presently to the shadow of a great rock, which overlooked the sea, and she sat with her head

Yolanda Takes Center of Stage 249

against his shoulder, and all the night was a glory round about them. And there they talked of their plans. She was to go home and tell Mary and Joel and Yolanda. And as soon as possible, she and Kit would be married, and have their honeymoon at Kit's camp in Maine — a long rest and a holiday before they were off for India.

"I am so glad you asked Joey to be with us in Maine. It will be the hardest thing to give up Joey. He's like my own little son, Kit."

It was late when they parted. He went with her as far as the garden, and there he picked a white rose which was silver in the starlight, and tucked it in her hair. The night seemed filled with romance. Joel's great house loomed dark in the white night. For so many years its shadow had fallen upon Jacqueline's soul. But now there were no shadows. The world was lighted by the radiance of her happiness.

"I'll come tomorrow," Kit said. He kissed the rose in her hair, and then her lips. "You are lovelier than ever."

"Really, Kit?"

"Really, blessed one. . . ! And now I must go. Can you hold me in your heart until tomorrow morning?"

"I can hold you in my heart — forever. . . ."

IV

When she entered the house Jacqueline went at once upstairs to see Mary. In the upper hall she was met by Miss Ogden. "Mrs. Hutchins is in great pain," she said, "you'd better not go in."

"Is she worse?"

"No. But she suffers, and she hates to have me give her an opiate. She wants to bring herself out of it. I've persuaded her to let me put on hot towels. That will ease things a bit." Miss Ogden had her cuffs turned back, and through the half-open door, Jacqueline could see a white pan set over an electric stove, its simmering burden of towels billowing up like great bubbles.

"Can I help you?"

"Not now." She turned back into the room but stopped to say, "How lovely you look, Miss Griffith."

"Do you like it?"

"It's just sweet."

Jacqueline smiled at her, and went downstairs again. The night was warm, so she took off her little coat, and stood bare-armed, looking out of the sunroom window. Under the great lamp that lighted the pier, she saw Stuart's boat arrive, and a little later he and Yolanda climbed the hill together. When, however, Yolanda came into the room she was alone. She gazed at her aunt, as Jacqueline turned to greet her. "For Pete's sake, Aunt Jack!"

"What's the matter?"

"What have you done to yourself?"

"Bought a new dress."

"It isn't just the dress. It's everything. . . ." Yolanda was puzzled. Then as her mind went back

Yolanda Takes Center of Stage 251

through the years, "You're shining, just as you used to be." She caught at Jacqueline's hand, "Aunt Jack, has Kit come home?"

"Yes."

"When?"

"I saw him for the first time tonight."

"Here?"

"No. On the bluff."

Yolanda was staring at her, "When," the words seemed to come with difficulty "When are you going to be — married?"

"As soon as possible."

"How soon is that?"

"Oh, a month, perhaps. It will take me that long to get ready. And then a honeymoon at Kit's camp — and then, India."

Yolanda was still as a statue, her face dead white in its frame of bright hair. "Oh, well you deserve all the happiness that is coming to you."

She went to the window and stood looking down at the lights in the harbor. "I think Kit's been marvellous," she said over her shoulder. "Not many men are like that — constant. Half of them don't know their own minds — they leave the women to make up their minds for them."

"It seems to me," Jacqueline said, "that if a woman had to make up a man's mind for him, he wouldn't be worth having."

"Our generation is different," Yolanda argued, leaning back on her hands. "In your generation the men wooed, and wooed hard. That was because the girls had oodles of proposals and could pick and choose. But now, the men are in demand, and the girls have to work for what they get."

"My dear," Jacqueline said, helplessly, "if you could only know how that sounds."

"I don't care how it sounds," Yolanda said, "it's the truth."

She returned to her survey of the harbor, and Jacqueline was aware that Yolanda's eyes were watching something or somebody on the pier. She crossed the room and stood beside her niece. Stuart had gone back to his boat but had not boarded it. He stood talking to one of the girls who had been at Yolanda's supper party — Kitty Jenks. There was another man and another girl, and a somewhat sumptuous automobile. It was evident Kitty was urging Stuart to join them. He shook his head, however, and waved his hand as they drove away, and when the sails of his ship again lifted, he was alone on deck.

Yolanda breathed a little sigh of relief. "Stuart's got a job," she said after a moment. "He's planning to live in New York next winter. His mother is closing the house on the Neck. She and Stuart are going to Wales next month with a party of friends. She has asked me to go with them."

Silence, out of which Jacqueline said, "Of course you can't."

"Not if you are going to be married."

Jacqueline opened her lips, but before she could

answer, Miss Ogden came running down. Her left arm was wrapped in a towel, her face was flushed and drawn. "I have burned myself," she said, "badly. I was lifting the pan and let it slip, and the boiling water poured over me. Mrs. Hutchins doesn't know. I didn't make a sound, and her face was turned the other way. But one of you must go right up to her."

"You go, Yolanda," Jacqueline directed, "I'll look after Miss Ogden and get a doctor."

"You'd better telephone for another nurse," Miss Ogden advised, "I won't be able to do anything for Mrs. Hutchins tonight. I've put on a lot of ointment, and the pain isn't so bad. But I must have a doctor."

The doctor came, but another nurse was not to be had until morning. "Miss Meeker will be here then," the doctor asserted. "Do you think you can get along tonight, Miss Griffith?"

"Of course." Jacquline wondered if he had forgotten that for seven years she had nursed the invalid with only old Hannah's help.

Having made Miss Ogden comfortable in one of the guest chambers, Jacqueline went in to Mary. The room was lighted faintly by a low lamp, and by that faint light Jacqueline saw that things had been left exactly as they were at the time of Miss Ogden's catastrophe. The white pan was still on the tiny stove, its towels cold and soggy. The rugs were wet and an overturned bottle of witch hazel gave an aromatic scent to the atmosphere. Yolanda, in a Chinese coat, sat in a big chair with her feet under her, apparently oblivious of the confusion about her. She had made no effort to reduce the disorder. And she said as Jacqueline came in, "Is Marta up? You might tell her to straighten things a bit."

"She went to bed long ago. I'll do it, Yolanda." Jacqueline bent over her sister, "Better Mary?"

"Yes. I wanted Miss Ogden to let me alone, but she wouldn't. . . ."

"I told Mums about Miss Ogden's accident," Yolanda stated, "she asked me, and I'm not very good at hiding things."

"I wish people wouldn't ever try to hide things," Mary said, vehemently, "it makes me feel shut away from life . . . and I've been shut away so long."

Jacqueline began to wring out the towels. Yolanda protested, "Don't do that, Aunt Jack."

"My dear, I'd rather. But I think I'll change my dress."

Back in her own room, her mirror reflected the white and charming frock, the waved rumpled hair. But Jacqueline had no eyes for it. She got into a wash frock and tied on an apron, and when Joel arrived a little later, he found her in Mary's room on her knees, sopping up the water with a sponge. Yolanda was still curled up in the big chair talking to her mother.

"I'm sorry I'm late," Joel began, then uttered a startled exclamation. "What's happened? And where's Miss Ogden?"

Yolanda told him.

Joel leaned down and kissed Mary. "I should have

been here, dearest. But we went for a sail after supper. It's a gorgeous night."

"Yolanda was sailing, too," Mary said, "Joel do you think I shall ever go sailing under the stars?"

The wistfulness in her voice brought her husband to his knees, "I thought of you a dozen times tonight, sweetheart, and wished you were with me."

"Did you, Joel, really?"

"Really Mary."

It was decided that Jacqueline should sleep on the couch in Mary's room, and that Yolanda was to keep an eye on Miss Ogden.

Yolanda and her father went downstairs together. "Do you want anything to eat, Daddy?" Yolanda asked. "There's lobster left over from supper and sandwiches."

"Not a thing, my dear. If I don't look out I'll lose my figure. And the Gilmans had a feast for the gods."

"What did they have?" Yolanda asked, idly. She didn't care in the least about the Gilmans' supper, but she had to say something, and lounged in one of the long chairs in the sunroom while Joel with the zest of the true epicure answered her question. "There was chicken with curry, and a salad of chilled asparagus with cress and green peppers . . . and. . . ."

Yolanda broke in with, "Aunt Jack's going to be married."

"*Married?*" Joel's countenance had the dazed look of a man struck by a sudden blow.

"Yes."

"But who's she going to marry?"

"Kit, of course."

"But my dear child, their engagement was broken off years ago."

"It was never really broken, Dad. She let people think it, but she has always felt that when she was free Kit would come back to her."

"Free, what do you mean, Yolanda?"

Yolanda sat up straight and looked at him, "Free of us, Daddy. Free of the whole darned family."

"We're not a darned family, Yolanda."

"We are. We've been perfect pigs! But being us, we couldn't help it, and Aunt Jack being Aunt Jack couldn't help it either."

"But I can't quite see."

"Oh, well, she couldn't have been happy to think of us all at loose ends. So she has waited until I was out of school, and until Joey could go away. . . ."

Joel stuck his hands in his pockets and considered it, "Well, of all things, little old Jack," he had a vision of Jacqueline as he had last seen her, on her knees, sopping up the floor. "And she'll be making the match of the season. Howland's simply rolling in money."

"He is? How did it happen?"

"His Uncle Timothy died and left the business to him."

"That won't mean a thing in Aunt Jack's life. She doesn't care a darn, Daddy, whether he is rich or poor. She's made that way, she can't help it."

"I know it," Joel drew a deep breath, "we're going

Yolanda Takes Center of Stage 257

to miss her a lot. I'm afraid we can't ever repay her for all she's done for us, Yolanda."

"Oh, well . . . she's got Kit. . . ." Yolanda stood up, "I'm dead for sleep. If you hear Miss Ogden's bell, just call me, Daddy. I told her not to hesitate to wake me if she wanted me."

She kissed him on the cheek as she passed him, "Nice old Daddy." she murmured.

He caught at her hand, "Love me?"

"You know I do."

"I'm a bit — lonely sometimes, Yolanda."

Her arm went around his neck. "I'm not much at saying things, Daddy, but I'll try to make up for a lot. . . ."

He held her close for a moment, her bright head against his coat. "Yolanda, do you ever think of Patsy?"

She shivered a little in his arms. "What makes you ask me that — now?"

"Because if she had lived, the two of you might have been such pals —"

Yolanda's breath came quickly. "I have never forgiven God for taking her, I shall never forgive him," she said, stormily, "oh, Daddy, Daddy, hold me tight. I think I'm going to cry my eyes out."

"My dear girl . . . why?"

"It was seeing Mums, when I went up to her. In a perfect agony, Daddy, and trying not to let me know it. And I couldn't help . . . and I hated it. . . ."

"My dear child" — his tone was tense. Yolanda,

fighting against the net that was drawing her in, curbing her freedom, weighting her down with cares, was aware that Joel was already caught in the net. It had begun with the war, and then — Patsy, and then his leg, and then her mother's illness. Faintly she remembered herself and Patsy, heads up, singing: *"This is the way we march to war, march to war, march to war. . . ?"* and Joel singing with them.

And now she too, Yolanda, was caught. She wanted to go to Wales, wanted it more than she wanted anything in her life, and she couldn't go because Aunt Jack was going to be married. Fate had it in for her. But she wouldn't submit tamely. There must be some way out.

v

Upstairs, Jacqueline having set the room in perfect order, lay down on the couch. She was spent with excitement. The hours had been packed full since Kit had tucked the silver rose in her hair. The rose was still there, she had forgotten it in the midst of the old heart-breaking worries.

It was very still, the only sound the creaking of the boats at anchor, and, far off, the faint reverberation of a bell buoy. Silence in the room and darkness, except for the slight gleam of a street lamp through one of the east windows. And by that gleam Jacqueline saw presently, a strange sight. She saw Mary rise up in bed, painfully, slowly, to a sitting position, hold it for a few moments, and then lie down again.

She whispered in the darkness, "*Mary.*"

"Are you awake, Jack?"

"Yes."

"Then — you saw me?"

"Yes." Jacqueline rose and went to her sister's bedside, "Mary, I thought I was dreaming."

"No. I've done it before. I shall do it again. . . ."

"But why haven't you told us?"

"Because you'd all think it was that which brought on the pain. And it wasn't. It's something else — something I can't explain. I only know. . . ."

Jacqueline, knelt by the bed, "But it may be bad for you."

"No. Could anything be worse than lying here . . . day after day, week after week, month after month, year after year . . . without a ray of hope. But now. . . ! Jack, some day I'll stand on my feet. I don't know when, but I shall."

Jacqueline dared not shatter that hope by any word of hers. "Faith moves mountains, my darling. And there's no more reason why a miracle should not happen today as well as yesterday."

"That's the way I feel about it. But don't tell anyone, not anyone, Jack. They'll just weaken me by their arguments. And I want to do it — alone. . . ."

Jacqueline knelt beside her, until Mary fell asleep. Then she went back to her couch, feeling shaken and awed by her experience. She still seemed to see that strange figure rising up and lying down again. She felt she ought to tell someone. But Mary had made her promise.

She felt, too, that this hour with Mary had stolen

from her the keen rapture of those moments on the bluff. Was it too late for her ever to find happiness? Hadn't she been so long a part of this household that the tearing apart would be like the tearing of flesh? And could she ever leave Joey, the child of her heart if not of her body? The dark house seemed to hold her as in a prison. A prison from which she wished to flee, but to which she was held because of those others imprisoned with her.

Yet, before she slept, peace came in the thought of Kit. He was strong, wise. He would be a bulwark against the storms which had assailed her. She would go with him, curled up in his heart, hidden from all the cruel blasts in the nest that he would build for her.

CHAPTER TWELVE

Crumbs From the King's Table

I

THE next morning Jacqueline told Mary she was going to be married. It was very early in the morning, before the day nurse came, and while Miss Ogden was still sleeping. Mary was much better, and took the news calmly. "I shall hate having you go, Jack. But it is splendid to know that Kit has come for you."

Jacqueline outlined her plans. "It will be a very quiet wedding, Mary."

"I don't see why it should be. I should think you'd want to ring bells and sound cymbals after all this waiting. And we've got a big house and a lot of friends, and Yolanda could be your bridesmaid."

Jacqueline shook her head, "I'd rather put on a white dress and run around the corner to the little church, and come back and have a party up here in your room."

"But Kit's position demands a little more formality than that, dearest."

"I don't care anything about Kit's position. . . ."

"But you know he's rich now, Jacqueline."

"If he is, what matter? He's my same Kit."

Mary laughed and patted her hand. "You'll never grow up, darling. But whether you'll admit it or not, you're really making a grand match." She lay looking out towards the east. The sun had not yet risen, and the sky was suffused with the white pearl of the dawn. "I wonder what Sue will think of it," she said.

"She's probably forgotten that she ever cared."

"No. She hasn't forgotten."

"But she never speaks of him, Mary."

"Which shows how much he means to her."

Jacqueline weighed that, "It is strange," she said, at last, "that Sue has never married. She's really a rather wonderful person."

"I'm not sure she is so wonderful. She might be if it wasn't for Paula. Paula is a trouble-maker, and she's making Sue as worldly-minded as herself."

Remembering Paula's letter from India, Jacqueline was aware that Mary spoke the truth. She had told no one of that letter. She would never tell. Yet the fact of it had stood all these years between any possibility of a close friendship with Paula or even with Sue. And Paula knew it. She was sure Paula knew.

But Jacqueline didn't want to talk about Sue. Some day, perhaps, Kit would tell her, and she could wait for that.

She was glad, therefore, when Yolanda appeared in the doorway. "I heard you talking. How are you this morning, Mums?"

"Much better."

"I had a beastly night. Miss Ogden slept but I couldn't."

"Why not?"

"My little mind kept working, darling. And I'm not used to a working mind."

She sat down on the foot of her mother's bed and yawned. "Monday's an off day with me. Too much Sunday."

"If you'd go to church with your Aunt Jack, darling—"

"Why go to church when you can do anything else?" Yolanda rose and yawned again. "I'm going for a swim. I adore the water at this time in the morning."

"I don't like to have you out alone," Mary said.

"I shan't be alone. Stuart's coming."

"Stuart? How did he know?"

"I called him up. And we won't be back to breakfast. I'm taking bacon and bread, and a thermos of coffee, and we'll build a fire on the rocks."

"But my dearest...."

"Oh, don't be stuffy, Mums. You're going to say that we oughtn't to eat in our bathing suits, or that we ought to have somebody along to play propriety. But I shan't listen, darling," she crossed the room and cupped her mother's face in her hands, "Oh, Mummy, Mummy, you're such a back number."

"Am I, 'Landa?"

"You are. And you've got to trust your darling daughter to *not* hang her clothes on a hickory limb, or go too near the water," Yolanda straightened up and began to sing the words of the old song, accompanying them with a fantastic dance of waving hands and shuffling feet:

"Mother may I go out to swim?
Yes, my darling daughter,
Hang your clothes on a hickory limb,
And don't go near the water."

Her aunt and her mother gazed at her with eyes of women who admired, yet hardly dared approve. Yolanda was dressed for her swim in her sea-blue tunic, with a blue rubber *beret* hiding her hair. The stern line of the cap showed her profile as clear cut as a cameo, and its blue brought out the blue of her eyes. Her skin was as white as milk. She carried over her arm a beach coat of lacquer-red. The contrast was startling but effective.

"Please put on your coat, 'Landa," her mother begged.

Yolanda wrapped it about her, "I bought it the other day in Boston. Like it?"

"Yes," Jacqueline said, "You have the art of choosing things. I shall want you to go with me to Boston and help me buy my wedding clothes."

"Not to Boston. New York."

"But why desert our home town?"

"Because Stuart will be in New York next week and the week after, and he says he'll give me the time of my life if I'll come. And you know Mums and Dad wouldn't let me go alone. So we'll kill two birds with one stone. Wedding clothes, n'everything."

She kissed the tips of her fingers and fluttered them in a gay "Good-by." She had, as she had told them, spent a dreadful night. But now she was going to meet Stuart. And nothing else mattered.

Jacqueline followed her, presently, downstairs, and had Marta bring a cup of coffee to the sunroom. From the window she watched Yolanda and Stuart. They swam about for a bit, then climbed into Stuart's motor boat and were off. There was a stretch of quiet beach at the lower end of the Neck. They would sweep out of the harbor into the open sea, find a landing place among the rocks and build their fire. And they would be as far away from the world as if it were a desert island. Some morning, Jacqueline decided, she would do it with Kit — go off that way together and build a fire on the rocks.

Old Simon, the parrot, who had his cage in the sunroom ruffled his feathers and made sharp demands on his mistress for his own morning crusts and coffee. Jacqueline rose and filled his cup. "I'm going away," she said, as she watched him eat, "will you miss me, Simon?"

He cocked an inquiring eye at her and went on eating. Joey's cat rising from a rug, stretched and came forward. Jacqueline gave him the rest of the cream from her pitcher. And then the telephone rang, and Marta came to say it was for Miss Griffith.

Kit was at the other end of the line. He was stopping at the big hotel on the town side, and he was wondering if he and Jack couldn't run away and have breakfast together. He simply couldn't wait until later to see her. "I thought I could, but I can't. And I know a wonderful place on the North Shore."

"Kit, I've just had my coffee, and the day nurse hasn't come, and the night nurse burned her arm, and Yolanda's gone swimming."

"Anything else?"

"Nothing that I can think of."

"Well, not any of it counts with me. You're going to have breakfast with me, Jack. I'll be there in fifteen minutes."

"But Kit . . . !"

There was no answer. He had hung up the receiver. Jacqueline was thrilled by his high-handedness. She flew upstairs, stripped off her morning frock of blue linen, and got into a skirt and sweater of white wool. She had bought everything in white for Kit's coming, and there was even a white *beret*—not worn as severely as Yolanda's, but with a wave of hair pulled out over each ear and the effect was charming.

She gave breathless orders to Marta about the family breakfast. "I'll not be back. You and the cook must see to things. And Miss Meeker will be here in a moment. And you will hand this note to Mr. Hutchins?"

The note told Joel that Kit was home again. "I intended to let you know last night, Joel, but so many things happened. Kit is carrying me off to have breakfast with him, and will see you tonight when he dines with us. And please forgive my announcing it this way. I've talked it over with Mary and she'll tell you all about it."

Jacqueline felt sure that Joel wouldn't like this way of announcing things. Joel stood always, quite definitely on his dignity. But it wasn't Joel she had to think of now, but Kit.

She had someone else, however, with whom to reckon, for as she stepped out of the front door, she met Joey. He, too, had been for his morning swim, and was wrapped in his bath robe, with his pale gold hair plastered close to his head.

"Darling," Jacqueline said, all flushed and radiant, "I'm running away."

"Where are you going?"

She put her hands on his shoulders, "Joey, you remember I told you last night I had a secret. Well, this is it — I am going to be married."

So absorbed had she been in her own happiness that she had not considered the effect of her abrupt announcement on Joey. He had been smiling his bright confident boy's smile, but her words swept the smile from his face — "You mean —" his voice caught, "you are going to be married — now?"

"Oh, no, Joey. But Kit has come back and I am having breakfast with him this morning."

"I don't think I — like it. Does it mean you're going away?"

"Yes. To India."

"When?"

"In a month or two. And Kit wants you with us while we are at his camp for our honeymoon. Then we can have those last days together."

He shook his head, "I'm not going with you on a honeymoon."

"Why not?"

"I couldn't Aunt Jack. You wouldn't belong to me any more."

"I shall always belong to you, Joey." She had her arm about him, "always...."

And then he said a strange thing for a child to say, "My heart aches." But Joey had the maturity of the poet-mind. And this was no pose. Not another soul would miss her as would this slender lad who had been for so many years so close in spirit. Dear Joey, who would always be hurt, but who with all his sensitiveness had a strength which was surprising. And now he said, "Oh, well, Aunt Jack, you've got to be happy." And when the car came he shook hands with Kit, and said, with his odd air of maturity, "The only thing I've got against you is that you're going to take Aunt Jack away."

And Kit said, "What about your coming out to us some day?"

"To India?"

"Yes. It would be a tremendous lark, wouldn't it?"

Joey was lighted up, "I'll say it would."

"Well, then that's settled. Our boats are always going back and forth — a slow voyage, but a stunning one. We'll plan for next year — it won't hurt him to lose a few months from school, will it, Jacqueline?"

"No, he's far ahead of the boys of his age."

"Well, then . . ." Kit smiled at Joey and started his motor. "We might even hunt elephants."

"I don't want to hunt anything. But I'd like to see the elephants."

The big car slid away, with Joey waving, and when they were out of hearing, Jacqueline said, "Kit — how do you do it?"

"Do what?"

"Settle things with a gesture. Joey was so unhappy, and now he'll dream all day of coming out to us."

Kit laughed, "If I could have settled you with a gesture, I'd have done it long ago. To even things up, I'll have to rule you for the rest of your life."

"I shall love it," Jacqueline declared, "I always thought that Goldilocks was a most ineffective person, but now I see the sense of her. Why wash dishes and feed the pigs when there was a cushion to sit on and strawberries and cream if one crooks her finger?"

"That sounds well coming from you."

They laughed together, light-heartedly, and Jacqueline looking up and seeing her lover so tall and straight beside her, sighed, "Oh, Kit, you're so — beautiful," and Kit said, "Hush, woman, or I'll be wrecking the car. . . ."

They came at last to the place Kit had chosen, the house of a retired skipper, who cooked himself the food he served his guests, and there they had Rhode

Island corn bread, and crisp small pan fish and clear strong coffee, and Jacqueline told Kit about Yolanda and Stuart on the rocks. "We'll do that some day."

"We'll do everything some day," he told her ardently, "but why talk about Stuart and Yolanda when we have ourselves to talk about?"

So sitting there in the sweet and shining little room, with the sound of the sea in their ears and the sight of it in their eyes, Kit poured out his heart. It was a long history of a man's loneliness, of a man's constancy, "Now that I look back, I wonder how I did it. I wonder why I didn't come and carry you off. But something always warned me. There was a part of you which didn't belong to me, that would never belong until you called me back, and so — I went on living as best I could — and waiting — and there has never been any other woman."

And then, before she knew it, she was asking. "Did you ever love — Sue?"

He gazed at her in silence before he asked, "What makes you ask that?"

"Well, there's that heart by the fireplace in your old house, and your initials and Sue's in it."

"Who told you I carved it?"

"Miss Phoebe."

"Why did she tell you?"

"I don't know."

"And you — thought I had — cared?" there was a touch of sternness in his voice.

"What else could I think?"

Crumbs From the King's Table 271

His face softened, "I know. And here's the story. It was Valentine's Day and Sue and I, just boy and girl, were popping corn over the coals, and making rhymes to fit the day, and Sue borrowed my knife and cut the heart, and I put in the initials, and we laughed, and it was all a great joke, and that was the end of it. I never thought of it again, until one night Sue came to the library and —" he stopped.

"And what, Kit?"

He laid his hand on hers. "She wanted to dig up what she called our old romance . . . and there wasn't any . . . never had been," he shook his shoulders as if he shook the thought away from him, "but why should we waste our time with this, my blessed one? It's past and gone — forever."

II

Stuart would not, under any circumstances, have called Yolanda, "my blessed one." He didn't think of her that way. He thought of her as challenging, charming, arousing his man's sense of conquest by her sudden flares of independence. But of that spiritual quality which drew Kit and Jacqueline together, he knew nothing. He was apt in his most melting moods to call Yolanda, "Dear Thing." It was the best he could do, and he did it now. "Dear Thing, what about the New York trip?"

"Aunt Jack is going down to buy clothes. And I am going down to sell myself to you!"

The impudence of her! He shouted. "If you meant that you wouldn't say it."

"I do mean it . . ." she stopped long enough to warn him: "Stuart, the bacon's burning . . ." then as he lifted his stick, on which a slice of bacon was impaled like a pennant, beyond the reach of the flames, she continued. "You've changed a lot, Stuart. You're spoiled. And you're too good to go to waste like that. What you need is a friend who knows your faults and tells you of them. But you don't look upon me as a friend . . . you just list me with all the other lovelorn lassies who wait for your smile . . ." she shrugged her white shoulders, "and I'm not. That's why I've got to sell you the idea of friendship, with a very large F. It is really a lovely relationship, Stuart."

"But just what do you mean by it?"

"Oh, companionship, confidences, but no kisses."

"Nothing new about that — but it isn't my fault if you go to your grave unkissed."

"No," she had been tending the toast, and now accepted his offering of bacon on a slice of it. "No . . . nothing new. But something — defined. Otherwise we might drift."

"Drift where. . . ?"

"Away from each other, precious," she tossed a crust into the flames of the little fire, and gave him a long level glance from beneath her lashes, "away — away — away." Her white arm seemed to wave him to some distant spot on the horizon. "Another girl for you. . . ! Another boy for — me!"

Crumbs From the King's Table 273

"There isn't going to be any other girl for me."

"Isn't there? Well, there might be another boy — for me."

"Cut that out, Yolanda."

"Why?" coolly. "It can't go on this way, Stuart. Crumbs from the king's table. You've been handing out your favors to me lately, as you handed me that strip of bacon, casually. And I won't have it."

"Oh, look here, Yolanda."

"No. I'd hate not having you in my life. But when you act like a — Turk, I'm not going to be a part of your harem."

"When have I acted like a Turk?"

"Well, last night on your boat. Four girls — one every fifteen minutes and saying the same things to all of us."

He laughed, "Jealous?"

She nodded her head, soberly, "Yes. I missed the friend who used to be mine."

There was a shake in her voice, which brought him to his feet. "Dear Thing," he said, "you're not really feeling it?" His finger was under her chin, turning her face up to him.

"Yes," tears dripped under her lashes. Modern as she was, she was using woman's oldest weapon. He drew her to him, "Look here, old girl, you know how I feel about you?"

She moved away from him, but left her hand in his. She was not sure how he did feel. When he was with her alone, he was all hers. But he had been so wonderful in the old days. So simple, so utterly without vanity. She told him the truth with a touch of wistfulness. "Things will never be quite the same. You were such a nice boy, Stuart. But now you are Cock o' the Walk and you know it."

"I am all yours, if that's any satisfaction to you," he was very much in earnest, his fair face flushed, "that's why I want you to go to Wales . . . why mother wants it. She likes you a lot," he drew a deep breath, "and I want you to marry me, Yolanda."

She sat still as a statue for a moment, then turned to him and said, "You darling . . ." and wept a little on his shoulder, as her mother and grandmother had wept before her.

III

In the days that followed, Jacqueline saw little of her niece. The child was forever up and away, going and coming in a sort of rushing excitement — dances, dinners, beach parties, boat parties, and always with Stuart and his crowd. And it was not until the two of them were in the train, on their way to New York and their shopping adventure, that she noticed Yolanda was very pale and very quiet, burying herself in a book and saying very little. Even when they reached the fine old hotel by the Park, and came into the rooms which Joel had engaged for them, and which were quite unexpectedly splendid, she showed little enthusiasm. Yet when the telephone rang and she found Stuart at the other end, she was lighted as by

Crumbs From the King's Table

a flame. "He's downstairs, and wants me to have tea with him, Aunt Jack."

"You might tell him that Kit has invited the three of us to dine with him."

"Here?"

"Yes."

Yolanda having relayed all this to Stuart, went down to meet him, and Jacqueline stood looking out of the window at the peaceful scene below. Except for the noise, and the castellated line of skyscrapers beyond the Park on the west, she might have been miles away from the metropolis. The trees were all in their summer green, and the line of little ducks swimming serenely across the lagoon seemed to belong to a pond in some serene countryside, so intent were they on their own business and oblivious to the pulsing life of the city streets about them.

Jacqueline told Kit about it all later. "As I stood there, Kit, I wondered if some day we could have some little ducks."

"You can have anything you want." He had come up to her sitting-room, and they were waiting for Yolanda, who was not dressed, and for Stuart who had not arrived. Kit's presence in New York was due to the fact that he had refused to be separated from Jacqueline. "Do you think I'll let you out of my sight for a moment?" he had demanded, "I have a feeling that some day you'll slip away from me."

"No such good luck for you." And they had laughed together. And now Kit was saying, "You can have anything you want," and she was saying, "We might have a summer place with a pond . . . and when I am tired of living in state and elegance we can run away."

"We are not going to live in state and elegance."

"Yes, we are," she was thoughtful, standing there by the window, and looking out with him over the sea of lights. "Yes, I shall be a Howland, darling, and there will be traditions to keep up. Nice traditions of dignity and everything. Yolanda laughs at me when I talk of dignity — but I like the sound of it. . . . There's something stable about it — and steadfast. . . ."

A door opened, and they turned to find Yolanda in the room. The room was lighted only by lamps, but Yolanda shone with an effulgence which spread a glory round about her. She wore orchid velvet in a pale shade, and earrings of amethyst and pearls dripped from her ears — her satin slippers were orchid, and a shoulderknot of orchids lay on her neck. She carried a wrap of summer ermine, and slipped her arms into it as she spoke to them. "Do you mind being called a heavenly host, Kit?" she asked.

"It sounds," he told her smiling, "like something in the hymn book."

"Aunt Jack says we're going on to a play afterwards. You were a dear to ask Stuart."

"I did it in self-defense. No Stuart, no Yolanda."

"It's not as bad as that. Aunt Jack and I are going to run around alone all day tomorrow."

"No, you're not. Your Aunt Jack is going to lunch with me at India House, and nobody is asked but ourselves."

At dinner, a little later, Yolanda told Stuart, "I am open for a luncheon engagement. Uncle Kit is going to carry off Aunt Jack."

"My dear child," Stuart protested, "why spring it on me like this? You told me you wouldn't and couldn't, and I've gone and made an engagement."

"Break it. . . ."

"I can't do it, old girl."

"Oh, well, if you can't, you can't. . . ." Yolanda swept away from the subject serenely, and during the hour that followed she was brilliant, gay, whimsical. Stuart delighted in her. In the dining-room and in the theater, people turned to look at her. And she knew it, and played up to their admiration with the somewhat regal air of remoteness which she affected.

After the theater, she and Stuart went off to dance, and Kit and Jacqueline had a few minutes alone in the lounge of the hotel. "Mayn't I go up with you, Jack?"

"Too late," she said, "and I shall see you tomorrow morning."

Once more in her room, Jacqueline undressed slowly, but she had been for a long time in bed before she heard Yolanda come. She did not open the door between the rooms, and Jacqueline fell asleep thinking of the child's affair with Stuart. It was fast and furious. But nothing would surely come of it. They were both so young.

When she waked in the morning, she went in to see Yolanda who was also awake, and propped up on her pillows. Bound about her head was a length of amber tulle, and she wore a padded satin jacket of the same honey-colored hue. A band of sunlight, falling through the open window turned all of her amber to gold. "I've ordered orange juice and coffee sent up for both of us," she told her aunt, "and toast for you. If I am going to lunch with Stuart, I won't dare eat anything now."

"I thought Stuart had an engagement."

"I made him break it."

"Wasn't that a bit high-handed?"

"No. It's the only way to keep him in order," she hesitated then went on. "Aunt Jack, I've got to tell you. I'm going to marry Stuart."

"*Marry — Stuart!*"

"Yes. Oh, Aunt Jack, haven't you seen what was coming? I love you and I love mother. But I love Stuart more than either of you. And Stuart isn't like Kit. He loves me, but if he can't have me . . . he'll find somebody else. And I won't — lose him. . . . And there's no reason why if I get married, you should have to stay at home. I know you'll say that mother needs one of us. But it isn't mother's life we are thinking about, is it, but yours and mine. Of course if mother means more to you than Kit, then you'll have to stay with her. But Stuart means more to me than anyone else in the whole wide world, and that's why I'm going to marry him!"

CHAPTER THIRTEEN

A Call to Adventure

I

It seemed to Jacqueline that, when Yolanda ceased speaking, the room still echoed with the clang of her words. And there was another echo of long ago, "*London Bridge is falling down, falling down, falling down. . . .*"

Then through the clang and clamor, she heard a knock on the sitting-room door. She went at once to answer it, and admitted a waiter, who brought in their table, bright with silver and snowy with damask, with toast hot under covers and orange juice cool on crushed ice. He placed the table in front of the window that overlooked the Park. He was a red-cheeked Frenchman, expert, expressive. He spoke of the weather. "A beautiful morning, Madame."

She stood by the window. "I like to watch the little ducks."

He flashed a glance at her. Not many of the women who breakfasted in their rooms spoke of the ducks. Nor were many of them as crisp and composed at this hour of the morning. He liked the little Madame's chiffon négligé of faint blue, with the knot of violets at her breast. A lady, undoubtedly, but he thought she looked sad. Too sad for such a shining morning.

After he went away, Jacqueline still stood by the window, gazing down at the ducks, and wondering what she should say to Yolanda. There didn't seem to be anything to say. Yolanda had always had her way, and she would have it now.

She spoke presently through the open door. "Do you want to eat in here? Or shall I bring your breakfast to you?"

"I'll come." And Yolanda appeared presently, wrapped in her amber robe, her toes stuck into gold slippers with a fluff of feathers.

They sat down and Jacqueline poured the coffee. Then she looked at the headlines of the morning paper. It was Yolanda who finally broke the silence, "Listen, Aunt Jack. . . ."

"Yes?"

"It's like this," she was flushed, eager. "Stuart isn't Kit's kind. I've told you that. You can see for yourself. When I'm with him, I can wind him around my little finger, but when I'm away he does things. Like making that engagement for luncheon today. He wasn't going to break it even when he knew I was free until I got him in the right mood. And it was with another girl."

"Another girl!"

"Yes. Oh, that's Stuart's philosophy — to take second-best rather than not have anything. He really doesn't care a snap of his finger about anyone but me

A Call to Adventure

—but he isn't going to be left high and dry without somebody to amuse him. And that's why I'm going to marry him. . . ."

Jacqueline stopped her, "Oh, let's not talk about it." She rose and stood by the window.

Yolanda's eyes followed her, "You're making me feel like a worm of the dust, Aunt Jack. If you'd only be sensible. Mother's and Dad's happiness isn't any more important than ours, and there's no reason in the world why you should go on making a doormat of yourself."

"Why say it all over again, Yolanda?"

"But Aunt Jack—*Listen*. . . !"

Jacqueline turned suddenly and faced her niece. "No, I won't listen, and I'll tell you this, Yolanda. I may have been a doormat and a lot of other things that people have called me. But I wouldn't take at my lover's hands what you are taking from Stuart!"

Yolanda stared, and as she stared she saw a thing which astounded her. She saw a firmness in this tiny, flaming creature which more than matched her own. "It is that which has held her to it all these years," Yolanda told herself, with sudden illumination, "she is a strong little thing. Stronger than I am. Stronger than I shall ever be."

"I know," she said, and was suddenly swept by a storm of tears. "I know. But I can't give him up, Aunt Jack. I can't. You don't understand how I feel about it. I care—such—an awful lot. . . ."

II

Neither Jacqueline nor Yolanda finished her breakfast. Yolanda, having cracked the outer shell of youthful self-assurance, showed herself soft within like any girl in love. She argued and wept, and wept and argued again. But she came around always to a desperate summing-up: "I've got to marry him now or lose him."

Jacqueline was conscious of rather hating it all. Love as she knew it was something very different from this thing of which Yolanda was talking. Love in her life and Kit's had been a matter of high idealism, a belief, each in the dignity and integrity of the other. She tried to tell Yolanda something of the kind. "You may be making Stuart less than he is. . . ."

"He used to be different, Aunt Jack. He has changed. . . ."

"Then hold him to his best. Demand things of him."

"I'm afraid. . . ." Her eyes did not meet her aunt's.

The waiter came and took away the table. Yolanda went back to her room and looked in her mirror. She was, she declared a sight and a fright. She declared, also, that shopping was out of the question. She called up the hotel beauty shop, and went away presently to have the ravages of her emotional disturbances effaced by expert treatment.

Jacqueline put on her hat and coat and walked in the Park. There she watched the little ducks at close range. She watched, too, the people walking with

A Call to Adventure 283

their little dogs. The dogs were on leash and it all seemed very futile. Jacqueline reflected that freedom was something that belonged to a dog. It belonged, indeed, to every living thing. None of them should be caged or tied. But then, civilization was just that — caging and tying. She stopped at the parrot house and murmured things to the brilliant birds as she had so often murmured to Simon, and they seemed to understand and to ask something of her. . . .

"They want to fly in the forests," she told herself, and stood for a long time looking at them, "and they will never fly. They are caged — forever. . . ."

After that she could scarcely bear to look at them — these birds which were caged — forever!

An hour later, she told Kit: "I can't marry you."

She sat opposite him at a table in the dining-room of India House. He had shown her all the sights of the fine old place — the great stairway guarded over by a figurehead from a Yankee clipper, which seemed to strain and lift in this still air as it had once strained and lifted to the rhythm of wind and waves; the ship's lanterns whose lights now shone on models of vessels and the many trophies of that trade which began in America with Cathay; the old prints and paintings which gave the life of those days when steam and oil and electricity were unknown as motive powers, and when men steered their courses by the stars, and were carried across the waste of waters by bulging sails.

And Jacqueline, heavy-hearted, had followed Kit up

and down, until aware at last of her white face and lagging footsteps, he had said, "Tired?"

"A little."

"Hungry?"

"Not very."

"Late breakfast?"

"I didn't eat any."

"Why not?"

"Oh, because. . . ."

"Which isn't any answer. And you are going to eat right now."

So they had ascended to the dining-room, and Kit had ordered something with curry and something devilled, because that was the sort of thing the chef did very well, and "it will be a foretaste of India."

And it was then Jacqueline had said, "I can't marry you."

The waiter had gone, and they were alone in the big room, and Kit's hand had caught hers in a hard clasp. "What do you mean?"

"Oh, Yolanda's going to marry Stuart, right away. And go with him to Wales. She told me this morning."

The blood flew up in Kit's face. His grip on Jacqueline's hand hurt her. "The little slacker! Does she think she can get away with it?"

"She doesn't know she's a slacker. She wants her happiness. And I don't blame her." Jacqueline spoke with sudden passion. "I don't blame her, Kit. She's young . . . as I was young. . . ! I don't believe I could do it over again. I don't believe I could do it."

"Yet you are going on with it?"

"Yes. I've got to. There isn't any way out."

Dead silence between them. The waiter came back and set forth the delicious food. "I don't want anything," Jacqueline said, desperately, as the man departed. "Kit, I'm going home . . . now," she rose, and he rose with her.

Then suddenly she came to herself, "Oh, I'm afraid I'm making a scene." She sat down again. "You eat, Kit, I can't."

She made a pretense of it, however, and drank a cup of coffee at Kit's stern insistence. "I can't have you making yourself ill, Jack."

They had little besides that to say to each other. She attempted a wavering apology, "I'm sorry."

He did not look at her. "Nothing you can say will make it right with me. Perhaps the less said the better. I've fought for you all these years, but I've come to the end. I'm a man, Jacqueline, and I want you. I can't be content any longer with a shadow."

"I know. I'm not asking you to wait."

"And you can send me away like this?"

"I'm — sorry."

Another long silence, and then he said, "I can't think that you really mean it. One of our ships is sailing in three days. I am needed in India. There is unrest among the workmen and I have had several cable messages urging me to come. But I would not — because of our wedding. But now there is nothing to keep me. I'll give you the three days, Jack. If in that time you change your mind, I'll stay. Otherwise, I'll sail — and I shall never come back to you."

He looked up then and saw the despair in her face, "My darling. . . !"

"Oh, Kit . . . don't. . . ."

III

Jacqueline never quite knew how she got back to the hotel, or what she said to Yolanda.

Yolanda had come in, radiant: "Stuart and I had a gorgeous time. Such eats! Brook trout and new melons . . . and. . . ."

She had stopped suddenly, "What in the world are you doing, Aunt Jack?"

"Packing my trunk."

"*Packing*. . . ?"

"Yes. I'm going home."

"*Home*. . . ?"

"Why not? I'm not going to be married. And I shan't need wedding clothes. And that's what I came to buy."

"Aunt Jack, don't be a *fool*. . . ."

Jacqueline turned and faced her, "Why should you call me that?"

"Because you are taking it this way."

"How should I take it?" The golden air seemed

A Call to Adventure

to beat and throb between them, their cheeks were red, their eyes blazing. "How should I take it, 'Landa?"

"Don't be so — upstage. Nobody has asked you to give up Kit."

"You have certainly made it impossible for me to marry him."

There had followed a torrent of words. There was no need, Yolanda had asserted, why they should not both marry. With nurses, and Joey away at school. "I believe Mother would adore being alone with Dad. For years there has always been a third person."

"A third person? What do you mean, Yolanda?"

"A third person to come between them. You've always been there, Aunt Jack."

Yolanda had the cruelty of youth. She had wanted an argument and had taken the first one that came to her hand, but she had not dreamed of its effect on Jacqueline. She saw a change in her aunt which seemed incredible. The small, serene person she had always known was transformed into a raging fury.

"You can say that to me?" Jacqueline demanded, "after all these years? When your father begged me and your mother cried? When Kit came and went away because there was always something — to hold me back from happiness. Oh, I don't want to talk to you, Yolanda. Go on and marry Stuart. I wouldn't have him as a precious gift. A man isn't worth loving who can't do his own — wooing. . . ."

With that, she began flinging things into her trunk. As a rule she was exact and orderly, and it seemed to

Yolanda that her very disorder in flinging stockings and handkerchiefs and powder puffs and hairpins right and left and letting them fall where they would had in it something frightening and sinister.

"Aunt Jack," she protested, "I should think you'd be ashamed to act like this."

The small fury stopped for a moment, "If I had acted like this years ago," she said, "it might have been better for all of us. And now will you please go away, Yolanda? I want to finish my packing."

When she was at last in the train and speeding towards Boston, Jacqueline's mind went back to Yolanda and her protests.

"But you *can't* go, Aunt Jack. Not tonight."

"Why not?"

"Because I have an engagement with Stuart."

"There is no reason why you shouldn't keep it."

"But Mother and Daddy will have a fit if I stay here alone."

"Why should they?"

"Oh, well, you know they will."

"Chaperones are out of fashion. You told me that yourself. And anyhow I'm done with chaperoning you, Yolanda. You can live your life and I'll live mine. It isn't that I don't love you, but I can't be bothered. I've got too much else to think about. So that's that . . . and why talk any more about it?"

Yolanda, staring and subdued by her aunt's fire, had stammered, "Gracious, Aunt Jack. I didn't know you had it in you."

"I have a great deal in me that you don't know

A Call to Adventure

about. I've gone around like a timid mouse when I've felt like a raging lion. The psychologists say that periods of repression are followed by explosions. Well, I think this is my explosion. You can make your plans in your own way, Yolanda, and now, *please* let me go on with my packing."

So Yolanda, wordless for once in her life, had departed, and Jacqueline, turning back to her task, had caught a glimpse of herself in the long mirror, and had gasped at the sight. For here was a new Jacqueline. Her hair was a rumpled halo, her skin was clear red and white with the excitement of the moment, and the rosy slip she wore showed bare arms as slim as a child's. But it was not skin or hair or clothes which held her gaze. It was, rather, the look in her eyes. They burned with a reckless light. It was as if her soul had waked suddenly to a sense of adventure hitherto unknown in her ordered life. She looked younger by ten years than when she had sat white-faced opposite Kit at India House.

And with that sense of adventure still upon her when she reached North Station, she bought a ticket for Salem. She had decided not to go home that night. No one would miss her. Yolanda would think of her as safely with Joel and Mary. And Joel and Mary would not dream she had left New York. She did not want to face Joel and Mary — not yet. She wouldn't know what to say when she saw them. They would ask why she had come, and why she had left Yolanda, and she would have no answer ready. And anyhow, if Yolanda was right, they might even resent her coming back so soon. They might be enjoying to the full their moment of freedom. What was it Yolanda had said? "There's always been a third person to come between them. You've always been there, Aunt Jack."

That was the dreadful thing about it — to think that, perhaps, after all, they had not needed her. Had not, indeed, wanted her. That they might have muddled along in their own way and have been happier. . . .

When she reached Salem, she went to the hotel and had dinner served in her room. She found herself hungry. She had eaten nothing all day. She had soup and a salad and fruit. It was all delicious. She was still warmed by the excitement which had pervaded her since her conversation with Yolanda. She wondered what Yolanda was doing. The engagement had had to do with dinner at the Clairmont, and a drive into Westchester. Stuart had some friends there, and Yolanda would not get back to the hotel until morning. She would go upstairs alone, all lovely and shining in her orchid satin with her dripping pearls. And there would be no one to watch over her.

Jacqueline wondered at her lack of any sense of responsibility. But she was utterly without a care as far as Yolanda was concerned. She told herself, with a touch of whimsicality, that if anyone needed a chaperone at the moment, it was herself. Here she was alone in a hotel. A runaway. Hidden from her little world.

A Call to Adventure

She rose and went to the window. The dark had come and the moon was high. There would be a moon when three nights hence, Kit would sail for India.

Three nights! Three days! What was it Browning had said. ... *In three days and just one night ... but nights are short...?* But why think of Browning? It was of Kit she must be thinking. She had told Yolanda she would not marry him. Yet in the background of her mind had been the hope that she might harden her heart to those she loved and leave them. If only she could harden her heart ... not think of Mary in her bed ... or of Joel's poor leg ... or small Joey's wistful eyes.

Joey would go lonely to school, and Joel would sit alone at his table, and Mary would lie alone in bed ... and she and Kit would be sailing ... sailing ... under the moon...!

Three days...!

What if Yolanda and Stuart decided to be married tonight or tomorrow morning? It would be like them, and Yolanda was afraid to wait. She wanted her happiness and would take it.

Well, everybody wanted happiness, but they could not take it at the price of unhappiness for others. And Mary *couldn't* get on without her — not if Yolanda went. There would always be that fear at her heart of Joel's coming into an empty house and going off to seek gayer company.

Three days...!

If she said no word, Kit would sail without her. And it would be the end. They had not really said "good-bye" when he left her at the club. How could they say it in the great dining-room with the waiters coming and going? And Kit at the very last when he had put her in a taxi, had held her hand for a moment in a tight clasp and then dropped it: "I shall not see you again unless you send for me."

And then she had driven off, looking back at him and waving.

Three days. . . !

She found herself putting on her hat and coat, and presently she was out in the moonlighted streets. She walked and walked until she came to Kit's house. She had the key and entered. She dared not light a candle lest the Gilmans should question and investigate. Yet the moon illumined the rooms faintly as she made her way to the library. The shades were up and the windows of the big house across the way were golden squares. She wondered if the Gilmans were having a party. They liked to entertain in the early summer and serve coffee among the roses in the perfumed garden. And Sue would pour, with her sheer sleeves falling back from her white arms. . . .

Three days. . . !

The wide glass doors of the dining-room were thrown open and people came out on the porch. They went down into the garden, and the light from the door showed Sue among them in a picture frock of crisp pale green, and back of her was — Joel. . . !

A Call to Adventure

So Mary was alone ... alone in her white bed, with only a nurse for company. And Joel was finding his pleasure with Sue. Oh, what a fool she had been to think she could leave Mary!

She groped her way to Kit's desk, and sat in his chair. And all at once it seemed as if his arms were about her ... and she found herself weeping — great hot tears which fell on her hands and seemed to burn them.

Oh, Kit, Kit — here in this house with its ghosts of the past, its dreams of the future ... you and I, dearest, here by this hearthstone, with children's laughter all about us, and with little children's feet going up and down...!

When her storm of emotion had subsided, she left the library, and ascended the great stairway. She was not afraid. All the ghosts were friendly ones as they pressed close. The moonlight streamed through the high window on the first landing and fell in a flood of silver down the stairs, and Jacqueline, bathed in its light, was like a silver statue.

She had taken off her hat and coat for the night was warm, and when she reached Kit's room she opened a window, and a soft air with a tang of saltiness blew in. And that salt air came from the sea — the sea on which Kit was to sail — in three days...!

She made her way to the bedside table, where she found that for which she had come — the little prayer-book which long ago she had given Kit. She had felt she must have something tangible, something that

Kit had touched. Kit wouldn't care if she took it. Perhaps he wouldn't even know. Or, if she went with him, she would tell him about it, and they would read their evening and morning prayers — together. Kit was so wonderful about such things. She remembered he had said to her once, "Our love would be less than it is if it were not linked with love of God." Not many men were like that . . . and she was letting him go out of her life!

With the little book pressed to her heart, she breathed an agonized petition, "Show me the way. . . ."

After that, she went from room to room, hating to leave and return to the hotel. She wondered if she dared stay for the night. She could curl up on one of the beds, and no one would be the wiser. There was the great canopy bed in the guest room, or the low wide one in the room which had been Kit's mother, or the narrow hard bed which had been Kit's. It would be like Goldilocks in the nursery tale, "Who's been sleeping in *my* bed?"

But they might wonder about her at the hotel . . . the sensible thing was, of course to get back to electric lights and the radio and the jazz band in the dining-room, and away from the glamour and fantasy of this moonlighted house.

As she came once more to the high window on the landing, she stood looking down. She could see the Gilmans' garden and all the people sitting about in low chairs. They had finished their coffee, but Sue still lingered beside the table on which was the coffee

A Call to Adventure

service. She was talking to Joel who, even as Jacqueline watched, rose to say "good-bye." He held out his hand, but Sue stood up and walked away with him. She wore a flowing gown in the new fashion, which gave her the effect of unusual height and stateliness. But Joel was taller than she. He still limped but with his shoulders and military carriage, he seeemed a splendid mate for Sue as they walked together.

And Mary would never walk. . . !

Jacqueline turned from the sight, and descended the stairs. She went into the library for her hat and coat, put them on and started to leave the room, then drew back as she heard the faint rustle of garments, and someone entered. Someone who passed without seeing her, and went to the window. And the someone was — Sue!

Jacqueline among the shadows stood very still. She hoped Sue would go away without discovering her. But why had Sue come?

As if in answer to her unspoken question, Sue turned and knelt by the hearth. The moonlight shone on her head, and on her outstretched white hand, as her fingers sought the outlines of the crude heart carved on the baseboard beside the fireplace. And when they found what they sought, Sue still knelt, her face uplifted, tears streaming down her cheeks, her quick breath sounding in the stillness.

And it was then that Jacqueline spoke, "Sue."

Sue flung herself about to face the sound, "Who's there?"

"Jacqueline."

They stood now in the darkness, close together, "Jack, what made you come?"

"I'm running away."

"From what?"

"From myself."

Sue put her hand on Jacqueline's shoulder and drew her forward, so that the moonlight fell upon her, "You've been crying?"

"Yes."

"Why?"

"I'd rather not talk about it."

Sue did not withdraw her hand, but stood looking down: "Once upon a time you would have told me. But now you are keeping me at arms' length. And I want to be friends. But of late you haven't seemed to want my friendship? Nor Mary. I have an idea she thinks I'm vamping Joel. But I'm not. He's all Mary's, and I know it. And there's only one man for me. . . . I came here tonight to keep a tryst with him. He doesn't love me. He doesn't even know that I keep a tryst. And that's why I cried. Every night in all the years, I have come to have this moment with my dreams — of Kit. . . ."

She said it with a pride which scorned to keep anything back. The moonlight shining now full upon her showed her head held high, her hair a burnished crown, her shoulders white as silver, her green dress sheathing her like the calyx of a flower. She was very beautiful, but she was more than that. Jacqueline felt the fineness, the courage of her confession. She felt,

A Call to Adventure

too, a sense of awe in the knowledge of a constancy which asked no return but this mystical resurrection of the past.

"You have come every night, Sue?"

"Every night. And I want you to know it, because you are going to marry him, because I love you dearly, Jack, for your own sake, and because you are Kit's."

"But I'm not Kit's."

"What do you mean?"

"He's going away without me."

"Do you mean you are sending him?"

"Yes."

"Why?"

"Yolanda's going to be married. And we can't both leave Mary."

For a moment Sue did not speak, then she burst forth, "And Kit is letting you do it? If he had a bit of red blood in his body, he'd *make* you go...."

"Sue!"

"Oh, I suppose if I were like the girls in the movies, I'd be thinking that I could get him. But no one will ever get him but you, Jack. Can't you see it? He's that kind. But he's too good to you. If he'd been a bit brutal — hurt you as you have hurt him...."

"Sue...!"

"Oh, I'm telling you the truth, Jack. I've wanted to do it for a long time, but I thought things were going as they should. But they aren't and you might as well hear it. You've treated Kit abominably. You've thought of everyone's happiness but his.

You've thought of Mary's happiness and Joel's, and the children's! And in doing it you've wrecked Kit's life. But I don't blame you now. I blame him. He is stronger than you, if he chooses to use his strength. And you know it. You know that if he came to you in the full tide of his passion, and said, 'I won't take no for an answer Jack'—you'd marry him. But he's been such a lamb . . . letting you lead him about with a blue ribbon. . . !"

Jacqueline gasped, "Sue, how dare you."

"I dare anything. I want him to be happy. I think sometimes that I love him more than you do. For you make him suffer. . . ."

Jacqueline still had Kit's prayer-book in her hand. Upstairs she had prayed, "Show me the way." Was Sue showing it? Was Sue tearing away the veil of self-delusion in which Jacqueline had shrouded herself? Had the sacrifice of all these years been simply a self-satisfied gesture?

But Sue had not finished. "I'm not saying you weren't right in the beginning. You were. Mary needed you, and you felt you had a debt to pay. But you've paid it long ago. But by the time Joel's prosperity came you'd become obsessed with the idea of immolation. And you'd grown so into Mary's life that it was like tearing flesh to break away. But you should have broken. And if you let Kit go—and he goes because you tell him, I shall be done with both of you. . . ."

Her hands were on Jacqueline's shoulders, and she

gave her a little shake. "Are you mad, my dear, to lose the fullness of life when you might have it? Do you know how I envy you your chance? I, who shall never have it?"

Jacqueline clung to her, "Sue, darling."

"No, I'm not a darling. And I'm not big or fine or anything that you're thinking I am. I can't have Kit, and I'm not a dog in the manger. That's why I'm fighting for his happiness. But, why should I have to fight for his happiness, Jack, when you have it in your hands?"

It seemed to Jacqueline then as if a mighty wind swept through the still house, blowing away the doubts which had assailed her. "Sue," she said, "Kit has to sail in three days . . . and I am going to sail . . . with him. . . ."

She was in Sue's arms now, her head against that silver shoulder, and a great sense of peace upon her. It was all decided.

After a time, Sue said, "Surely you aren't going home tonight. . . ?"

"I've got a room at the hotel. No one knows I'm here. Yolanda thinks I'm with Joel and Mary and they think I'm with Yolanda. . . ."

"I'll send for your bag and you can stay with us."

"There'd be too many explanations. Sue, I'd like to sleep here. . . ."

"Why not? I'll telephone that you're spending the night with me, and that you'll call for your bag in the morning. Or do you want it sent up?"

"I'd rather not. . . ."

Sue bent and kissed her, "I shall envy you, sleeping here, with all your — dreams."

"I know. . . ."

"Sure you're not afraid, Jack?"

"No."

"I must be getting back, or they'll be wondering."

"Sue you've been so sweet—"

"Don't my dear. . . ." Sue bent again and kissed her. "And now, why can't I take you over tomorrow morning in my motor boat. Early. And we'll get a cup of coffee on the way."

So it was settled. And when Sue had gone, Jacqueline went upstairs. She chose the guest-room, because it was in the back of the house and there she dared to light a candle. The canopy of the bed was brocade of a faded rose, and the bedspread was of the same soft color. Sue had wanted to bring over fresh linen for the bed, but Jacqueline would not have it. "I'll slip out of my dress and wrap up in a blanket, and sleep like a top."

But she found she couldn't sleep. After she extinguished the candle, she lay in the moonlight, thinking it all out. When she went to the hotel in the morning for her bag she would call up Kit . . . and tell him. . . . And she would tell him, too, that she didn't want to wait for a big wedding. They would be married at once, and sail in three days. Nothing else mattered . . . but that she was to be his

A Call to Adventure

wife and would go away with him, and they would have their happiness on the high seas!

Then, as soon as she got home, she would tell Mary! When she reached that point in her thoughts it seemed as if a cold hand clutched her. She tried to tell herself that Mary would be glad. And that Joel and Mary and Yolanda and Joey would somehow make a go of things. But she couldn't. For so many years she had brooded over them, that now it seemed as if they hung about her, making demands. And when she slept it was to dream of them, calling out to her, "*Jack . . . Jack!*" and "*Aunt Jack . . . Aunt Jack*" in a dreadful clamor.

When she waked in the morning, dawn had come into the room — a delicate, rosy dawn. All the furniture, the bed on which Jacqueline lay, seemed to float in that light as on an opalescent sea. Shaking off the weird dreams of the night, she sat up and looked about her. What a peaceful old room it was, with its mellow mahogany, its serene portrait above the mantel of Kit's grandmother, fresh-faced in her white cap, with fine white lace on her flowing silk gown. She seemed to smile at the little figure on the bed, in the brief pink slip with the length of silken stockings. And Jacqueline smiled back. "What a darling you are," she said, aloud, and her voice woke tinkling echoes in the high-ceiled room.

Outside a bird was singing. Through the open window came the fragrance of dew-drenched flowers. A lovely world. And why should Fear enter into it. Yet Jacqueline was afraid, afraid of those voices she had heard in the night: Mary's voice: *"Jack . . . Jack. . . !"* And small Joey's *"Aunt Jack . . . Aunt Jack!"*

Sue's voice sounded in the hall and Jacqueline ran to open the door. Sue had brought hot water in a pitcher, towels, soap. "It was great fun getting it over without anyone finding it out." Then as she came in, "You look like a child with your hair loose like that. What a pretty thing you are, Jack."

They talked while Jacqueline groomed herself and got into her clothes, then left the house and walked to the hotel. Few people were stirring. Sue waited in the lobby while Jacqueline went to her room, and called up Kit's New York club. As she waited for an answer, she trembled. The words which would go over the wire, would be irrevocable. The things which she said now to Kit would bind her forever. She did not tremble because she was afraid, but because she was happy. It would be wonderful to say "Kit, I'm coming. . . !"

But Kit was not there. He had left, she was told on the midnight train for Boston. She called his club in Park Street. He had not come.

So that was that! Jacqueline hung up the receiver and went down to Sue. "I can't get him in New York or Boston. He took the midnight train."

"He's probably motoring madly to see you."

Jacqueline shook her head. "He won't come to me

A Call to Adventure

this time. He said I must come, or it would be — the end."

Jacqueline's bag was light, so the two girls walked to the restaurant by the waterside where Jacqueline had once come with Kit. The old Skipper knew Sue and liked her, and found a table for her by a window with crisp white curtains and a glimpse of the harbor. He wouldn't listen when Sue ordered coffee and toast. "I'll give you more'n that," he announced. "I've got somethin' here that'ull zest your appetite."

He set before them presently a hearty breakfast of English bacon and new-laid eggs. His coffee was perfect, the toast hot and crisp. Sue and Jacqueline ate everything he set before them, and were rewarded by his air of triumphant satisfaction. "I know you wanted more'n you thought. And that bacon's straight from a pig in Devonshire."

He went with them to their boat, and squinted an eye at the sky. "Clear enough, but it has the feel of a storm."

"Are you trying to scare us, Skipper?" Sue demanded.

"Nothin' scares you, does it?" He laughed and waved as they moved off, and it was not until sometime later that they recalled his prophecy, for the harbor stretched before them shining and still, and as Sue's boat went pip-popping out to the sea, the keel cut little frills of white on the smooth surface; the white gulls swung languidly, up and down, in the golden air, and Sue, all in white, stood at the wheel, her bare head flaming in the sun. Jacqueline, watching her, thought of the figurehead at India House, which had strained and lifted to the rhythm of wind and wave. So Sue seemed to breast the air — a Winged Victory with her draperies blown back.

It was when they came at last to the open sea that they were aware of a shadow on the waters, and of black clouds boiling up above the horizon. "The Skipper was right," Sue said, "there's wind in those clouds. But we may not get it."

They did get it, but not at once. They drove for a time through a stillness which was ominous. The gulls poised above them gave out shrill piercing cries. A bell buoy, far out, seemed to toll a warning.

But Jacqueline was not alarmed. She loved the sea, and she loved the wind — the wild wind — which had brought Kit to her in those days of war. She began to talk to Sue about it. "Sue, the war gave us something we shall never lose — a kind of courage — I've never been afraid of death since."

Sue said, sharply, "What made you think of death — now?"

"I don't know. I just — did."

The wind was upon them. The black sky pressing down. "It's going to rain pitchforks," Sue announced, "hand me my slicker, darling."

There was another slicker for Jack, and the girls in their waterproof coats were like two yellow birds on a precarious perch. Sue drove her boat strongly through the waves, "It's glorious," she gasped, "just sit tight, Jack, and we'll get there."

"I'm not afraid," Jacqueline told her, and meant it. The only things she was afraid of were those voices in the night.

CHAPTER FOURTEEN

An Angel on the Stairs

I

MARY had been alone for two days. The nurses had been very attentive. And Joel and Joey. She had said once to Joel, "Things are really running very nicely without Jack." And he had said, "Yes," and had gone down presently to dine with his small son and to wish that Jack were there or Yolanda. "A man needs a woman opposite him at the table."

But Mary did not know and was happy in her ignorance. And when the third morning came, and there was a letter from Yolanda, she opened it with anticipation. It was a special delivery letter, and there clung about the envelope a faint whiff of Yolanda's favorite perfume. Yolanda's script was firm and square, and the letter began, "Darlingest Mums—!"

Mary read a few lines, then gave a little cry. The nurse hurried towards her, "What is it?"

"Yolanda's married!"

"Married! Oh, Mrs. Hutchins!"

"Listen," Mary's voice ran on hurriedly. "Darlingest Mums, when you read this Stuart and I will be married. We decided it just after Aunt Jack left this afternoon for home. She's probably told you all about it, and that she's giving up Kit. But, listen Mumsie, you mustn't let her. It is time she lived her own life, and anyhow you and Dad will *adore* being alone. I told her that. . . . I thought she really ought to know. . . .

"Stuart and I are going to his friends in Westchester, and you needn't worry. All the proprieties will be observed. We've telephoned out, and I'm to stay there tonight, and as soon as possible in the morning we'll get the license, and I'm going to wear my orchid satin. It seems queer doesn't it, to be married in orchid. But Stuart says he loves it. . . .

"And, darling, I love you. And you'll forgive me because this is the only way out of it all, and I'm just being sensible, and taking things as they come to me. Dad will rage of course, but you can smooth him down. Oh, yes, and we're going to honeymoon on a *yacht*. One of Stuart's friends is lending it. And it will be *gorgeous. . . !"*

Miss Meeker, listening to that hurried voice, reached for a bottle of sedative. Mary was excited, shaking. Her cheeks red. "How dared she . . . and yet . . . she has what she wants, Miss Meeker . . . and Stuart's wonderful. . . ." There was a hint of complacency in her voice not missed by the astute Miss Meeker. Stuart Carleton with his wealth and his background was a match for any woman. And Mrs. Hutchins knew it.

Mary re-reading the letter, stopped at the third line. "She says that Jack left New York yesterday. What can she mean? She hasn't arrived."

"She probably stopped over in Boston."

"But why didn't she tell us, and why didn't she come up this morning, or telephone?"

"She may have told Mr. Hutchins."

"He'd have told me . . . you'd better call him up, Miss Meeker. And see if he has heard."

But Joel hadn't heard. He said that Mary was not to worry. He'd get Kit up in New York. Jack was probably safe and sound at the hotel. But what was that Miss Meeker was saying about Yolanda. *Married. Great guns! What a girl! Going off like that!*

Yet even as he protested, Miss Meeker was aware of that note of gratification which she had detected in Mary's voice when she heard the news. But her words showed no hint of what was in her mind. "I think you'd better come home if you can, Mr. Hutchins. Mrs. Hutchins is taking it very well. But of course it's a shock. And she's worried about Miss Jack."

"Tell her not to worry. Jack's all right. Yolanda was so excited, she probably didn't know what she was talking about."

As Miss Meeker went back to her patient the curtains of the windows in the hall streamed in the wind. She called down to Marta who was in the lower hall. "You'd better shut things up tightly, Marta. There's going to be a storm."

An Angel on the Stairs

Mary still lay with Yolanda's letter in her hand. But her mind was not on her daughter. "What did Joel say about Jack?"

"He says you're not to worry. That she's undoubtedly in Boston or New York. He's going to get in touch with Mr. Howland."

Mary drew a breath of relief. "Kit will know, of course."

"Mr. Hutchins is coming down as soon as he hears from Mr. Howland," Miss Meeker went about closing the windows of Mary's room. "I wish you could get a little rest, Mrs. Hutchins. Shut your eyes and relax a bit, can't you?"

"No, I'm too keyed up. It's all very well to say not to worry. But I shan't be easy in my mind until I hear from Jack."

The rain was streaming now against the windows. "I hope Jack isn't out in it," Mary remarked.

"Of course she isn't," Miss Meeker was soothing. "She has too much sense."

Mary, her hand under her cheek, lay looking off into space. "Jack's a darling. She has been more than a sister to me. The tie that binds us is very strong."

The tie that bound them was so strong, that as the moments passed, Mary grew restless. More and more she was oppressed by the feeling that something was happening to Jack. And if anything did happen could they ever forgive themselves? For, in all the long years since the war, had any of them been really concerned about Jack's happiness? Hadn't they taken all that she had to give of youth and strength without a thought of what it might mean to her?

"She's a darling," Mary said again to Miss Meeker, and then burst suddenly into tears. "It's been an hour since you called up Joel . . . and we haven't had a word. . . ."

"He's coming now." Miss Meeker rose and stepped into the hall. Joel said something to her in a low voice, and went on to Mary.

"Oh, Joel. . . ."

"Cheer up, old girl. You mustn't break down like this."

"Have you heard anything from Jack?"

"No."

"Something has happened to her Joel. I'm sure of it."

"Nonsense. What could happen. And now let me see Yolanda's letter." He swept Mary away from the subject of Jacqueline. And Miss Meeker went downstairs. For Joel had said in the hall: For God's sake go down. Howland's there. He drove me out — sixty miles an hour. We broke all traffic rules and got away with it."

Miss Meeker found Kit in the sunroom. He turned quickly as the nurse spoke to him. "I have just called up the Gilmans. They told me at the club that just before I arrived this morning there was a long distance from Salem. Miss Paula says that Miss Sue went out early in her boat and that Miss Jack was with her. One of the maids saw them from an upper window."

An Angel on the Stairs

"Then they are on the water — in this storm?"

"Yes. Miss Meeker, will you tell Hutchins that I'm going after them?"

He did not wait for slicker or hat. The wind blew his rough curls about as he ran down to the pier. The whole world was dark with the storm. He could hear men shouting across the harbor, and the wind was shouting and shrieking — the wild wind — that Jacqueline loved.

In the meantime, Mary upstairs grew hysterical. "Joel, are you keeping anything from me?"

"No." But he knew he was keeping this, that he and Kit had called up Jacqueline's hotel in New York, and had learned she had left, bag and baggage, and not a trace of her had been found.

Miss Meeker, coming in, once more urged rest for Mary, and Joel finally went away, to be followed presently by the nurse, "She'll sleep a bit now, I hope. And Mr. Howland left a message for you, Mr. Hutchins."

But Mary did not sleep. As a rule she had no fear of storms, but there seemed something horrible and frightening in all this crash and clatter at mid-morning. She knew if she touched the bell by her side that she could summon Miss Meeker. But she dreaded the platitudes with which Miss Meeker would try to soothe her. And there were no words to meet this dreadful uncertainty. It was not like Jack to hide herself away. From everybody. Even from Kit.

She tried to compose herself. She shut her eyes and

repeated all the formulas for sleep she had learned throughout her years of inactivity. There was one — making little marks on a sheet of paper — which rarely failed.

She reached for a pad and pencil which lay on her bedside table, then stopped with hand uplifted — for strange sounds were coming through the crash and clatter of the storm. The sound of hurrying feet, of opening doors, of suppressed and anxious voices.

She rang the bell. There was no answer. She called. And no one replied. She was filled with a sense of her impotence, and rang and called again, raging. Why didn't they come? The nurse? Joel? Marta? They always came. They knew she was bound hand and foot. Helpless! And still those sounds went on — of hurrying feet, of whispering voices! Something had happened! To Jack!

Frantic, and driven by her fears, she found herself sitting up. The last time she had raised herself in bed, Jack had been there to see . . . and they had spoken of it, and had clung together. . . !

The wind shook the house and screamed like a thousand furies, as Mary moved to the edge of the bed and put her feet to the floor. They were bare feet, and she had no slippers. Why should there be slippers for one who never wore them? She had no dressing gown — for a woman who never left her bed needed none, and so when at last, shaking but triumphant, she stood on the rug, she was thinly clad in bedjacket and night-

An Angel on the Stairs

robe of rosy crepe, and her two long fair braids hung to her knees.

Slowly, clinging to this piece of furniture and that, she made her way to the hall and looked down. A group of people had gathered there — Joel and Miss Meeker and Marta, and two unknown men, and Sue Gilman dripping like a rat.

But it was not at any of these that Mary looked. For in the center of the group, held in the arms of Kit Howland who was on his knees, was Jacqueline, her little sister. And Jack's face was as white as death, and she lay as one dead, and Kit was saying hoarsely, desperately, "Open your eyes, my darling, open your eyes, and look at me."

II

Jacqueline, far off in the darkness, heard faintly the call of her lover. But clearer than that call and close at hand, was another voice. A child's voice:

"*If I only knew more about it, Aunt Jack.*"

"*About what, Yolanda?*"

"*Heaven.*"

She smiled, and those who bent above her, said, "She's coming back." And Miss Meeker who had brought something in a cup said: "If we can only get this down."

But Jacqueline was again far away in the darkness:

"*The woodman came, and he said, 'You're a naughty*

wolf, and just for that you'll have to go without your supper.'"

"*Patsy!*"

"*So he didn't eat Red Riding Hood, and he didn't eat her grandmother . . . an' he was put to bed with bread and milk. . . !*"

They were forcing something down her throat, and now the child's voice drifted into silence . . . and warm waves seemed to wash over Jacqueline . . . and she felt herself rising up from deep waters, and she opened her eyes and saw . . . Kit! And she felt the strength of his body as he held her to him, and tasted the salt on his lips as he kissed her!

And then she remembered. . . !

The boat had gone over in the midst of a whirling sea. And she and Sue had managed to cling to the wreck and keep their heads above water. Sue had been wonderful! She had laughed at the thought of danger. "It's only a matter of keeping cool until someone comes."

It was Sue who had talked and had kept Jacqueline talking. About a lot of things. Intimate things. Of that time in India. "Paula made me think that Kit cared . . . but he didn't."

"She wrote me that he did."

"Paula?"

"Yes. That's why I let Kit go. I didn't want to hold him."

"You held him by more than any vow, Jacqueline.

An Angel on the Stairs

It is something in themselves that makes men constant, Jack. Not the women they love."

"Darling Kit...." Jacqueline had felt suddenly chilled and weak. Would she ever see him again? The water had seemed to weigh her down with heaviness.

Sue had spoken sharply. "Jacqueline! Hold tight! If you let go now, you may not be able to swim back."

Jacqueline had not been sure that she cared to swim back. If she could just float off somewhere ... away from this heaviness of waters.

She had heard Sue's frantic voice, "Jack ... Jack!" then darkness had swept over her and oblivion.

And now the world was filled with golden light, and she was aware that Sue was saying, "If Kit hadn't come just then! Kit, you looked like Lohengrin or Tannhäuser or some of the old gods, standing up in your boat, with your hair blowing back, and the light breaking through in the sky above you."

But Jacqueline didn't want to hear what Sue was saying. For she was in Kit's arms, and he was whispering, "Dear heart," and she whispered back, "In three ... days ..." and somehow couldn't finish. So he said it for her, "In three days we will sail away — together?"

And she smiled again and was content. For everybody was about her, making her for once the center of things; Joel, laughing in his relief, and Miss Meeker urging that she be put to bed, and Sue with hot water bottles and blankets, and Kit, hearing nothing, seeing nothing but the face of his beloved and loth to let her go.

Then all at once, they all turned from her, and gazed upwards — staring. Even Kit stared and his arms loosened. And Jacqueline following the direction of their eyes, saw Mary, all pink and gold like a radiant angel, coming down the stairs!

Temple Bailey's Charming Novels

May be had wherever books are sold. Ask for Grosset & Dunlap's list.

THE RADIANT TREE. Unusual short stories in which Miss Bailey shows her knowledge of character and her skill in romance tales.

ENCHANTED GROUND. The story of the love of young Dr. Peter Ferry for Mary Hamilton, with her bright beauty and her desperate need of his protection and care, is here presented in all its power and pathos.

LITTLE GIRL LOST. Youth, beauty, the adoration of two men were Araminta's. Barney offered marriage, Janney insisted that friendship would fill her life. Out of this conflict came the gripping climax.

WILD WIND. A girl's sacrifice for the children of her sister is the keynote of the heart-stirring love story.

BURNING BEAUTY. Beautiful Virginia Oliphant is loved by two men; one tempts her with millions, and the other tempts her with nothing more than his devotion.

SILVER SLIPPERS. Days of delight and disillusionment until Joan Dudley's knight actually came.

WALL FLOWERS. They were twins, they were "Wall Flowers" perhaps—but they were beautiful, and young and *real*.

THE BLUE WINDOW. Hildegarde finds herself transplanted from the middle western farm to the gay social whirl of the East.

PEACOCK FEATHERS. Jerry, the idealist, loves Mimi, a beautiful spoiled society girl. A conflict of wealth and love.

THE DIM LANTERN. The romance of little Jane Barnes who is loved by two men.

TRUMPETER SWAN. Randy Paine came back from France to the monotony of everyday affairs. But a girl showed him the beauty in the commonplace.

THE TIN SOLDIER. Derry wishes to serve his country but is bound by a tie he cannot in honor break. Jean loves him and shares his humiliation to help him win.

MISTRESS ANNE. Into the life of Anne came two men; one is weak and the other strong and they both need Anne.

CONTRARY MARY. An old fashioned love story that has a very modern application.

GLORY OF YOUTH. An old question yet ever new—how far should an engagement of marriage bind two persons who find they no longer love?

GROSSET & DUNLAP *Publishers* **NEW YORK**

FAITH BALDWIN'S
Delightful Stories of
ROMANCE AND YOUNG MARRIAGE

May be had wherever books are sold. Ask for Grosset & Dunlap's list.

She writes about the people you know—The girl next door, the man who rides down the elevator with you, the people in your office—their loves, their ambitions, their dreams—these are the people about whom Faith Baldwin writes. In her stories you will come to know them better than you have ever known them before.

- PRIVATE DUTY
- THE PURITAN STRAIN
- THE MOON'S OUR HOME
- AMERICAN FAMILY
- HONOR BOUND
- WHITE COLLAR GIRL
- BEAUTY
- SELF-MADE WOMAN
- DISTRICT NURSE
- WEEK-END MARRIAGE
- GARDEN OATS
- MAKE BELIEVE
- TODAY'S VIRTUE

GROSSET & DUNLAP   *Publishers*   NEW YORK

The Novels of Sinclair Lewis

May be had wherever books are sold. Ask for Grosset & Dunlap's list.

Within the space of a few years, Sinclair Lewis has become one of the most distinguished of American novelists—and the first American to win the Nobel prize for literature.

ANN VICKERS

Ann Vickers is a product of the twentieth century—a woman, fearless and dauntless, who set out to do things. Mr. Lewis draws a frank, enduring picture of Ann, one that has life and color and speed against a background teeming with the questions and causes of the day.

DODSWORTH

Dodsworth is another Main Street, sophisticated and matured, with a new problem, but the same broad pages full of the most excellent reporting. No one who is interested in American life should miss it.

ELMER GANTRY

By successful advertising methods in the best Babbitt tradition, Elmer Gantry, Methodist Pastor, hypocrite and voluptuary, becomes a power in a large community.

ARROWSMITH

The story of a country doctor whose search for the truth led him to the heights of the medical profession, through the tests of love and marriage and to final peace as a quietly heroic laboratory worker.

BABBITT

Every man will recognize in the character of George Babbitt something of himself. He was a booster and a joiner, but behind all of his activities was a wistful wonder as to what life holds.

MAIN STREET

An absorbing drama of real life in the average small town as seen through the eyes of an impressionable young girl who married the local doctor.

GROSSET & DUNLAP   *Publishers*   NEW YORK